Love Finds You™

IN

Sun Valley

IDAHO

Love Finds You™
IN
Sun Valley
IDAHO

BY ANGELA RUTH

summerside
PRESS™

Summerside Press™
Minneapolis 55438

Love Finds You in Sun Valley, Idaho
© 2010 by Angela Ruth
ISBN 978-1-61129-447-7

Scripture taken from the Holy Bible, New International Version®. NIV®. Copyright © 1973, 1978, 1984 by International Bible Society. Used by permission of Zondervan. All rights reserved. References not noted in the text: Chapter 9, Matthew 5:45: "He [God] causes his sun to rise on the evil and the good, and sends rain on the righteous and the unrighteous." Chapter 26, Isaiah 55:1: "Come, all who are thirsty, come to the waters." Chapter 26, Matthew 14:31:"You of little faith…why did you doubt?"

The town depicted in this book is a real place, but all characters are fictional. Any resemblances to actual people or events are purely coincidental.

Cover Design by Garborg Design Works | www.garborgdesign.com

Interior Design by Müllerhaus Publishing Group | www.mullerhaus.net

Photos of Sun Valley provided by the Sun Valley Resort, www.sunvalley.com. Used by permission.

Summerside Press™ is an inspirational publisher offering fresh, irresistible books to uplift the heart and engage the mind.

Printed in USA.

Dedication
....

To Kevin and Rebecca,
for showing me what love is again

Acknowledgments

My mom—for being my first editor and biggest cheerleader.

My dad—because of his heart for a good story and for me.

My kids, Jordan, Caitlin, and Lauren—
for their ideas, enthusiasm, and faith.

Grandma Ellie—for letting me stick her
in my novel (upside down).

The River Company—for helping me get into character.

My critique partner Christina Berry—how did I get so lucky?

"Perpetual Editor" and friend Becky Lyles—
for making me sound half-intelligent.

My first official editor, Ramona—
for making me feel half-intelligent.

My agent, Tamela—for her foot that got me through this door.

All my favorite authors—you know who you
are, and hey, my stalking paid off.

Family and friends—because your support was often undeserved.

God—for romancing me.

Many waters cannot quench love;
rivers cannot wash it away.

SONG OF SONGS 8:7

Sun Valley, Idaho

SUN VALLEY, IDAHO, BRINGS THE HIGH-CLASS DOWN-HOME. IN THE resort town of around 1,400, only a few are permanent residents, while many keep vacation homes or host meetings for corporations owned by Oprah or Middle Eastern princes. The hallways of the huge lodge are lined with black-and-white photographs of celebrities initially invited to help promote the area as the first destination winter resort in the United States. Located close to the Sawtooth National Recreation Area, Sun Valley boasts a variety of summer activities as well, including rafting, golf, fishing, roller ski skating, and even ice-skating on the year-round outdoor ice rink.

As for culture, the state-of-the-art Sun Valley Pavilion offers a free summer concert series, and the Opera House frequently shows the movie Sun Valley Serenade, filmed in 1941. Ernest Hemingway also penned at least one novel from the Hemingway Suite before buying his own home in the area. Sun Valley is a great place to visit, whether you want to rub shoulders with the rich and famous or just have an adventurous getaway.

Angela Ruth

Chapter One

Tapping the brakes to turn off the cruise control in her rented Ford Escape, Emily squinted to read another marker located along Hwy 21. The windy road transitioned from the forested mountains to the dry valley, where the pine trees grew taller as if wearing stilts. This meant she was getting closer to the river and her resort destination.

When she was growing up, Dad had always refused to take her to Sun Valley, Idaho. Said he'd rather avoid the snobs who vacationed there. Of course, he was referring to the rich and famous, the actors and actresses. Which ironically she now was. An actress anyway. Never a snob.

Should she feel guilty for staying in the swanky lodge? Nah. She needed a good night's rest before the flurry of filming swept her downstream—literally. Especially after spending a week with Mom in her hometown of Boise.

She also needed a bathroom and a hot meal. Spying a rustic restaurant snuggled next to a bend in the river, she pressed harder on the brakes before swinging onto the gravel side road leading to The Point. The log building looked as if it were in need of some sprucing up, but by the number of cars parked out front, the food must have made up for any lack of elegance.

Emily pulled the compact SUV into what might be considered

a parking space and leaned over the passenger's side to pull her purse from underneath a sweatshirt. Since it was July, she'd only brought summer clothes, but Mom had pretended to be practical for a moment and insisted she take the ugly orange Boise State hoodie. Guess it was always good to be prepared.

Behind her, the driver's side door jerked open with a squeak. The car rocked, and the sun baked her back, though that didn't keep goose bumps from popping up on her flesh. Reactively, she dug one hand into her purse for a can of mace as she whipped around to confront the intruder. Every muscle tensed as possible scenarios tore through her imagination. *Hijacker…mugger…crazed fan…*

Her makeup stylist? "Emily Van Arsdale, what took so long? Never mind. We'll say you got a flat tire. Or you got lost. Is that what happened? You got lost? Didn't you grow up around here?" Charlene didn't wait for a response before dragging the actress from her vehicle.

"Char?" Emily pulled her arm free and tried to reorient herself. The rushing river sounded similar to cars streaming down the freeway in L.A., but the scent seeping into her pores was a fresh mixture of dust and dry grass. "What's going on? What am I late for?"

Charlene paused, narrowing her eyes. Then, grabbing Emily's arm again, she took off toward the building. "Don't tell me you didn't get the text message. Bruce had us all come a day early. There's some kind of rodeo next weekend, and he's afraid we won't be able to get anything done with so many people in town."

Emily's quickened stride didn't even rival the pace of her heart. She wouldn't get a break after all. Groan. "We're starting today?"

The answer stared back at her in the form of a "honeywagon"

half hidden behind The Point. How had she not noticed the trailer the director used for an office? And of all the restaurants she could have stopped at, how did she accidentally end up where she was supposed to be?

She smothered a giggle at how she could have innocently been playing tourist at a historical landmark only a mile back, while everyone waited for her here. Char was in no mood to appreciate the joke, though.

No, her friend pulled her inside the oversized pine door before sticking one hand on her hip. "You didn't get the text." It was a statement, not a question.

Emily shook her head. Shoot, it was her fault. It would have been so much easier to blame somebody else. One of these days she'd remember to charge her cell phone.

"The first team is waiting for you, girl. Come on!"

Charlene rushed her forward through a sitting area in front of a massive stone fireplace and past the entrance to a dining hall with a balcony in the distance. The place was bigger on the inside than it had looked. They continued their trek down a flight of stairs into a musty-smelling daylight basement, which, Emily guessed, had been rented for the main actors, or "first team," as Char called them.

The makeup artist continued to rant. "Of all the days to be late, today is the day you have to wear the wedding dress and have your hair fancied up."

Emily squinted out a window—the interior of the building seemed dim compared to the bright sunshine. There they were. Bruce had a crew down at the water's edge. He looked at his watch, then yelled at someone hidden from her behind a tree.

"I'll be fast." Emily sighed before ducking into the restroom. She *hoped* the day would go by fast. At least there would be no stunts. She'd just have to look pretty—an idea that still made her dubious.

Grabbing the gown she'd been fitted for back at the studios, Emily ripped off her summer dress. The costume designer was ready and waiting to fasten the buttons up her back. Before the woman even finished, Char attacked her face, and the hair stylist began defining her short, dark ringlets with a curling iron and a shower of hairspray.

Good enough. She was as camera ready as she would ever be. Emily lifted up the hem of her scratchy tulle skirt and took off out the back door and down the hill still wearing her own shoes. She'd be barefoot in the rafting scene anyway. Skating on a pinecone, she leapt over a boulder as if she'd planned the move all along.

Scanning the crowd for Bruce, her eyes stopped on a man who seemed to have taken over. He wasn't anything like Bruce. He wore the same kinds of outdoorsy clothing, but the khaki cargo shorts and sleeveless shirt looked authentic on him. Long, lean muscles and sun-baked skin gave him the appeal that all her acting associates paid big bucks for, but it was the messy hair and laid-back posture that caught her attention. And then he flashed his smile.

* * * * *

Tracen Lake laughed and waved his employee away. It was comical to see the difference between the uptight film crew and the fun-loving raft guides. He was excited, though. Whitewater rafting was a rush in itself, but now he'd be orchestrating the direction of a movie through his rafting company. It would be great for business, and the position paid enough for him to finally build a log cabin on his riverfront property. If only the star would arrive so they could get the show rolling.

Tracen glanced up the hill to see if there was any sign of Wonder Woman. His scan of the area stopped the moment his gaze reached…a bride? The lady looked as delicate as a snowflake, but by the way she descended from above, she resembled a hailstone.

Tracen felt his brows draw together, and he forced himself to survey the rest of the area to see if anyone was with her. Not good.

Weddings had been held there before. After all, it was a beautiful location. But there was no wedding scheduled for today that he knew of. If there was, he could kiss his cabin good-bye. The embankment was supposed to be shut down for everyone except the movie crew.

His eyes traveled back to the woman in white. He knew her somehow. He couldn't place her, but she looked familiar. Her hair bounced to just below her chin. And he could see the brilliant blue of her eyes as she got closer. His mind scanned through the residents of Sun Valley. None of them fit.

Her sapphire stare landed on a spot behind him, and a smile exploded across her face, causing her cheekbones to stand at attention. Scenes from a movie played through his mind. Those features did belong to Wonder Woman. But she'd cut her hair off.

He let his gaze linger for a second longer before the anger took over. Not only had she delayed the filming for a full hour, but nobody had told him she'd be wearing a wedding dress. It was like she was taunting him. Like she knew his fiancée had run off to seek her fame in Tinseltown. And here she was, a famous movie star, showing up in his backyard dressed for a wedding.

Pushing away personal thoughts, he stalked over to Bruce to talk business. "Why is she dressed like a bride?"

Bruce peered up from a squatting position where he'd been in conversation with a technician who seemed to be measuring light. "What did you expect her to wear in a movie titled *Whitewater Wedding*?"

Even the lighting tech rolled his eyes at Tracen. They thought he'd asked a stupid question. But they were the ones being idiots. Or were they just incredibly ignorant?

Bruce stood and shook his leg as if to get rid of a cramp. It was obvious he wanted to get rid of Tracen, as well. "The characters are escaping from a forest fire that crashes their ceremony in the woods."

How could the director sound so condescending while explaining the ridiculous? "Right." Tracen shifted his jaw side to side, wondering how the clown didn't see the risk he was taking with his talent. "I agreed to let you shoot this scene without life jackets since the water is pretty calm here. But I didn't know your actress was going to be wearing an anchor."

Bruce scratched his balding head, looking past him. "An anchor?"

Tracen placed one sandaled foot on a rock and huffed. "What happens if she falls overboard? That dress will absorb enough water to pull her down like she's encased in cement." The analogy made his skin grow clammy.

Bruce shrugged. "She's not going to fall over the side unless I tell her to. She's an experienced stuntwoman. We'll be fine."

Stuntwoman? Tracen hadn't heard that before, but what

difference did her experience make? It was his responsibility to ensure nothing happened while rafting. "Listen. Either you have them put life jackets on or..."

Bruce tilted his chin up. "Or what?"

What else could he do? "Or put me in the raft."

Bruce's laugh sounded hollow. "That's not going to happen."

Tracen shot a glance toward the actress in question. *Mercy.* She had her skirt hiked up to her knees and was kicking off pink flip-flops. She had no clue of the possible danger downriver. Tracen cocked his head as he faced the director. "What kind of insurance do you carry?"

Bruce shook his head but, glancing at the activity around him, couldn't seem to find a rebuttal to Tracen's argument. "Fine. But you're going to have to put on a tux."

Tracen hadn't expected the director's response. He'd just become an extra in the film.

Chapter Two

. . . .

The chill of the water practically burned Emily's toes. She shivered as she climbed into the slippery blue raft banked in the shade of a couple of tall trees. How long until they could launch into the sunshine?

An arm snaked around her from behind. "I'll help you stay warm," offered the lead actor in a voice that could make most women across America swoon.

But Emily found its rich tone to be arrogant and fake—like him. Ugh. She untangled herself from his arms. "Save the romance for the kissing scene, Jack."

Jack winked as she scowled over her shoulder. "Just getting into character."

Emily turned her back and settled on the side of the raft, like Bruce directed. The rest of the groomsmen followed suit.

Bruce cleared his throat. "We're taking long shots this morning. I need you to float around the bend in the river. Later we'll get action and dialogue."

Emily grabbed a paddle. "All right. Let's go." The sooner they got this over with, the sooner she could relax in a hot bubble bath. Her body needed a breather between the workout her mother gave her and the stunts she would be doing soon. She arched her back, hoping it wouldn't feel as tender the next morning.

Bruce glanced at his watch. "We're waiting for Tracen."

Emily scanned the faces of her fellow cast. Nobody else seemed confused by this statement. "Who?" She thought she'd been the last one to arrive.

Bruce grunted. "The rafting guide insisted on being on the raft when he saw what you were wearing. Supposedly your dress is a safety hazard."

Emily's lips curled up. It was sweet that some guy worried for her safety. There weren't many men like that where she came from. But what made her smile was the fact that she could take care of herself. The guide was going to have his hands full trying to keep up.

Emily scanned past the director. She hoped "Tracen" was the tall, tanned guy. Sure enough, the man in question strode down the hill, though he didn't look quite as comfortable in a tux as he had in shorts and sandals. He even frowned at her grin.

His giant stride didn't slow until he was standing in the water beside the paddleboat. He assessed the seating arrangement. "I'll be seated in the stern. When I say paddle right, that means everyone on my right. Same thing for the left. If I say hard right or hard left, you need to paddle hard. If I say full back, both sides need to paddle backwards. Any questions?" He didn't sound like he really wanted to hear any.

Emily lifted her eyebrows at Tracen's stern expression. Did she mistake him for laid-back earlier? The man had turned into a slave driver.

"And Ms. Van Arsdale, I need you to straddle the side of the raft." He didn't even look at her as he said this. But he must know she was wearing a dress. She would remind him in case he hadn't considered the fact. "I'm wearing a dress."

Now his hazel eyes met hers. They held a golden glint of challenge. "Your dress is the whole reason I'm here. My job is to keep you safe. And you will be better balanced with a leg on each side. I'm sure your skirt is big enough to keep you decent."

* * * * *

Tracen considered the dress. Her skirt poofed big and fluffy now, but if it got wet, it would cling to her body like fur on a drowned kitten—and that's about how well she would be able to swim. He watched her blink, then turn around smoothly. She had the grace of a cat, as well.

Emily swung one long leg into the water.

She couldn't be more than five-foot-two, so where did the length come from? Then the leg disappeared underneath yards of white fabric, and Tracen adjusted his bow tie, trying to refocus on his goal.

He didn't like being put in this position. Not only did he have to wear layers of stiff clothing (some of which were now sticking to his wet calves), but he had to ensure the safety of six others in a very unsafe situation. Rafting was supposed to be a wild adventure. This was more like a controlled disaster.

"I'm pushing us off, Bruce."

Bruce nodded his permission, though he really didn't have much of a say. He hurried away to monitor filming around the bend.

"All forward," Tracen called, pulling sunglasses out of his breast pocket as the raft drifted into the sun. He only sneezed once before sliding the shades over his ears and, more importantly, his eyes.

"God bless you," the token female on their journey offered, glancing back. Then she turned more fully, as if to study his sunglasses.

"Thanks," Tracen muttered. He hoped she didn't question the addition to his "costume." He didn't want to explain his sun sensitivity.

The woman smiled at him, but it wasn't the most reassuring of smiles. It was rather smug, as if she thought he was wearing the sunglasses so he could watch her without her knowing it—which wasn't a bad idea. After all, he was responsible for her, but it bothered him that she didn't ask, just assumed. Of course, she was from Hollywood, wasn't she?

A couple of actors in the front of the raft splashed each other. Tracen peered over his shoulder at the other rafting guides helping the crew still on shore. If they were the ones water-fighting, he would have joined right in.

A light voice broke into his thoughts. "How gorgeous!" Emily Van Arsdale studied the mountains looming ahead.

Jack Jamison—the only other actor Tracen recognized—studied Emily. "My thoughts exactly." It was obvious he wasn't thinking about nature.

Tracen felt a pinch of pleasure when Emily ignored Jack's attempt at flirting. She placed her hands behind her on the raft and leaned back, lifting her face to the sun and closing her eyes. Tracen found himself staring, just as Jack had.

Tearing his gaze away, Tracen chided himself. Not only was he imitating Jack's behavior, but he'd done so from behind his glasses, just as Emily's smile said she'd expected him to. Tracen pulled at his tie. How had he gotten into this position again? To make it worse, he was sitting between two feuding lovers, if the scene he'd witnessed from the window of the restaurant was any indicator.

He wouldn't let himself get sucked in, though. He'd declined the lure of Hollywood before, and this wasn't even an offer.

Jack glanced at him. His smile had "gloat" written all over it. He addressed the bathing beauty across from him. "Emily, do you realize you are the only girl in the group?"

Emily's curls bounced as she turned her face away from Jack and began to row. "Good thing I'm a tomboy."

Jack continued to ogle. " I don't see anything boyish about you."

Emily didn't respond, and her discomfort drifted back toward Tracen. The roar of the river had never seemed so quiet. He racked his brain for something distracting to say while using his paddle like a rudder to direct them.

"How *did* your character become the only female left behind after the fire at her wedding?" He'd been given the screenplay but hadn't been able to get into it. He preferred non-fiction.

Emily's eyes lit up as she twisted in her seat to face him. They were the lightest blue he'd ever seen, surrounded by an outline of navy. He reminded himself to focus on her words. "A helicopter rescues the wedding party, but the groomsmen let the ladies be flown to safety first. I, naturally, refuse to leave my groom, so I stay behind with the men."

"Naturally." Tracen heard the teasing drop in his voice.

Emily played along, overdoing the drama. "The fire rages faster than we expect. The deserted raft is our only chance of escape. But through this miserable experience, I realize I'm not in love with my groom after all, but his best man. Isn't that the most romantic thing you've ever heard?"

"And realistic," Tracen quipped.

Emily's giggle delighted. It wasn't humoring or overly loud. Just real and contagious. Tracen smiled.

Jack added on to Emily's explanation. "I'm the best man." Or maybe he was marking his territory.

"Here we go, guys!" the Asian groomsman called from the bow. "The cameramen are filming. Act upset and depressed."

Tracen was new to the acting thing but figured he could simply act like himself. It was upsetting to feel responsible for the lives of six clueless rafters and depressing to be reminded his ex had left him.

The talking quieted. Tracen wondered if anyone would recognize him in the movie. The footage was being taken from quite a distance, so he could be any lanky extra.

Tracen refused to glance at the camera. He had to appear natural. Well, what would he naturally be doing? He would be watching downriver. Shifting his gaze from the other actors, he focused straight ahead and jerked to attention.

They were headed straight for a giant rock.

"Hard left!" Tracen broke character, but that was better than breaking his neck. This part of the river was calm—if you stayed away from Bird Poop Island, as his employees called it. None of them had ever hit it before. Where was his head?

"What?" called one of the guys up front.

"Left side paddle hard!"

Nobody else felt his panic. The river remained a ribbon of silk as far as they were aware.

Jack shook his head in what looked like pity. "We're not supposed to be rowing now, Rafter Boy."

Though his jaw shifted side to side—once for the name and once for the ignorance—Tracen remained focused on the danger ahead.

Emily's paddle dug deep underneath the surface, but everybody else stared at him in confusion. It was too late. The bow hit the rock, and the current that had appeared lazy hoisted the entire raft up on top of the boulder. There wasn't anything to do except pray the raft didn't capsize. He snatched Emily's wrist just in case.

The paddleboat plunged back into the river, the middle sucked down the deepest, folding the raft like a taco. Tracen lost his breath at contact with the freezing waves, as if his lungs were filled with dry ice. Too late he saw Jack's head coming toward his. He tried to brace himself, but the impact on his skull was the only thing he experienced for what seemed like eternity—even numbing the chill from the river.

Of course it happened in the fraction of a second, but that's all it took for him to lose his grip on Emily. Water rose around his neck and gurgled into his mouth and up his nostrils. A scream sounded from a distance, but he had brief comfort from the knowledge that it was too low to be a female voice.

The raft slipped sideways, roiling in the whitewater, spitting them out like the shells from sunflower seeds. He grasped futilely for Emily again before he too went flying. He couldn't reach her now, but she seemed better off without him.

Emily was on her feet, on the side of the raft as if she were a log roller. While the raft continued its rotation, she ripped off the fluff from her skirt in one smooth motion and dove past him with another. If he hadn't seen it happen before he was submerged, he wouldn't have believed it.

Had the vicious slap of the water messed with his mind? Or maybe because he'd lost his glasses, it had all been a trick of the sunlight. Twisting underwater, he let out air from his frigid lungs and scissored his legs to propel himself back to the surface. He broke free, gasped, then felt the sneezing attack.

Between sneezes he thrashed around, looking for Wonder Woman through watery eyes. Even if she'd gotten rid of her skirt, she would still have trouble making it to land through the current. The river carried him past the camera crew before he was even able to start swimming. But where should he go? Who needed him?

Not Emily Van Arsdale. Tracen blinked to make sure he was really seeing her on the shore, wringing water from her hair, the under layer of her skirt clinging to her legs. Tracen took off swimming toward her before realizing that another actor might need help.

Yep. Jack clung to another rock downstream. Hopefully he hadn't been thrown into it. But if he had… Tracen shook the thought away. Yeah, he wanted the guy to learn to respect the river. But he didn't want anybody to have to learn the hard way—the way he had.

Chapter Three

....

"Absolutely brilliant!" Bruce raved over her performance. "If only you had swum back with your skirt in hand. But I guess you'll be wearing this number for the rest of the filming, anyway."

Emily huddled in a towel and looked down at what was left of her dress. She hadn't planned to rip her dress apart, but the rafting guide's fear had seeped into her, causing her reaction. And she was lucky she hadn't been tossed from the side of the raft the way everybody else seemed to be. Sometimes her body surprised her with what it could do.

The other surprise was Jack. The tough guy wasn't so tough after all. The rafting guide—Tracer? Taylor? What was his name?—had to swim out and save him. She hoped the meal of humble pie would fill Jack up enough to keep him from salivating over her.

She watched as both men stumbled up the bank. The rafting guide had already rid himself of the tuxedo jacket, vest, and tie, and now he pulled at the buttons on his shirt. Jack merely fell to the ground panting.

The guide's shirt was halfway down his broad shoulders when a sneezing fit doubled him over. Another rafting guide—a thicker man who didn't appear to be a fan of shaving—ripped a pair of sunglasses off his head and handed them to her guide. Immediately the sneezing stopped.

"What's that all about?" Emily wondered from a distance.

A female rafter with a long braid and no makeup chuckled. She reminded Emily a little of her mom. "Tracen has sensitive eyes. It's actually called the Achoo Syndrome."

"Achoo?" Emily echoed. So maybe he hadn't put the glasses on to check her out inconspicuously after all. "As in the sound you make when you sneeze?"

The woman with the braid nodded. "Well, it stands for some technical term, I think, but yeah, the name sounds like a sneeze. Isn't that adorable?"

It was. A macho Sun Valley outdoorsman who couldn't control his own reaction to the sun. "Yep, he is."

The woman lifted a bushy brow. "I meant the name of the syndrome, not the man."

Emily grinned at her misunderstanding. "Oh."

"Tracen is adorable too. But he wouldn't be interested in you."

Emily paused in surprise. It had been awhile since she'd heard words like that. In fact, since she'd become well known for playing the role of Wonder Woman in last summer's blockbuster, every guy she met seemed a little too interested in her. What would make this guy different? She opened her mouth to ask but was interrupted by Bruce's assistant.

"Miss Van Arsdale, we've got a ride for you back to the restaurant. We'll continue shooting after lunch."

Thank goodness for food. And warmth. Weren't those basic needs for life? And here she was, a famous actress, without either.

Yet Braid Lady's words held her back. Emily turned to ask for an explanation, only to find the woman headed down the hill to help out the very man she wanted to talk about.

She hesitated, waiting to see their interaction. Maybe Braid Lady and Rafter Boy were a couple. But Braid Lady hadn't seemed defensive, and she was obviously older. She patted Rafter Boy on the back—not a romantic touch, but…

"Thanks, honey," Rafter Boy said.

Maybe he went for older women. The two did have a common lifestyle. It made sense. Whereas an actress from L.A. and a small-town outdoorsman did not. So it shouldn't bother her. But then why was she still staring?

Rafter Boy was shirtless now, that's why. And he seemed much more comfortable with this state of dress. Most males would be, with ripped abs like those. Emily squinted at his stomach. She saw shadowing between muscles in his six-pack, but there was also a lighter line along his right ribs. Could it be a birthmark? Or a scar of some kind? He became more interesting every minute.

"Miss Van Arsdale?" the assistant called again.

Stomach growling, Emily trotted up the hill to a Suburban. She planned to ignore the craft table with its array of junk food and order a real meal. But back at the restaurant, she hunted for Charlene first. She had to share her rafting experience—and she might have to ask about Rafter Boy too. Why couldn't she remember his name?

Char found her first. "Why are you all wet, girl?"

Emily rolled her eyes as her friend rubbed at her with the towel as if she were a child. She stepped out of the damp gown and into her favorite floral halter dress. "Nothing major. We capsized the raft, that's all."

Char shrieked. "Did Tracen have to save you?"

Tracen. *Tray-sun*. He was allergic to the sun, lived in Sun Valley, and had the word *sun* in his name. She could remember that. "Not me. He had to save Jack."

Charlene gasped. "You're kidding! Oh, I'm selling that story to the tabloids!"

"Char!"

"Just kidding. I wouldn't accept money from those rags. I'll merely let the story leak out accidentally."

Emily laughed. If it were gossip about anybody else she'd argue, but Jack liked publicity. "Come have lunch with me."

Charlene started organizing her makeup cases. "Already ate. The pulled pork is awesome."

Emily felt her stomach complain again. She was hungry but not excited about sitting with the other actors. Maybe she could join the rafting guides. Hmm...

Char snapped her fingers in front of Emily's face. "Did you hear me say the pulled pork is awesome?"

Emily blinked. "Oh, yeah. Thanks. Let's do dinner later."

"Sure thing, girl."

Emily headed up the basement stairs to her car. She was starving but needed a sweatshirt to comfortably enjoy her meal. The sunshine peeked through the trees, leaving a checkerboard of light. Now she was warm. Now she wasn't. She wondered what it would be like for the rafting guide to walk through the trees like this without his sunglasses. He'd sneeze every other step.

"Wonder Woman!" A raving fan interrupted her thoughts. "I knew I would see you here. Nobody else believed me."

Emily slowed her pace as a chubby middle-school-aged boy joined her. Her fans came in all shapes and sizes.

"Hi." She smiled kindly before clicking the unlock button on her rental remote and grabbing her mom's bright sweatshirt.

The kid frowned at her. "You look different."

She looked normal. But, for a celebrity, normal was boring.

"I like different." He grinned now, his pudgy face reminding her of the Pillsbury Dough Boy. "I'm kind of different too."

That he was. She held out a hand. "You can call me Emily, instead of Wonder Woman. I left my red boots at home."

A fleshy hand grasped hers hesitantly. "Emily Van Arsdale, I know. You were a great Wonder Woman. I love Wonder Woman. I love all comic book heroes. In fact, I'm named after a character in a comic book."

Emily turned back toward the restaurant. The kid strolled with her. What might his comic book name be? Peter Parker? Clark Kent?

"My name is Jor-El."

What was it with names of Sun Valley residents? She couldn't even remember what the rafting guide was named, so how was she supposed to remember Jor-El?

They stood at the door now. Emily swung it wide, and Jor-El followed her in.

"I can see you don't recognize my name," he continued in a scholarly fashion. "It's the name of Superman's father."

So that's where it came from. "Well, it was nice to meet you,

Jor-El. I'm going to have lunch now. I hope you come see *Whitewater Wedding* when it's in the theaters."

"You bet I will, Emily. Emily? That sounds weird. I've always thought of you as Emily Van Arsdale. I can't believe I'm talking to Emily Van Arsdale. Can I get your autograph? Nobody is going to believe me if I don't." The kid stuffed his hands in his pockets, probably looking for something for her to sign.

Emily sniffed the air and got distracted by the spicy scent of barbecued meat. "I'll leave an autograph for you at the front desk when I'm done eating. Is that a deal?" She still hadn't gotten used to being a celebrity. Rarely could she walk down a sidewalk anonymously anymore.

Jor-El nodded so hard his double chin jiggled.

Without another word, she turned toward the trembling hostess waiting to seat her. Goodness, she wasn't a real superhero. Only human. It was always astonishing to her the nervousness she caused in others. And what else could she say to Jor-El? "See you later" wouldn't work, because he'd actually expect to see her later.

The hostess led her toward the table with the other actors. Catching the woman's arm, she conferred quietly. "I'd rather sit by myself, if you don't mind. I'm exhausted and need some peace and quiet."

"Yes, ma'am." The woman jerked her head back and forth looking for an empty table. "How about outside?"

Emily sighed, grateful it hadn't been a big deal. "Sure."

The tittering of excited patrons followed her advancement across the room. She nodded pleasantly as she passed. Maybe she had grown up in Idaho, but nothing was the same anymore. They stepped onto the weathered deck.

"Will this work?"

"Perfect." Emily sank down onto the bench and swung her legs underneath the table, hoping she didn't just give herself a splinter in the butt. She gazed out over the river, then caught sight of the cute guide rinsing off a raft.

The hostess followed the direction of her gaze. "Did you meet Tracen?"

Tracen. "Yes." She smiled to herself at the thought of how much better the man had gotten acquainted with Jack than her.

Tracen turned then and headed up the hill. Emily had to admit her curiosity was piqued. "How long has he worked here?"

The hostess didn't seem too eager to get back to her other customers. "Practically all his life. That's how he got the scar on his torso."

So it was a scar. Emily faced the hostess so the rafting guide wouldn't catch her staring. "It's a big scar." Emily quickly decided to edit her words. She didn't want to seem judgmental. Funny thing, though, she was usually the one being judged. "It adds personality. Otherwise he'd be too perfect."

The hostess's jitters seemed to calm. She spoke quietly. "Well, don't get yourself interested in him. You're not his type."

Emily tucked a stray curl behind her ear. This was the second time she'd heard the warning within the last hour. "Is he single?" She wouldn't have even thought to ask this before, but with every statement meant to discourage her attraction, she became more fascinated.

The hostess pressed her lips together. "He is. But like I said, he won't have anything to do with you."

"Huh." Hadn't he laughed with her on the raft? And grabbed her arm in an attempt to save her? What was it about her that the Sun Valley residents thought he'd find so detestable?

"I'll be right back with some water and rolls."

She shouldn't let it eat at her. "Okay. Only, I don't…"

The woman retreated, leaving Emily to the breeze and the birds. A chipmunk chirped from a tree overhead. Then the sound of voices from the lobby filtered through the white noise of the river.

"I met Wonder Woman." The pre-pubescent voice had to be Jor-El. Yes! She remembered his name.

"You did not, dork."

"I did too. I shook hands with her, and she is going to leave me her autograph after she eats."

Emily tilted her head to rub the tension out of the back of her neck.

"Prove it, fatty. Go talk to her right now."

Emily closed her eyes. Kids could be so cruel. And it wasn't just one kid's voice she heard. They were ganging up on Jor-El. So that's what he meant about being different.

"I can't do that. She's eating." Jor-El's voice sounded whiny and desperate.

"Whatever. You're afraid, because you really don't know her."

Jor-El sniffed—an I'm-not-going-to-let-you-see-me-cry sniff. "I just met her. And I don't have to prove it now. I'll show you the autograph when I get it."

Laughter erupted from the inside of the open sliding glass door. It was the laughing-at kind, not the laughing-with.

"I'll bet he fakes the signature."

Enough was enough. Emily stood up and headed toward the door, the heels of her flip-flops slapping against her feet. She was going to teach those bullies a lesson. She sent up a silent prayer, thanking God she remembered the kid's name.

Tossing her half-dry hair out of her face, she stepped into the doorway. The arguing stopped.

"Hi, boys."

All jaws dropped. But the jaw Emily noticed first didn't belong to a boy. The rafting guide stood at the cashier's counter watching her.

* * * * *

Tracen had been ready to interrupt the bullying when Emily Van Arsdale arrived. Her eyes only flicked up to his for a second. Then she turned coldly toward the brats who mocked Jor-El.

She'd changed from the ripped costume into a floral dress that wrapped around the back of her neck. It matched her pink flip-flops, but not the BSU hoodie she wore over it. Her hair was a rat's nest of dark curls and not a trace of makeup remained after her swim, but she looked regal standing there. He briefly wondered why she wasn't sitting with pretty boy Jack Jamison. Then she spoke and gave him a whole new set of questions to wonder about.

"Jor-El," she began, speaking with familiarity, "would you like to join me for lunch?"

Her right cheek twitched as if she were trying not to smile. So the kid wasn't lying when he said he'd met her.

Jor-El jumped up from the couch in front of the fireplace. "I would love to, Emily."

Emily? Not Ms. Van Arsdale? Not Wonder Woman?

Emily lowered her eyes to the boys still on the couch. "Jor-El is a great name, isn't it? Very strong and unique. He knows who he is, and he doesn't have to make fun of others to feel better about himself."

Ouch. The brats wouldn't likely forget that lecture. It reminded Tracen of the end of his favorite cartoons when he was a kid. G.I. Joe would show up and give a short lesson in tooth brushing or talking to strangers. *And knowing is half the battle.*

The actress paused to wait for Jor-El to walk across the room toward her. Her eyes met Tracen's again. He gave a salute, still thinking of G.I. Joe. The actress's lips quirked up, but it wasn't quite a full-on smile. She seemed to study him before turning and looping her arm through Jor-El's.

The kid didn't know how lucky he was. And the woman wasn't what he would have expected.

She gave all her attention to the boy. "Would you like my rolls? The hostess said she was bringing me some, but I can't eat them."

Darn, a Hollywood diet. Maybe she wasn't that different from his ex, after all.

Chapter Four

....

The night of sleep brought the rest she needed. But it also left Emily stiffer than she expected. She rolled her head from shoulder to shoulder before climbing into the rafting van.

Today they would be shooting on more treacherous waters downriver. The thought sent a delicious chill up Emily's spine. Her mother would be proud of the way she had learned to manipulate her body in a fall.

The other actors climbed into the van. Rafter Boy took the wheel. Today he was definitely aloof, the way Braid Lady and Hostess had predicted, but at the restaurant yesterday, he'd saluted her. Maybe the gesture was empty. She had to find out for sure.

Sitting behind him, she couldn't catch his eye in the rearview mirror because he was wearing sunglasses again. She slipped her own onto her nose and, for a brief second, thought she spotted the same little smirk on his face that she had given him yesterday—the look that said, "I know you're watching me from behind your shades." He was right. But had she been?

The drive took them back the way she had driven yesterday. Sun Valley was located close to the Salmon River and an abundance of alpine lakes. Though Dad had never taken her snow skiing in Sun Valley, she'd once gone on a youth group wakeboarding trip to Redfish Lake. The memories were some of her favorites.

Water was a powerful substance. It could bring life or destruction. *Living water. River of life. His rule will extend from sea to sea.* Water was actually what covered the earth on the first day God created it. Interesting. She'd never put all the verses on water together before. She'd have to do a Bible study on it, since it seemed to be a current theme in her life.

The van rumbled to a stop. She glanced into the rearview mirror to find another pair of sunglasses already reflected there. Maybe he was looking at her, maybe he wasn't. But the chill that ran up her back earlier turned warm.

"Let's go, people!" Bruce pulled open the van door. "Have a once over with makeup, then get down to the river."

Emily followed the others out. Rafter Boy stopped each one by one to check their life vests, which their characters had conveniently found stored in the raft cooler the next day. He sauntered over as Emily climbed out.

"Are you cinched up tight?" he asked.

Emily paused for inspection. "I think I'll be fine. But you might want to double-check Jack's vest."

The guide gave a little snort as his deft fingers squeezed each of the clasps across her torso. Emily looked up at him. He was taller then she remembered, but then she hadn't stood face-to-face with him before. He slipped fingers underneath the vest above each of her shoulders and lifted. It stayed in place.

"You're good to go," he commented without making eye contact —or would that be glasses contact?

So maybe Hostess was right. He wasn't interested. But that's what Emily found so intriguing.

He turned to leave. At least she could be polite. "Thanks, Sonny."

Sonny paused and turned back toward her. Oh, no. His name wasn't Sonny. What was it?

"Sonny?" An eyebrow lifted above the frame of his Oakleys. "I thought only old women used that term."

Shoot. "Um, what was your name again? I remember it had the word *sun* in it because you're allergic to the sun."

He carelessly pulled his shirt over his head and grabbed a life vest of his own. "So you know what I'm allergic to, but you don't know my name?"

He made her sound stuck-up. Like she didn't care to remember people's names, only their shortcomings. Well, she'd definitely remember that scar along his ribcage, though she didn't consider it a shortcoming at all. He had her all wrong. "I remember your allergy because of the cute way you were sneezing yesterday. But I can't seem to remember your name because I've never heard it before. So can you refresh my memory…Sonny?"

A deft hand ran through the sun-bleached strands of his sandy brown hair. "I suppose I've been called worse. And we haven't really been introduced." His hand continued through his hair to extend towards Emily. "The name is Tracen."

"Tracen." She slipped her smaller hand into his. How could she forget a name like Tracen? It was strong and unique, just like Jor-El. But she should still connect it to another word besides sun—just in case. "Like tracing."

Without thinking, she pulled her hand out of his and reached toward his scar. Her finger traced the line down the muscles covering his ribs.

* * * * *

Tracen's hand caught her soft one, and he removed it from his skin. What was she thinking? Well, he probably knew exactly what she was thinking. And now she had him thinking the same thing. "Can you remember my name now?"

"Oh. Yeah." She snatched both her hands toward her chest and clasped them over her heart. "I'm sorry." She apologized for the touch but continued infringing on his personal life. She motioned to the scar with a nod. "What happened?"

Tracen gave what he hoped resembled a distracted shrug. "Rafting when I was younger. I got cocky and thought I could handle a class six."

Emily nodded, and he felt her studying him through her glasses. "So that's why you're so uptight about safety."

Uptight? He'd never been called *uptight* before. "You've figured me out."

"Actually"—the actress crossed her arms—"there's something I can't figure out."

Tracen had a sudden urge to retreat. First, she was making up nicknames for him. Then she was touching him. Now she was asking deep questions. Did he mention she had touched him? What next? "Really?"

"Yeah." Emily quirked her full lips.

She probably had this effect on all men. He knew Jack Jamison was already bewitched. This was not what Tracen needed.

"See, I had two different people tell me yesterday that you would not be interested in me. Now why would they both say that? Just because I told them I think you're adorable. Maybe I think you're adorable like a puppy dog. Yet they acted like they needed to protect you from me."

He didn't know exactly who Emily had talked to, but he knew exactly why they would respond that way. And it wasn't something he wanted to talk about.

Emily now played with her springy ponytail. Was she nervous? Did she really think he was puppy dog adorable, or was it more than that? Did it matter?

Before he could respond, Emily continued. "What is it about me that would automatically get my name crossed off your to-date list?"

Tracen ran a hand across his mouth to hide a smile. Yes, he was smiling. It was funny how she phrased the question. What was not funny was his answer. He looked down at her and tried to think of a different excuse. Man, she was short. His answer to her question came out of desperation. "Your height."

Emily didn't move. He guessed she was just as stunned as he was by what he had said. Too short? Now there was a lame excuse. Abort! Abort!

Tracen turned to walk down the path the way everybody else had already gone.

Emily's small strides rushed to match his. "Height? You're telling me everybody in town knows you don't date short people?"

Tracen gave a noncommittal toss of his head. "Weird, isn't it?" It was more than weird. It was untrue. But hopefully it would keep her away.

Emily rubbed the back of her neck. "Yeah, it is. You're prejudiced."

That stopped him. "Not really. I don't hold anything against you.

I simply think that when God made the perfect woman for me, he made her my size." Oh, now he was pulling God into this. He sent a short prayer up to heaven. *My bad.*

Emily's glasses came off. "So you've never been attracted to a petite woman?"

Her eyes bored into him like lasers. And as much as he wanted to tear his gaze from hers, she held him entranced. What had she asked? And why were the apples of her cheeks starting to grow larger the longer he stared at her? She had amazing cheekbones. The perfect size to stroke his thumb over...

Perfect size? Isn't that what he had just said she was not?

Emily tilted her head. "I think I have my answer."

Chapter Five
....

Emily's cheeks hurt as she tried to control her smile. The guy was attracted to her all right. Only he wasn't pursuing her the way most men did. For some reason she found that fact as refreshing as a dip in the river.

"What?" Tracen's voice held a hint of amusement. "You don't have enough lovestruck fans already? You want me to join in and declare my adoration?"

His sarcasm was delightful. "Maybe."

"Emily Van Arsdale!" Char's commanding voice called from her makeup station nearby. "What is taking you so long, girl? Do you want to delay another day's shooting schedule?"

Emily glanced over her shoulder to mentally calculate how much time she had before the makeup artist dragged her away by her hair. Subtlety wasn't one of Charlene's strong suits.

She grinned at Tracen. Dang those dark glasses. They kept her from reading his expression.

Tracen finally gave a nonchalant shrug. "Come on, we've got work to do." As he stepped past her, he added, "Anyway, you know you're cute. Why do you need to hear me say it?"

But he did say it, and the words warmed Emily like sunshine. He thought she was cute. She wanted to giggle, which was definitely out of character. She watched Tracen strut away.

Charlene's face appeared in front of Emily. "What are you smiling about?"

Emily pressed her lips together but couldn't keep the corners of her mouth from turning up. Oh well. She might as well tell Char why. "Tracen said I'm cute."

"Pshah!" Char waved a hand with attitude. "Cute? Babies are cute. Girl, let's get you glammed up."

Emily followed obediently and sat down in a swivel chair completely out of place in the forest surrounding them. The foundation Char spread on her face had the consistency of frosting and smelled dry and sterilized. If this was what it took to be glamorous, she'd go for cute any day.

"Char?"

"We'll use waterproof mascara. I don't want you to have raccoon eyes when you get wet."

"Uh, great." Emily watched Tracen direct the placement of the raft at the river's edge. "Do you think Tracen is too tall for me?"

"What? Who's too tall?" Char rummaged through her makeup brush collection. "You're talking about the rafting guide again?"

"He said he doesn't date petite women."

Char paused. "You asked him out?"

Emily laughed but wouldn't meet Char's eyes. "No."

"Ah!" Char clapped, causing powder to puff up from the fluffy brush in her hands. "But you want *him* to ask *you* out. This is fantastic. My little Emily finally has a crush on a boy."

Emily reached out to hold her friend's hands still. "Stop. You didn't even answer my question."

Charlene went back to work, rubbing the soft bristles across

Emily's forehead and chin. "What question was that? You wanna know if the rafting guide is too tall for you? Of course not. Look at Will and Jada."

Will Smith. The makeup artist read too many tabloids. Or maybe she'd actually met the couple and "glammed" them up.

Emily's glance returned to the water. Now Tracen was talking to Jack—not the best combination. She hoped Jack wasn't trying to stake claim to her again.

Char followed her line of sight. "He *is* ruggedly handsome."

A sigh escaped on Emily's breath.

Char must have felt the heavy exhale as she swiped on Emily's lip gloss. "Uh-oh. What are you thinking? You gonna buy some platform shoes to make yourself taller?"

Emily shot her friend a wry smile. "Yes, I'm going to wear platform shoes on the raft."

Char chuckled. "Why not? They already have you in a wedding dress. You can do anything in the movies these days."

Bruce's bullhorn interrupted the conversation. "Attention please. I need my actors. Gather round."

Emily rose from her chair and headed toward the director. Jack and Tracen came from the other direction, Jack's arm wrapped up and over Tracen's shoulder. *That* was unexpected. She tried to catch Tracen's attention to share the humor in his situation, but as soon as his gaze met hers, he turned and shot up the embankment. Emily watched in confusion until Bruce's voice drew her attention. Tracen was probably just after another safety device of some sort.

"Emily? Are you ready?" Bruce asked.

Emily squared her shoulders, adjusting her mindset to the day's activities. "Yes."

Bruce pointed out over the water. "See that first peak of white-water? After the raft hits it, I want you to fall out to the right side. Just make sure you arch back so it looks like you are out of control, then hinge at the hips so you land fanny first."

"Right." Emily studied the location on the water, imagining herself going through the moves.

"Jack's stunt double will jump out after you," Bruce continued. "Just act as if you're drowning, and let him drag you to shore."

Emily nodded at the stunt double. Jack wouldn't even have to get wet until the next scene. *My hero.*

Bruce barked into the bullhorn again, sending grips scrambling. Emily climbed into the raft and straddled the side the way Tracen had instructed her the day before. Where was Tracen, anyway?

* * * * *

Tracen conferred with the director before setting up the raft's location. Apparently they were filming a stunt, and he'd only have to guide the raft through one rapid before beaching it again. A snap compared to the catastrophe he'd created the day before.

Jack Jamison even had a stuntman filling in for him. Tracen breathed easy. Surely the double knew what he was doing.

Tracen glanced over at Emily in her makeup chair. He'd told her she was cute. He shouldn't have done that. But it was more than her appearance that he found alluring. She had an adventurous personality blended with an unexpected sense of dignity and a contagious smile. Good thing she was short, or he might not have come up with an excuse for snubbing her. Only…her size somehow made her even more of an anomaly. He wanted to protect her, while knowing full well she was capable of looking out for herself.

"Tracen, my man."

Tracen glanced up in time to see Jack trotting down the hill toward him. Jack slapped a hand on his back.

Tracen arched an eyebrow. The famous actor suddenly wanted to be buddy-buddy?

"Hi, Jack." Tracen scanned the area for somebody who might resemble the actor. "I didn't think you had to be here this morning. Don't you have a stuntman filling in for you?"

"Oh, yeah." Jack dragged his words out in a gravelly voice, exuding enthusiasm. "But once my double makes it to shore, I get to take over."

Tracen flipped the raft to dump out excess water before repositioning it. "Sounds like a cushy job."

Jack even laughed with enthusiasm. "Oh, I couldn't do what you do. You were amazing yesterday. You saved my life. I seriously thought I was going to get knocked unconscious by that huge rock, and y'all would find my body downstream next week." Jack spread a hand across his chest as if gratefulness came from his heart. "And after the way I acted yesterday…"

"No kidding." Tracen grunted. "If they hadn't been paying me to keep you safe, you'd still be out there."

Jack slapped his thigh. "I'm sorry, man. I've been kind of irritable because Emily won't go out with me. Let me make it up to you. I'll buy you a drink at The Point tonight."

Who was this guy? And was he telling the truth about Emily?

Tracen found the satisfaction that came with Jack's story to be disturbing. Well, it didn't matter. The cast and crew would all be headed back to Hollywood within a month.

A bullhorn blared. "Attention please. I need my actors. Gather round."

Tracen hesitated at Bruce's call to action. He wasn't an actor, but he'd be on the raft. Should he join in? Emily would be there, so maybe he shouldn't.

"That's you, man." Jack wrapped a friendly arm up around Tracen's shoulders and pulled him toward the small group gathering.

Yep, there she was, glowing with cosmetics. Her makeup artist had turned her into the image of perfection, but Tracen preferred her fresh-faced. He looked away.

A flash of color by the road caught his attention. He squinted into the sunlight and focused. It couldn't be.

Jerking away from Jack's hold, Tracen scaled up the hill. He'd have to be quick because they were filming soon.

"Jor-El?" The kid was on his unicycle. Unbelievable.

Jor-El dropped to the ground and grabbed the seat of his unicycle in one smooth movement. The coordination was impressive but also out of place.

Security stopped the kid at the road. "You can't go down there."

"It's okay." Jor-El tried to step past the crewmember. "I'm friends with Emily Van Arsdale."

The security guy blocked the kid's progress with arms crossed. "I didn't get any authorization from Miss Van Arsdale."

Tracen huffed with exertion by the time he reached the road. "The kid's with me," he said between gulps for air.

Jor-El's eyes grew wide, then he glared back at the security guard as if to say, "I told you so."

Pulse slowing, Tracen shook his head and walked the boy away from the film location. "But you're not joining us, Jor-El."

"What? I rode all the way out here—"

"I see that." Tracen eyed the unicycle. "Not your wisest idea."

"Please, Tracen. Emily would let me. You saw how she invited me to eat lunch with her yesterday." His voice turned whiny.

"Well, today she's working." Tracen continued to walk the boy away from the crew.

Jor-El stopped. "You want me to go home?"

"Yes."

"I can't. This is my dream come true. A real, live comic book hero has come to town. I can't let this chance pass me by."

Tracen wrinkled his brow and shook his head in exasperation. "A chance for what?"

"I don't know."

"Look." Tracen motioned toward the film crew. "Emily can't let every comic book fan join her. You got to eat lunch with her yesterday. That's more than most people get to do."

"Please, Tracen, I'm not going to get in the way. I just wanna watch. I don't have anything else to do today. I'm sure—"

"You need to leave right now, Jor-El." Tracen crossed his arms, feeling much like the cold security guard who already tried to get rid of the kid. He could do better than that for a neighbor, couldn't he? "But I'll talk to Emily and see if there's another time you can watch the filming."

The kid's face lit up. "Awesome. This is the best summer ever. I can't wait to—"

"Go!" Tracen pointed down the road. "And don't let me catch you riding your unicycle out of town anymore. These roads aren't safe."

Tracen descended back toward the raft. Emily sat straddling the right side. She wasn't relaxed the way she had been before. Her spine held her body tall, and her head whipped around with the excitement of a puppy dog's tail. When she spotted Tracen, she bounced up and down in her seat.

* * * * *

Emily's heart raced with the high of preparing for a stunt. She felt alive, as if her skin could barely contain the adrenaline that surged within. She was ready to go. If Tracen didn't get there soon, she was going to shove off and demand he be written out of the scene. Of course, it would be more fun if he were there to share the excitement.

Oh! There he was. Her thighs flexed and relaxed in preparation, causing her to bounce on the inflated raft. This is when her actions became uncensored. Since she'd deliberately be putting herself in harm's way, she had to switch off the filter that would keep her acting sensibly.

Waving a paddle, she taunted, "One might expect you to get here faster with those long legs of yours."

Tracen hopped into the paddleboat and sat down in one motion. "Are we talking about height again, Shorty?"

Emily's guffaw turned into a grin. "Actually, we're talking about timing. Where've you been?"

Tracen motioned toward the hill with his head. "Jor-El wanted to watch the show. I told him he needed to get your permission first."

Emily peered up past the trees. No Jor-El. Too bad he'd already left. Stunts were what she did best and what a comic book fan would enjoy the most. "Do you have his phone number? I'll have to call him."

Tracen gave a belly laugh, causing Emily to frown. "What?"

Tracen grabbed an oar as he shot her a smile. "The kid's in love with you, that's all."

Emily rolled her eyes. "No, he's in love with Wonder Woman. Most men are." Everybody except Tracen. "You didn't see my first movie, did you?"

"I fell asleep at the theater."

Emily gasped. "You did not."

Tracen chuckled but didn't have a chance to respond.

Bruce's bullhorn blared. "Ready?"

Emily pushed away thoughts of Wonder Woman and Tracen. She nodded once at Dave, Jack's stunt double. They'd already rehearsed how he was going to grab her after she "fell" overboard, though you never really could plan a stunt. Whatever happened, happened.

"Rolling!"

Tracen pulled his oar up from underneath the water. He'd been using it to anchor them in place. The waves came without warning. Emily squeezed her inner thighs against rubber. She didn't want to get tossed until she was supposed to.

The raft bobbed and spun, the current fighting itself to pull them under and forward at the same time. The stinging cold water frothed around Emily's right leg, the slapping of its waves a warning of what was to come.

She marked her spot downstream, ignoring the present pounding she was receiving from the river. It would all happen so fast. She had to be ready.

Flexing every muscle in her body, she crouched, ready to spring. Time was up. Dramatically throwing her body forward, she reversed directions as if her torso was a pendulum, arching her back and pushing against the bottom of the raft. Letting go of her paddle, she surrendered to gravity and folded herself into a loose pike so her hips hit the water first. She barely had time to catch her breath before the rest of her body was sucked under as well.

The roaring water gave way to a peaceful gurgle underneath the waves. Her hair floated around her head, dancing to a silent melody. The tranquility shattered as her life vest yanked her back up to the surface. With hair plastered to her face, Emily fought the current that juggled her. The waves snaked their way up her nostrils and down her throat. She choked and sputtered, looking for Dave. Hopefully he could reach her within range of the cameras.

"Help!" She raised one hand overhead. Pretending to drown didn't take much acting at all, but she didn't want to have to do it for longer than necessary.

Catching sight of the raft, she saw Dave lean toward her in preparation of the rescue. Thank goodness they weren't too far away. But before Dave could dive out, Tracen shoved him back in his seat and, with one mighty pull on his oar, steered the raft adjacent to Emily's body. In the next instant he had his hand on her vest and was dunking her under the surface of the river. Emily didn't have a chance to catch her breath this time.

Water burned her nose, her throat. She clawed at Tracen's arm.

He must have meant to pull her up, not push her down. Though he shouldn't have touched her at all.

Then she was shooting out of the river like a rocket. Tracen had only pushed her under so the life vest would propel her up with more force. He caught her the moment she reappeared and jerked her to safety. Together they slipped down to the bottom of the raft, Emily cradled in his arms.

Coughing, she wiped strands of hair out of her eyes. She leaned back, shivering against the side of the raft and gulping oxygen. Tracen looked just as beat, which was weird since he'd been in the paddleboat the whole time.

The rest of the actors maneuvered them toward shore, jabbering about what had happened. Their voices faded into the background as Tracen flipped his sunglasses onto his forehead.

"You okay?" he asked, his eyes roaming over her face in search of any indication that she needed medical attention.

Emily let out a breathless laugh at her predicament. She was okay—more than okay. But not for the reasons he was asking.

"Dude, *I* was supposed to rescue her," Dave admonished. "You ruined the scene."

Tracen's gaze went hard. He glanced up at the stuntman before locking eyes with Emily. "I must have missed the memo."

Emily made no effort to climb off Tracen's lap. Her limbs still hung limp, recovering from the adrenaline rush. She sprawled sideways, body growing heavier. Tracen didn't attempt to move either, and she couldn't resist shooting him a knowing smile.

Chapter Six

....

Tracen had to run the rapid a couple more times. First so they could reshoot the stunt from a distance. Then they had to do it close up. Now the director was busy arranging cameras for the scene where Jack would drag Emily up to shore. The idea of Jack Jamison rescuing Emily was a joke, but the way Tracen had accidentally rescued her earlier was no laughing matter—though the other rafting guides seemed to find humor in it.

Why couldn't somebody have filled him in on the fact that Emily was planning to throw herself overboard? He knew she used to be a stuntwoman, but he figured now that she'd made a name for herself, a double would be doing anything dangerous.

Well, it was too late now. He couldn't take back his mistake. And he couldn't erase from his memory the expression Emily had shot him when he'd pulled her into his arms. That was the worst of it. Of course, he would have done the same thing for anyone of the crew—it was his job. But he wouldn't have felt the same way with them sprawled across his lap. And she'd known it.

It was a ridiculous attraction. She'd pretty much told him that all men wanted her. The question was, did she treat all men the way she was treating him? The smiles she sent him seemed intimate somehow. Or maybe that was wishful thinking. Or perhaps she really only saw him as a challenge the way he'd suggested. Good thing she would be leaving soon. He didn't need such a complicated distraction.

The other actors bantered back and forth behind him as they carried the raft upstream. Emily and Dave had already swum to shore—for the seventh time. The idea of making movies used to seem like such a glamorous lifestyle, but in reality it was nothing but repetition. And waiting. Waiting for more repetition. At least he got a little break.

The actors dropped the raft and took off for their lunch break. Tracen grabbed his water bottle and joined the other guides, who were only there for the show. Yeah, he'd been the entertainment.

"Where's your girlfriend?" teased Howie. The big man more closely resembled a logger than a rafting guide.

Honey joined in, her braids tucked under a baseball cap today. "You better go make sure she doesn't need any more rescuing."

Tracen sank onto a stump. "Nah. She's a superhero. She'll be fine."

Honey tossed him her bag of trail mix. "Are you gonna be fine?"

Tracen slanted his eyes toward the middle-aged woman. "Why wouldn't I be?"

Honey stood up and wiped pine needles off her rear. "For some reason I thought you'd be avoiding Hollywood starlets. I even told Wonder Woman you wouldn't be interested in her."

So that's who Emily had been talking to. "You know? She mentioned that."

Honey gave a toothy grin. "Am I right?"

Tracen groaned. "You're ridiculous. What are the chances that a movie star would come to a small town like Sun Valley and fall for a local?"

This shouldn't be a big deal. Everyone was making too big of a deal out of it. Out of nothing. Yeah, he'd been hurt before. But he'd learned his lesson. And it wasn't like he even had a chance with the actress.

"Come on." Honey headed toward the river. "I'm in the mood to go pick some huckleberries."

Tracen knew what Honey wanted. Her favorite huckleberry bush was most accessible from the water. He climbed to his feet to take her downstream. "Are you coming, Howie?"

"What?" Howie's low tone teased. "You afraid I'm gonna stay here and make a move on your woman?"

Tracen chuckled at the image of Howie making a move on Emily—the only funny thing about his whole situation. He shook his head and followed Honey. The guide could join them if he wanted, but Tracen wasn't going to stick around to be the butt of any more of his jokes. Turning a corner in the path, he slowed at the sight of Emily seated on a rock in the sunshine. He couldn't get away from her. It was as if his thoughts conjured her up every time. Hopefully she hadn't heard his conversation.

The actress had changed into shorts and a tank top, but her skin still glistened with moisture. Her smile was just as slick. She gestured past him toward Howie, who had apparently decided to follow.

"Who are you going to make a move on?" she asked him sweetly. *Mercy.* She'd overheard and was feigning innocence.

Tracen's best bet was to feign innocence, as well. Though he really felt like kicking something—Howie's backside would do. He tilted his head toward his friend and pasted on a smile. Emily couldn't see the dare in his glare. "Yes, Howie, who are you making a move on?"

Howie's normally ruddy face now resembled a ripening tomato. "Uh, nobody?"

"Oh, that's too bad," Emily purred. "You're a handsome guy. Some woman out there is going to be awfully disappointed."

Tracen rolled his eyes heavenward and shook his head at Howie's reaction. The rafting guide's chest puffed out far enough to rival his beer belly. Flattery would get Emily anywhere with him.

"Do you want to come pick huckleberries with us?" Howie's invitation exploded like a bomb before Tracen could defuse it.

Maybe he could still prevent the disaster. "Emily is working, remember?"

Howie looked down, as if he were a kid being chastised. "Oh, yeah."

"Actually…" Emily's one word drew all of Tracen's attention. He held his breath. "One of Bruce's cameras just broke. He's sending a grip into town to pick up another part. That gives me plenty of time to pick huckleberries."

* * * * *

Emily saw Braid Lady (now Baseball Cap Lady) send Tracen a questioning look as they joined her at the raft. The man shrugged his wide shoulders, waiting quietly for Emily to hop in. The other two guides sat together, and Tracen swung a leg up to straddle the raft behind her. The awareness of his proximity felt like static electricity. And he leaned even closer to push them away from the bank.

"So, you like huckleberries?" Baseball Cap Lady asked Emily.

Emily turned her head to face the woman. She could respond, have a normal conversation. All she had to do was block out any thoughts of Tracen. "Mmm...yeah." Huckleberries. She was talking about huckleberries. "I especially like taking a raft to pick them."

Baseball Cap Lady smiled. "I like you." She let go of her oar with one hand to reach across the raft and shake. "My name's Honey Christiansen. I know we spoke yesterday"—her eyes slid back toward Tracen—"but I didn't get to introduce myself."

Ah, that's why Tracen had called her "Honey." It wasn't an endearment—it was her name. So what was with the look she sent him?

"And I'm Howie Christiansen." The big man reached over to grab her hand, as well. His shake was firmer, almost painful.

Emily nodded. Honey and Howie. Howie and Honey. They had the same last name. Were they married? Or brother and sister? She opened her mouth to ask, but Honey spoke first.

"And you are Emily Van Arsdale."

"Oh, yes!" That was rude to assume they knew her name, even if they did. "Nice to meet you."

"Hard right," Tracen grunted.

Emily gripped her paddle with both hands and dug into the heavy waves. An inlet with water as smooth as glass rushed toward them. "Is that where we're going?"

"If we can get there." The current threatened to push them past.

Emily pulled on her oar, testing her shoulder muscles. Wasn't she freezing cold a moment earlier, and now the moisture on her skin was from beads of sweat?

The front of the raft kissed the mouth of the inlet, but the current attempted to pull them away. Emily whipped the oar in and out of the water, trying to resist the force of nature with greater speed.

Then she felt another force press against her. This time it was Tracen's warm, hard chest pressing into her back. She had no choice but to lean forward, straining her neck to get her head out of his way. What was the man doing?

"Grab on!" he growled in her ear, his arms reaching around her.

A tree branch scratched her arm—a tree branch Tracen was pulling. Emily mimicked his actions, grasping at leaves and stems and anything else that could be used like a rope to pull them towards the shore. The work took all her physical effort, but her mind still had time to wonder if the musky scent that surrounded her was from nature or the nature lover.

She didn't have time to figure out the answer before the paddleboat glided into the peacefulness of the alcove. After rafting the waves, she'd forgotten how silky a body of water could be.

The river raged by, but to Emily it seemed as if time stood still for the four of them. She held her paddle across her lap, floating aimlessly.

"Nice work, Shorty."

Emily twisted halfway around to give Tracen an unconcerned smile. "If I'd been any taller, you wouldn't have been able to reach over me for the tree."

"I could have pushed you out of the way."

Howie snorted. "Yeah, right. We know better than that, Tracen. We saw you rescue her earlier."

Honey glanced at Emily. "Huckleberries."

Emily echoed, "Huckleberries!" in good humor at the deliberate change of topic. She shot another knowing grin to Tracen.

Howie maneuvered them closer to an overgrown bush with easy strokes. The smell of the ripe fruit descended with a fog of memories. How long had it been since Emily had picked berries?

Honey pulled the baseball cap from her head and began filling it with the berries. "You boys are invited over for cobbler tonight."

Emily plucked a plump berry and popped it into her mouth. The sweet juice washed over her tongue, reminding her of the even sweeter treat. "My mom used to make cobbler."

Honey tossed a braid. "Well, you can come over for cobbler too, Emily. I just figured you'd be wiped out from filming."

Emily shrugged at the insincere invitation. "Thanks, Honey, but I can't eat cobbler anymore anyway."

"Huh."

Howie pointed overhead. "Look. Somebody put the rope swing back up."

All faces tilted toward the canopy of leaves overhead.

"All right!" Honey placed her hat full of berries on the bottom of the paddleboat and began rowing toward a level embankment.

Emily smiled to herself as she helped pull the raft to shore. She was by far the youngest in the group, yet they were all acting like kids. Picking berries. Swinging from ropes. This is why she had to get away from L.A. more often.

Tracen followed Howie and Honey toward a tree with wooden slats nailed to the trunk like a ladder. He looked over his shoulder at Emily. "You coming?"

Emily skipped to keep up with his long stride. "Of course." Was that a satisfied smile she saw on his lips as he began to climb?

Howie swung from the tree like Tarzan, yelling the whole way. Water splashed up, the tiny drips stinging like a snowstorm.

Honey's dismount from the rope involved a cannonball. "How old is she?" Emily asked in disbelief.

Tracen stepped out on a thick branch above her head. Finding his balance, he gripped both hands around the rope. "I believe we've celebrated her fortieth birthday three years in a row now."

"Amazing."

"You wanna see amazing?" Tracen grinned down at her. "Watch this."

Emily loved his desire for her attention. It was a little juvenile, like pulling on pigtails, but hey, they *were* playing on a swing. "I'm watching."

Tracen pushed from the branch, sailed as far as the rope would let him, then released with a twist that propelled him all the way to the middle of the lagoon.

"Woo-hoo!" Howie and Honey hollered while wading into a shallow area.

Emily pulled herself up to the thick branch that ran parallel to the ground. The tough bark pricked at her bare feet. Hanging on with one hand, she reached out to catch the rope as it swung back in her direction. Curling her fingers around its coarseness, she watched as Tracen swam to shore.

"Not bad," she called.

Tracen turned over on his back. "Try to beat it!"

The little butterflies that usually accompanied her when

performing stunts were back in her chest. The butterflies liked a challenge.

As if one with the rope, Emily pushed away from the tree and let gravity pull her toward the water. Reaching the lowest point, Emily began to swing up higher, and as she did she pulled her legs up, as well. The momentum caused her to rotate upside down. Letting go of her cramping grip on the rope, Emily continued her flip and sailed feet-first down into the river.

The water welcomed her like a blast from a fire hose. Blowing bubbles, she swam the breaststroke underwater toward shore. The shouts from Howie sounded distant until she reached the surface.

The big man pumped a fist in the air. "What was that?"

Honey turned toward the tree to jump again. "She's a stunt-woman, Howie. She gets paid to do stuff like that."

Howie high-fived Emily as she trudged to land, then raced to catch up with...his wife? sister?

Tracen sat in the raft, drying his face with the shirt he'd previously removed. "I guess I asked for you to show me up in front of my employees."

Emily wrung her hair out before joining him. "I didn't hurt your ego too much, did I?"

"Nah." He waved a hand dismissively. "Though I'm curious as to how you became a stuntwoman."

Emily took a deep breath, wondering how much she should reveal. It wasn't that she didn't want to get to know Tracen better, but Howie and Honey could pop back into the picture anytime, so she'd keep her answers simple.

"My first stunt was for a stupid TV show about lifeguards. I had to fall out of a boat." Emily leaned back and let the sun warm her skin. "I was so excited about that little part, even though it's nothing compared to what I'm doing now."

* * * * *

Tracen cocked his head. He had trouble reading her. If she was so ambitious, why was she hanging out with a bunch of river guides? "Yeah, you've really moved up in the world. Now you get to fall out of rafts instead of boats."

Emily's laugh made him smile inside. It was so light and carefree. "All in a day's work."

Tracen rubbed a hand along his prickly jaw. He needed to shave. How must he appear to her? Unkempt? Rugged? So very different from what she was probably used to. Her clear blue eyes watched him, waiting. They made him uncomfortable but a little excited at the same time. *Down, boy.* "What else can you do?"

Howie flew over their heads, attempting the flip and ending in a belly flop.

"Ouch." Emily cringed before leaning forward to answer Tracen's question. "Oh, I've fallen off lots of things. A building, a train, a cliff."

Tracen watched his rafting buddy kick toward shore. "So you're kind of a klutz, huh?"

Emily swatted at him. He ignored the impulse to catch her hand and pull her closer. It had been awhile since he'd felt this way about a woman. He liked the feelings, but the woman was too much of a risk.

He watched Honey climb the tree, afraid that if he looked directly at Emily, she'd be able to read his attraction. Though it wasn't as if he'd been doing a great job of hiding it. He smiled as Honey swooped through the sky like a hawk—much more graceful than her counterpart.

Emily smiled at his smile. "She's pretty good. If you're not careful, you're going to lose a rafting guide to Hollywood."

Tracen grunted. He knew all about losing someone to Hollywood. What had they been talking about before Honey caused the change in subject? Oh yeah. "What was your favorite stunt?"

"My favorite?" Emily paused, her eyes rolling toward the few clouds in the bright sky. "I love gymnastics work—back handsprings, tucks, layouts. But right before filming *Wonder Woman* I got to double in a wakeboarding movie. That had to be my favorite."

She seemed so sincere. As if she'd answer any question he asked. And she'd answer thoughtfully. It made *Tracen* think.

Howie flopped over the side of the raft like a fish. Tracen wanted to push him back out, but he should have welcomed the diversion. He looked his buddy over. "You okay?"

Howie rubbed his bulging gut and moaned. "I'm never jumping off a rope swing again." He angled his head toward Emily. "Did you say that you wakeboard?"

Tracen flicked his gaze toward Emily. Was there anything she couldn't do? He turned his back on their conversation to help pull Honey into the raft.

"You're the hero of the day, aren't you?" Honey spoke the words in a teasing voice, but her eyes brimmed with concern. She'd warned Emily away from Tracen for a reason.

"Cool!" Howie's exclamation caught their attention. His eyes crinkled at the corners as Tracen and Honey turned to catch up on the conversation. "Emily said she'd go with us to Redfish Lake tomorrow."

Tracen exhaled. Emily obviously wasn't taking Honey's advice to heart. It was going to be all his job to avoid her. "Don't you have a movie to make?"

Emily tilted her head, her sassy smile only for him. "Tomorrow Jack and my groom are going to be filming their fight scene."

"Perfect!" Howie clapped his hands together. "Emily can help you with your backroll, Tracen."

That's exactly what Tracen wanted—a cute woman teaching him how to flip around on a wakeboard. Those moves were supposed to impress the girl, but only after he'd perfected them.

Honey smashed her lips together and dramatically lifted her brows as if to say to Tracen, "You're on your own now."

Chapter Seven

....

"Hit it!" Emily called from her position floating in the water. She pulled her abs and legs in tight to keep the tip of her wakeboard above the surface. Elbows by her sides, she gripped the nubby rope handle.

The engine revved, matching the race of her pulse. The boat zipped away. The rope pulled taut. First her wakeboard pushed through the water like a snowplow, the board wiggling beneath her bindings. Then her body began to rise, waves slapping her face as if she were back on a raft. Finally, within a matter of seconds, she skimmed across the surface of the lake, the wind breathing life into her pores.

This was why she loved wakeboarding. The speed. The power. The unlimited number of tricks to try. It was all within her control.

And here on Redfish Lake, she had memories. This is where she'd gotten up on skis for the first time. From then on her dad had called her Water Woman. It was too bad he never saw her playing the part of Wonder Woman. He would have been her biggest fan.

Another boat crossed their path, causing Howie to angle his ancient craft closer to shore. Then they were all watching her again— Howie, Honey, and Tracen. It was hard to see them in the sunlight— as if she were looking at an overexposed picture.

She'd wait to get past the other boat's wake before she went for the backroll, but she could do a couple surface tricks in the meantime. Grasping the handle of the rope between her knees, she raised her arms overhead in a Vegas showgirl-like pose. Howie's arm pumped the air with enthusiasm for her no-hander.

The board jerked sideways, causing her arms to fly wide for balance. Okay, she was rusty. Wrapping her fingers around the handle once again, she turned her board at a 90-degree angle to grind the wake.

"Woo-hoo!" Howie hollered.

It was gonna take more than that to get Tracen's approval.

Shooting off toward the left side of the boat, Emily rode back toward the wake with purpose. Wind whipped hair into her face, but that was merely part of the rush. As soon as her wakeboard hit the swell, she pushed with her legs, as if bouncing on a trampoline. Popping off the water, she spun around, letting go with one hand to grab the smooth fiberglass board between her legs on the toeside edge, so she was facing away from the boat in midair. She soared with freedom, releasing her "Indy Grab," and once again gripped the rope handle facing the opposite direction from where she started. Then she let go with the first hand to help stabilize like a bull rider would as her board crashed back down. Knees bent, she held the burning squat until she could reorient herself without fear of wiping out. Not a bad backside 180.

Emily shot a grin towards the boat. Dang, Tracen hadn't even been watching. Howie turned the boat to head straight across the middle of the lake. This was it. She wasn't going to have a better opportunity for a backroll.

Cutting outside the wake, she waited for the board to naturally pull her back in. She held the rope close to her body and leaned away from the boat, the force of gravity adding to her speed. Standing tall, she edged hard until the wave kicked her up into the roll. No, throwing herself out of Tracen's raft had nothing on this rollercoaster ride. Looking over her shoulder and up, she watched the sky fly by until she was facing the water again. Spotting her landing, she came down with a splash. Delicious.

* * * * *

Tracen watched Emily take off. She rotated perfectly. What was he doing so differently that caused him to under rotate every time? Maybe it was their size difference. He had more length and weight to whip around, while she wasn't much bigger than the board itself.

"Ah, yeah!" Howie yelled back to Emily. He'd been watching her every move from the driver's mirror.

Tracen, on the other hand, was very conscientious about not staring. After her amazing backroll, he swiveled his head to take in the beauty surrounding Redfish Lake. In the distance behind the green hills, the Sawtooth Mountains pointed toward the azure sky. He drank in the splendor, letting the majesty fill his soul. How anyone could ever move away from Idaho, he didn't know.

The rumble of Howie's outdated engine quieted to a gurgle, causing Tracen to jerk his head toward the stern of the boat to see if Emily had bailed. Of course she hadn't. She'd simply let go of the rope to sail smoothly to a seated position on the dock by where they'd put in. The girl had wanted to dock start as well, but there had been too many boats around at the time. If she had, though, she would have wakeboarded without ever getting in the water. Now that was impressive.

Honey's eyes caught Tracen's. She'd been watching him watch Emily. "You ready?" she asked, and Tracen didn't know if she was offering him the chance to wakeboard next, or if she was referring to how he was feeling about Emily getting back in the boat with them.

Howie answered for him. "He's ready to drive the boat. I want to board next."

Tracen shrugged for Honey's benefit. "I guess I'm driving."

Howie pulled the boat next to the dock so Emily could hop in. She shook her wet curls like a dog drying off and took the towel Honey extended.

Tracen tried to keep his smile nonchalant. "Not bad."

Howie moved toward the stern so Tracen could take the wheel. He motioned for Emily to sit in the front seat as he plopped onto the backbench by Honey, wrestling to get his life vest fastened. "What Tracen means is that you were incredible."

Tracen narrowed his eyes at his friend. He could speak for himself.

Howie ignored the look. "I want to try that first trick you did, Emily."

Emily shivered and rubbed at the goose bumps on her legs. *Mercy*, the woman even made goose bumps look cute.

"The no-hander?" she yelled over the engine, as Tracen gave it more gas to speed out to an open area of the lake. Howie needed as much room as he could get.

"Yeah, the no-hander. You think I can do it?"

Emily nodded optimistically.

Cutting the engine, Tracen watched Honey help Howie climb down the back ladder until he was bobbing in the water. She plunked the wakeboard in next to him, then raised the orange flag overhead.

Tracen didn't know if Howie would be able to master the no-hander, but he did know that his friend's boarding would be an easy act to follow. Howie would make him look good.

Tracen turned to glance warily over at Emily as she leaned toward him. She smelled of coconut sunblock. How was it they ended up seated next to each other once again? And why could he always sense her proximity without even looking?

He had to remind himself that she was like the chicken pox he got when he was seven. The more you scratched them, the better they felt, but the longer they took to heal.

Emily motioned toward the back of the boat with her head. "Are they a couple?" she asked softly.

The question caught Tracen by surprise. He'd expected her to mention her maneuvers, seeking praise. Besides that, he'd never considered the idea of Howie and Honey becoming more than friends.

Tracen took a deep breath and leaned back in his seat. How could he explain Howie and Honey? "No, they're not a couple. They're like brother and sister. Actually they are brother and sister-in-law. Honey married Howie's brother, Edward. He died a few years ago. Cancer."

Emily's eyes darted away toward the mountains. Usually her eyes danced, but at the moment they seemed especially solemn. In fact, they glistened and reminded Tracen of runny egg whites. Was she going to cry? Tracen blinked and opened his mouth, hoping that something brilliant yet sensitive would come out. No words formed. With four brothers, he didn't have much experience with his sensitive side.

Emily faced him again. The glow of her caring smile left him wondering if what had appeared as a weakness had only been his imagination. "That's sad."

Tracen studied her a moment longer. "Yeah, Edward was a great guy." Tracen swallowed hard, remembering how Edward had joked and laughed until his very last breath. "Without him, Honey didn't know what to do with her life. So I offered her the job as a rafting guide."

Emily's gaze flitted to Honey and back. "What about Howie? How long has he been with you?"

"Howie." Tracen sighed with relief at the change of subject. He couldn't mention Howie without a grin. He ran a hand along the finger grooves on the steering wheel, trying to decide how much to share. After all, he didn't know Emily's faith status. "Howie— Howard—was our pastor when I was a kid. He was fresh out of seminary and full of pompous ideas of religion. I was kind of scared of him, actually."

"No. He was your pastor?" Emily waved away Tracen's words as if she wasn't able to buy them.

"Yeah." Tracen nodded, her disbelief making the story more fun to tell. "I think I was in eighth grade when somebody in the church gave him a jet ski. 'What am I supposed to do with a jet ski?' he asked. 'You could use it for a jet ski ministry,' they answered. So that's what he did. Every Sunday after church he would bring his jet ski out here and give rides to anybody who wanted one. The only catch was they had to listen to him preach about Jesus the whole time."

Emily threw her head back and laughed. "I love it."

Tracen loved her reaction—the way she exposed the graceful curve of her neck, the way her shoulders shook with mirth. She didn't reveal her own beliefs, but at least she didn't get tense at the mention of Christianity. "Yeah, he takes my dog for a ride on his jet ski sometimes too."

Emily's giggles were addicting. "You're kidding."

Tracen shook his head, trying to remember the last time anyone had been so entertained by one of his stories.

"Hey, Captain!" Howie's voice called from the water. "What are you two laughing about?"

Tracen felt Emily turn to look at Howie with him. "You," she said at almost the same time he did. Then her eyes caught his, and he couldn't look away. He had to study them closer to see if they were really a lighter blue than the sky. They belonged in one of his niece's Disney movies.

"That's nice," hollered Howie. "Take advantage of the fact that I'm freezing my tail off in the lake so you can blab all my embarrassing stories."

Tracen dragged his gaze away from Emily. "If you're ready to wakeboard, Howie, just say so. I need some more embarrassing stories to tell about you anyway."

"Shut it," Howie shot back.

Tracen held a hand up to his ear. "Did you say 'hit it?'" Before the older man could answer, he pressed on the throttle.

Emily doubled over, watching Howie try to get up out of the water. She wiped tears from her eyes as Honey raised the orange flag again, and Tracen circled around.

Her contagious laughter made Tracen chuckle as well. "He looks like a walrus trying to wakeboard, doesn't he?"

Emily's laugh turned silent. She could barely get enough air in to breathe, let alone make a sound. She shoved him on the shoulder as if he were the only one making fun of Howie. "You are so mean." She gasped for the next breath.

"I'm only repeating words that came out of his own mouth." Tracen grinned down at her. He could get used to this, but he better not. He motioned toward the back of the boat. "Why don't you go coach him?"

Emily did. And Howie got up on the third try—his average. He never mastered the no-hander, though Honey perfected her flag-waving skills. Between each brief run, Tracen finished the story he'd been telling Emily.

She plopped back into the front seat as Howie readjusted his board. "He's not a pastor anymore?"

Tracen shook his head. "Not in the traditional sense. After seeing how many non-believers he could reach on the lake, he decided to try the river, as well. He started the rafting company I now own. He didn't like the business side and offered me a great price to buy it."

Emily's humor had finally settled down. She studied Tracen with what appeared to be respect. "It's worked out well for both of you."

Tracen shrugged. That's not how Serena had seen his career choice. He revved the engine and pulled Howie another third of the way across the lake before the big guy bit it once again. Tracen ignored Howie's rant about "receiving an enema" to focus back on Emily.

"So what do you do in the winter?" she asked.

Tracen pointed past her to the jagged Sawtooth mountains, still boasting snow between each peak, even in July. "We teach boarding lessons."

Emily's lips hinted at a smile. "Howie too?"

"Howie too." Tracen pretended not to notice how much the rafting guide thrashed about in the water to reach the rope Honey threw him. "He's better on snow."

Emily ran a hand through her tangled locks and looked around. "I forgot how gorgeous it is up here."

Tracen knew how gorgeous the scenery was. It was Emily's pert nose and luscious lips that had all his attention. "You've been to Redfish Lake before?"

"Oh, yeah." Emily turned her attention back to Tracen, forcing him to monitor his expression. "I grew up in Idaho."

So she knew what she was giving up. Yet she chose the smog and traffic jams of Southern California over "Adventures in Living"— as the brochures advertised Idaho. She'd made her choice, just as Serena had.

Tracen stood, ripped off his shirt, and dove overboard, the cool splash of water almost knocking some sense back into him.

* * * * *

Emily blinked at Tracen's hasty exit. Was he hot? Was she supposed to dive into the lake, as well? Or was Tracen going to board with

Howie? That was always fun, though Emily didn't know if the engine to the tiny craft was strong enough to pull both boarders. Howie alone had been almost too much for it to handle.

Howie apparently thought so too. "Dude," he admonished.

"My turn." Tracen called dibs. "Honey, can you toss me a life jacket?"

Emily almost responded before she realized he hadn't been calling her honey. That would have been a little presumptuous.

Howie reached the ladder. "Was I really that painful to watch?" he grumbled.

Tracen stuck his arms into the vest Honey tossed him. He floated on his back and buckled the straps across his long torso, leaving a huge strip of skin above his trunks. He was fascinating to watch, but the sudden shift in behavior baffled her.

His attitude didn't improve much as she coached him on his back-roll. "You under rotated." She leaned over the edge of the boat after he crashed on his first attempt.

"I know." He didn't even look at her.

Maybe he was just humiliated that she could do the trick and he couldn't. "Do you know how to correct it?"

Tracen set up for another run. "Rotate more?" He sounded testy.

Emily stood tall and crossed her arms. "Just keep the rope in tighter." Okay, now she was getting testy. She shouldn't challenge him. Relaxing her posture, she added, "I had the same problem when I first started."

Tracen tossed his head as if shaking water out of his ear. Either he hadn't heard her, or he didn't care to respond. What had happened to the sweet man who talked of Christ and shared her laughter? Hello, Mr. Hyde.

Emily lifted her chin and took her seat. As Tracen attempted the backroll again, it was obvious he'd heard her advice. He landed the flip by holding the rope closer to his body. It wasn't pretty, but he pulled it out. The second time his landing flowed. The third time he owned the move.

Emily cheered along with Howie and Honey. Surely nailing the backroll would put him in a good mood.

But as Howie circled the boat back around in front of the campground, Tracen dropped the rope and mimicked the dock landing she'd previously performed. Only he didn't climb back in the boat afterward. He left the wakeboard and his vest resting on the wooden planks above the water and yelled to Howie that he was headed back to town with somebody else to help them finish painting their house. He didn't speak another word to Emily, and she couldn't tell if he even looked at her with his blasted glasses on. Not the ending to their outing that she'd expected. Not the ending she'd hoped for.

Chapter Eight

Not only had Emily gone wakeboarding when she should have been memorizing lines, but Tracen's early departure had kept her from being able to focus that evening, as well. She moaned the next morning while plopping into Char's chair.

Char gasped. "You've got puffy eyes, girl. I'm going to have to pull out the big guns." She opened a plastic drawer in her pink case to remove a tube of hemorrhoid cream. "Didn't you sleep last night?"

Emily flipped through her "sides" to find the scene with Jack. "I stayed up late trying to learn my lines."

"What?" Char was so full of drama, *she* should have been the actress. "You know them now, don't you?"

Emily bit her lip. "Not as well as I should."

Char's fists found their way to her hips. "Why not?"

"Oh…" Emily looked around the grove as if a good answer to Char's questions would appear. None did. "'Cuz I went to Redfish Lake yesterday."

"Goodness gracious, girl. I'm guessing you went with that Tracen fellow. Hope it was worth it." Char twisted the top off her tube of cream and smeared it under Emily's eyes. She continued her rant, not giving Emily time to respond. Or maybe Emily's response was too slow in coming. "Well, you look over your lines on paper while I take care of the lines on your face."

Emily ignored the herbal smell as she lifted the script so she could read it over Char's hand. She read a sentence then dropped the papers back to her lap. "Won't work."

Char continued to rub at Emily's skin. "Sure it will."

Emily tried to go through the lines in her head. What came next? Ugh. It was going to be a long day.

"I'll have to wait till you're done, Char. Even if I could see my lines over your hand, you know that with my learning style, I need to be moving to memorize something."

Char pulled away and huffed. "Go." She pointed toward the backwoods. "Swing through the trees like Tarzan, or do whatever it is you do when you learn your lines. I don't really buy that 'learning style' stuff, but I can put Jack's makeup on first if that helps you. And I'll be extra slow about it. That hemorrhoid cream needs time to work its magic anyway."

Emily pushed to her feet. She was going to have to cram to make sure she was ready in time. But she could do it. "Thanks, Char. I owe you."

"And don't you forget it. I don't know what you'd do without me."

Emily left Char raving about how if Wonder Woman had a superhero sidekick, she'd be the perfect fit. Escaping the craziness of the film crew, Emily found a clearing where she could focus without distraction. She paced from tree to tree, letting her lines spill from memory, pausing to look up the ones she forgot. As the scene began to form in her head, she found herself moving faster. She circled around a fat tree stump, bounding over the snakelike roots.

She could see the scene in her head. Jack would yell. She'd wave her arms as she argued. He'd grab her wrists to hold her still. Then she'd be in his arms, his lips hovering close to hers. His hazel eyes would caress her face, their golden flecks lighting with awareness. Then they would grow darker as they...*dang*. Jack had blue eyes. She'd been imagining kissing Tracen.

Even when she was practicing her lines, she was still thinking about the rafting guide. With a growl of frustration, Emily charged the largest tree. She didn't slow down as she neared it. Rather, she placed one foot on the thick trunk as if she were going to run right up it, kicked the other leg through, and tucked her body into a flip. Landing on her feet, she found herself face-to-face with Tracen. His startled eyes were definitely hazel.

* * * * *

Tracen swung the axe one last time and felt the satisfying split of the log becoming firewood. Even though Idaho summers were warm, the mornings usually started out chilly. And a roaring fire was always a sure hit with customers hoping for an outdoorsy adventure.

Dropping a couple more sticks for kindling into his pack, he headed back toward The Point, surrounded by the woodsy scent of cedar and pine. He needed the day off from filming. Not only did he have a backlog of bookwork and phone calls to return, but he could use a distraction from the actress with the irresistible smile.

He'd only known her for three days now, but during those three days, she'd been everywhere he went. It was intoxicating. That's why he'd run away from Redfish Lake the day before. Yes, a friend had asked him to help paint his living room, but if his friend hadn't been there, he would have found another excuse for taking off. He felt bad for leaving Howie to remove the boat from the lake by himself, but he was sure Honey understood.

As for Emily, he'd definitely sent her mixed messages, which was another good reason he was glad he wouldn't have to face her today. He needed time to think about what he would say when he saw her again.

But his time was up, because there she was, flying through the air like a wood sprite, landing only a few feet away. Her lips parted in as much surprise as he felt.

This was the last thing Tracen expected when he left The Point to chop wood. The thought caused a chuckle to rumbled in his chest. "What are you doing?" Dare he ask?

Emily stepped backwards, as if embarrassed. The emotion made her even more endearing. "I'm practicing my lines."

Tracen glanced at the tree Emily had pushed off from before flipping through the air. "It looked like you were practicing for a stunt."

"No." Emily shrugged. "The stunts are easy. It's the lines I really have to work on. I can't remember them unless I'm moving while I practice."

Tracen swung his pack to the ground, the weight too much to support while standing still for a discussion. It would have been a good excuse to keep going, but his curiosity kept him from continuing to the lodge. "Shouldn't you know your lines by now?"

"Yeah." Emily's cheekbones popped out as she smiled. "Yeah, I should. But, see, I went wakeboarding yesterday instead of working."

Tracen clicked his tongue. "What'd you do that for?"

Emily's smile turned mischievous. "Well, there was this one guy I wanted to help with his backroll."

Tracen crossed his arms. "Did he get it?"

Emily's eyes lit up as if delighted Tracen chose to play along. "He did." She tilted her chin up. "Then he took off without saying good-bye."

So she'd called him out on the floor, and it wasn't as bad as he'd expected. The words he thought he'd have to take time to consider came easily and truthfully. "He should have at least said thank you."

Emily wandered away, running her fingers through the leaves that waved in the trees. "That would have been nice. Though I don't think he was thankful. He seemed kind of resentful."

Tracen wanted to follow but instead rested one hand on a branch overhead and watched her. "Maybe the guy was dealing with something else you know absolutely nothing about." Oops. That was more than he had wanted to say.

Emily rounded a tree and came back to face him, the teasing twinkle gone from her mesmerizing eyes. "It would have been nice if he had told me, instead of keeping me awake all night wondering."

Tracen had trouble absorbing her words. He'd been up all night too, but he never expected Emily to feel the same way. Wasn't he just a challenge for her? While he ached to hear her words, he needed to ease away from getting his emotions tangled with hers. "I'm sure he'll make it up to you if he can." There. He'd taken the conversation to the tangible.

Emily stopped moving—a rare sight. "Really?"

Her one word caused him to freeze, as well. "What do you want?"

* * * * *

What did she want? She wanted to know what Tracen was dealing with, but obviously he was hesitant to tell her. He just wanted to fix the problem. He'd offered to make it up to her, but how far was he willing to go? The way he grew still when asking what she wanted gave her the impression that she'd do better to ask for something little.

Taking a step forward, Emily moved closer to Tracen. "I know what I want."

Tracen's eyes went on alert. What was he afraid of? What did he think she would ask? She took another step forward. His face turned to stone.

He was shutting down, like he had before diving out of the boat. Could the mysterious "something else" he was dealing with have to do with another woman? Is that why he put up his guard every time she got too close?

The closer Emily got, the higher she had to lift her head to focus on his face. Tracen's gaze was wary.

He cleared his throat, causing his Adam's apple to bob. "What?"

Emily waited a moment before lifting her script between them. "I want to learn my lines. Will you read the scene with me?"

Tracen's nostrils flared as he inhaled. He took the script from her hands, careful not to touch her. "I can do that."

Emily decided not to let him off so easily. Grabbing his free hand, she pulled him toward the stump. His skin felt warm and rough, hinting at the strength it must have taken to split the logs he'd been carrying. His grip was light, but protective at the same time, making Emily think he was hesitant to overdo another rescue. Reluctantly she let go, wishing he would want to continue touching her as much as she wanted him to. Wishing he would cradle her cheek in his palm or run his fingertips along her arms. Her toes tingled at the thought.

"Okay." She stepped up onto the tree stump so her eyes were level with his chin. "Second page."

Tracen looked down at her a moment before lifting the script. "Who am I? Where do I read?"

Emily leaned forward. "Right there." Tracen's breath lifted a curl from her forehead. He was so close. "Right, um…" The warmth spread through her face and down her spine. "It's, uh, Jack's character. I think…" How could she talk when her senses kept her so distracted?

Tracen snapped to attention. "Got it."

Emily straightened, as well. "I'm ready." *Yeah, right.*

Tracen's eyes focused on the paper. "Where's your fiancé?" His voice sounded stiff as he read the line.

Emily made sure she spoke naturally. "He's patching the raft."

Tracen took time to follow the written dialogue. "How are you?" he finally asked.

"I'm scared," Emily answered. "Do you get scared?"

"I'm scared right now." Tracen plodded along.

Emily gave a disbelieving laugh. It must have sounded real, because Tracen looked up to gauge her expression. "What are you scared of?" she asked.

Tracen looked back down. "I'm scared"—he paused as if reading to himself—"that I'm falling for you."

Tracen's words startled her. She hadn't thought this far ahead when she requested he read the script, though he probably thought she did. Her next line popped out. "What?"

Tracen glanced up, then back down. "I've been trying to hide it—especially from myself. But I've had some extra time to think lately. And now I'm thinking that maybe we're here for a reason."

This was just how Emily had imagined it. His hazel eyes with the golden glimmer met hers.

"You and me?" she asked, heart in her throat.

Tracen looked back down at the script. "I know. It doesn't make sense. But can you deny that you feel something for me?"

She couldn't deny it. There was something there. But this is where she flailed her arms and gave excuses. "We're friends. That's all. You've been my closest friend lately. And with all that's gotten our adrenaline pumping, it's natural for feelings to arise. It's just a ridiculous attraction."

Tracen's head lifted. Apparently he was prepared with his next line. "So you are attracted to me," he stated, tone deep.

Goodness, she was attracted to his voice, as well as everything else. She found it hard to breathe. "Yes."

Tracen's eyes searched hers, as if looking for the truth. Jack would do the very same thing, only he would be acting. Tracen's gaze wandered down to her lips. They suddenly felt dry, so Emily licked them. Jack would kiss her here. Had Tracen read that far ahead? Was he going to kiss her because it was in the script? Or was he feeling what she felt?

Tracen blinked and bowed his head to return to the script. So he hadn't read ahead to the kissing part. He'd simply felt the connection between them—as if they were Lady and the Tramp sharing a strand of spaghetti.

Oh no! When he looked back at the script, he'd discover that she blew her line. In the movie her character would lie and respond that "no," she wasn't attracted to Jack. Emily knew the line. What had she been thinking? It was probably obvious to Tracen that she was attracted to him, but she didn't need to be so brash about announcing it.

Hopping down from the stump, she tugged the script out of Tracen's hand. "Thanks!" She made herself sound chipper.

Tracen rocked back on his heels. "Is the scene over?"

A little laugh spilled out of Emily. A nervous laugh that she hoped sounded light. "No." She took a step backward, feeling the air around her grow colder as the distance expanded between them. "But I'm sure you wouldn't want to rehearse the kissing scene." Another giggle. Okay, she needed to go for a mature, teasing tone, not schoolgirl giddy. "Since I'm too short for you and all."

Chapter Nine

....

Bruce's loud cursing from the hotel room next door woke Emily early the next morning. Apparently the director was so used to California sunshine that he hadn't been watching the weather forecast. Beyond his ranting, the dull tap-dancing of a summer drizzle could barely be heard.

At first Emily curled up tighter under the warm covers, planning to sleep the day away, but the caress of rain down the windowpane reminded her of the Bible study she had been wanting to do on the subject of water. She could use some extra time off to catch up with God. And being that she was so close to "home," she should spend another day with her mom, as well.

Emily threw on her favorite yoga pants, grabbed her Bible and journal, and headed to The Point to study in front of the fireplace with a cup of hot tea. She curled into the plush microfiber sofa, wrapped her hands around the steaming mug, and watched the gray world grow soggier through the glass doors. She'd always hated the rain, but this morning it brought needed relief from filming. She couldn't help wondering what Tracen was doing and if he enjoyed rain. He probably did, being the nature boy that he was. The thought brought a smile to her lips. Flipping her Bible open to the concordance, she decided to begin her study with verses on "rain."

The first rain came with the flood. It purified the earth. The second mention of rain came when Elijah prophesied a drought. The lack of rain was a punishment. But then in the book of Matthew, when Jesus spoke about loving your enemy, He used rain as an example: "God causes his sun to rise on the evil and the good, and sends the rain on the righteous and the unrighteous." The whole idea boiled down to the fact that God was in control. Emily grabbed her journal.

Sorry it's been so long, God. How are you? Oh yeah, you're awesome. I knew that. I'm doing pretty well. Just exhausted. Not physically. It's more emotional. You know why. Thank you for your rain. I can really use the rest.

Emily paused and chewed on the tip of her pen. God knew why she was exhausted. He knew more about Tracen than she did. And He was in control. There was nobody better for her to talk to about the rafting guide.

Okay, here's the deal. I can't stop thinking about Tracen. I'm not sure why. I'm usually so focused and independent. But...

Emily grinned at her notebook. She wasn't seeing the college-ruled lines. Memories of every single conversation she'd had with Tracen paraded through her mind.

He makes me laugh. He's so strong, and I don't just mean

physically, though you did a fantastic job when you created him, God. Tracen uses his strength for good. He gives. He saves. (Wasn't that funny when he had to rescue Jack?) He's loyal and steady. And I'm pretty sure he's one of your friends too.

Emily sighed and sank back into the couch cushions. She'd always thought it was silly when girls got all dreamy like this over members of the opposite sex. But there was something different about Tracen. Something that drew her to him.

If God was in control, then He'd planned for her to meet Tracen, right? Or was this infatuation her own creation? She sat back up and propped her notebook on her knees.

A little help here, please. What do you want me to do? Is there a future for me in Sun Valley? Am I supposed to get to know Tracen better? He's a little hesitant for some reason, though oh my goodness, he looks at me like there's nobody else around. Give me some sign, if this is your will.

* * * * *

Tracen pulled the baseball cap lower over his forehead before rushing through the rain from his truck into The Point. He had to put in an order for babyback ribs to be ready when his brother came home from Iraq. And then he needed to spend the day cleaning his house. If his mom found so much as a hand towel out of place, she'd spend her visit reorganizing his linen closet rather than celebrating Sam's return from overseas.

Stepping into the dark entryway, Tracen wiped icy water droplets off his jacket. The smell of sizzling bacon and freshly ground coffee kept him from being completely thorough in his attempt to dry off. He strode through the lobby, knowing he had permission to seat himself, since Gigi would probably be working double duty as hostess and waitress. There weren't many customers, however. Only one woman occupied the lobby. Tracen glanced her way, and his steps slowed down.

Emily sat curled by the fire with a book on her lap and a mug in her hand. She looked so tiny and content, like a little girl on her daddy's lap.

The urge to join her tugged at Tracen, but he continued on his mission, even when she smiled sweetly at whatever it was she was reading. Then she scribbled into a notebook. Maybe she was working on memorizing her lines for the next day. Again, Tracen considered joining her. He'd helped her with her lines the day before. Yeah, that had ended well. He'd almost kissed her.

Tracen took a seat at the bar facing the side wall. Scratching his face, he was able to peek over his hand at where Emily was sitting without looking too conspicuous.

"Take a picture. It will last longer." Honey rattled a shiny white mug against its saucer as she set it on the bar in front of him.

Tracen averted his eyes and scratched up closer to his temple so he couldn't see Emily anymore. "What?"

Honey shot him a disapproving glare.

Tracen focused on his coffee. It took a moment before he realized he'd been served by Honey. "Why are you serving coffee?"

"Gigi's sick." Honey handed him a long, sticky, plastic menu.

Tracen bowed his head as if reading about the steak and eggs, but out of the corner of his eyes he checked to see if Emily was still reading. Maybe she would come over and join him for breakfast.

He heard Honey sigh. "Did you know she was going to be here this morning?" she asked.

Tracen looked up with wide eyes, planning to pretend confusion, but Honey's expression said she saw right through him. "No," he admitted, letting the muscles on his face relax. "I thought she'd be sleeping in."

Honey rubbed at the counter with a rag. "Think about her a lot, do you?"

"I'm trying not to." Tracen shifted in his seat. "Though I am curious as to what she's reading this early in the morning."

"The Bible."

Tracen felt his eyebrows shoot up. "Really?"

"Yup." Honey placed one hand on her hip. "I took over her tea. We talked about it."

"Hmm." Tracen spun his stool so he was now directly facing Emily—not exactly subtle.

Honey tapped the pads of her fingers on the scarred wood countertop. "Did you want to order?"

Tracen nodded distractedly. "I need some ribs for the family reunion." He stood. "But I'll phone the order in later."

A stinging snap of Honey's towel to Tracen's arm drew his attention back. "Hey!" She knew he fought dirty and that she better not start anything.

But Honey had already started her retreat into the kitchen as if afraid he'd Frisbee his saucer at her. "I just want to make sure you know what you're doing."

Tracen rubbed the growing welt on his arm. She sure was feisty this morning. "I've ordered ribs before, Honey."

Honey pulled two plates of biscuits and gravy out from under the warming lamp as the cook rang the bell. "That's not what I'm talking about, Tracen, and you know it." She motioned with her head toward Emily before her swinging hips carried her away.

Tracen grunted. "I know what I'm doing." But did he? "I'm only going to talk to her about the Bible—like you did."

Honey's mouth drew into a grim line as she shot him one last glance before turning on her charm for the young family seated by the window. The couple and their toddler were probably rained out from their campsite. Sun Valley was a tourist town. Nobody ever stayed. Not even for love. Tracen knew that fact all too well.

He must have stood there longer than he realized, contemplating the wisdom of joining Emily, because Honey returned and handed him a pot of hot water. "Make yourself useful, Tracen. Go refill her tea. Then at least she won't know you're approaching her out of interest."

Tracen looked down at the half-empty pot. It was an excuse. "Thanks, Honey." She probably understood his risk better than anyone. After all, she'd also loved and lost before.

Emily was completely absorbed in her notebook as Tracen strode over. She looked so cute in her concentration that he hated to disturb her. He cleared his throat. "Are you ready for a refill?"

Emily glanced up for a second. "Oh yes, thank—" She did a double take. This time her eyes grew wider—if possible. "Oh, thank you. I didn't know you work here too." She slapped her notebook closed.

Tracen leaned over the coffee table to refill her mug, the hot steam collecting on his skin as he poured her tea. "I have my office here for the rafting company, so yes, I do work here, but normally I don't wait tables. I'm just helping out Honey because she's busy this morning." He motioned toward the breakfast bar, though he wished he hadn't. Honey stood still, chewing on a fingernail and staring into space. Real busy.

Emily looked past him to Honey, then smiled with amusement. "Good thing *you're* not too busy. Or I couldn't ask you to join me." She uncurled her legs and scooted to one side of the couch.

Why not? Despite Tracen's efforts to not make himself too available, she obviously knew he was seeking her company. And she was good company. He squatted back onto the sofa, the pot of water still in his hands. "What are you reading?"

Emily turned her slim fuchsia Bible so he could see the cover. "A love letter." Her answer was unexpected, but she probably had a lot of experience with love letters. Jor-El had written at least one that Tracen knew of. And that was before they'd even met this Wonder Woman.

Tracen played along. "A secret admirer?"

Emily waved a hand. "No secret. In fact, I bet you've got the same one."

Tracen nodded, his eyes locking with Emily's. It was like she knew him already. "I do. Though my letter isn't pink."

Emily laughed and relaxed back against the arm of the sofa. "I'm reading about rain. See, I've got this whole water theme going on in my life—rivers, lakes, and rain. I find that if I'm experiencing a particular event in my life, it makes it easier to relate to Bible characters who might have been going through the same thing."

She had a fresh perspective for everything. "I like it."

"And I bet you like the rain too." She did know him.

"Even though it's bad for business, I love it." It was so soothing and peaceful. It washed away dirt and grime. Gave everything a fresh smell. Brought life.

Emily tucked a stray curl behind her ear and focused on him. "So what do you usually do on a day like today? Since you don't have to work."

"Actually, I usually do work on rainy days. It gives me a chance to play catch-up on the books and e-mails. All the stuff I hate about owning a business." Tracen set the pot down. He was obviously going to be staying awhile.

"Usually?" She caught his keyword.

He gave a mysterious smile. "As in not today."

Emily nodded, then helped him along. "Because today you're…"

"Getting ready for my brother to return. The dummy signed up for Reserves during a war. He's flying back from the Middle East this week." Tracen sat up a little straighter. Being related to "the dummy" made him proud. "My whole family is coming out this weekend."

Emily sat up with him. Her expression would have made one think it was her brother returning from overseas. She reached out and squeezed Tracen's shoulder. The touch was electric, but its shock was overlooked because of Emily's excitement. She was being a friend. "Tracen, that's wonderful. I bet your family was worried about his safety. Where are they coming from? Do you have other siblings?"

Tracen made himself comfortable and crossed one ankle over a knee. She wanted to know about his family. She just wanted to hang out. He could do this all day. His mom might end up straightening his linen closet after all.

"I've got four brothers. Sam is the baby. He's going to be moving in with me for a while. The rest scattered after Mom and Dad sold the Christmas tree farm and moved to Florida."

Emily pulled her legs up to sit on her knees facing sideways. She still wasn't at eye level with him. "So you all grew up here?"

It had been good while it lasted. "Home sweet home."

"A Christmas tree farm would be fun."

Serena hadn't thought so. He could have bought the farm from his parents if she had stayed to help. "Christmas Trees by the Lakes," he mused. Now the property was a campsite for RV trailers.

"Oh, were you located up by the alpine lakes?"

"We were." Thoughts of Serena should have pulled him away from the actress. Instead he stayed. Her enthusiasm over his lifestyle kept his anger from taking over. It was silly to think that she was any different from the woman who had hurt him so much, but couldn't he just hang out with her until she confirmed his suspicions? What were they talking about? Oh yeah, the tree farm. "We were located between the lakes, but our last name is also Lake. I'm Tracen Lake."

Emily's energy subsided. Wonder shone through her eyes as if she'd been a kid at his Christmas tree farm. "Your last name is Lake?"

Isn't that what he'd said? Why would she be acting like he was the movie star and she a starstruck fan? "Yes, my last name is—"

Oh! Emily had just told him that water was a theme in her life. But that was merely a coincidence. She surely wouldn't see it as a sign from God or anything if his last name was *Lake*.

Emily bit her lip and scooted forward in her seat. "Do you want to come to Boise with me today and meet my mom?"

Chapter Ten

....

Goodness. She'd just invited Tracen to meet her mom. Yeah, his last name had zapped her like a lightning bolt right out of God's hand, but she shouldn't act as if Tracen had felt the storm, as well. The sign was an answer to her prayers, not his.

Tracen blinked. "You want me to meet your mom?"

"Yes!" Emily's laugh sounded half-crazed. She needed to take it down a notch. Tracen probably thought she was imagining him and her mom as in-laws. And maybe she was, but there were other reasons.... "My mom teaches one of the only university-level trampoline classes in the nation. She can strap a trampboard to your feet and teach you wakeboarding tricks out of water. It's safer and effective."

Tracen's head tilted. "That's how you—"

"She taught me everything I know." *Whew.* At least he hadn't run away screaming.

Tracen nodded thoughtfully. "Does your mom teach classes during the summer?"

"Yes. Her classes are in very high demand." It was too late to take back the invite. She'd enjoy having Tracen keep her company on the two-hour drive, but how would she explain his presence to her mom?

Tracen rubbed the back of his neck. "Would your mom have time to teach me if she's at work?"

"Um…" Emily twirled a ringlet around her finger. "I'll probably be putting on a show for her class today. Wonder Woman can draw a crowd, you know. So Mom will have plenty of time to work with you."

Tracen shook his head as if he'd forgotten he was speaking to a celebrity. A small smile played on his lips. "It sounds tempting, but I've got to get ready for Sam's return. I need to do laundry and mop and—and organize the linen closet."

"Okay," Emily responded quickly. She didn't want to sound desperate for his attention. Though now that she'd considered the idea of traveling with Tracen, the thought of leaving without him made the trip seem drab and lonely. "But if you want to come, I could always mop your floors for you." She didn't. Oh no, she did. What was wrong with her? She'd volunteered to help with housework! "I really hate laundry and organizing linen closets. But I don't mind mopping. I can mop." She was babbling now.

Tracen had a pasted-on smile as his eyes wandered her face in confusion. He squinted. Emily waited for the letdown. She'd probably scared him away for good this time. Finally he responded. "Wonder Woman can probably clean at super speeds, can't she?"

Relief rushed through Emily, forcing a laugh to burst out. This is why she was falling for him. "You have to see it to believe it."

Tracen rubbed his hands up and down his thighs and stared out the glass doors for a moment. "I can't let you clean my house. I like to give the impression that I'm one of those rare tidy bachelors, and seeing my place the way it is now would ruin the image."

Well, she'd tried. And he wasn't rejecting her exactly. In fact, his statement offered hope that she might be invited over to his place sometime in the future. That's the way she'd choose to see it anyway.

"Okay." She shifted forward to rise. Best to make a hasty retreat. "You're missing out." Was she talking to Tracen—or herself?

Tracen lifted a hand, motioning her to stay seated. "I'm not done."

Uh-oh. Maybe he really was going to reject her now.

"I didn't say I'm not coming with you. I just said you couldn't clean my house."

Emily scrunched up her forehead as she tried to follow Tracen's logic. "What?"

Tracen gave a sheepish smile. "My brothers. If I choose to clean my house instead of hanging out with Wonder Woman, my brothers will give me a bad time about it for the rest of my life. "

Emily instantly liked Tracen's brothers. "We can't have that." She stood up before Tracen could stop her a second time—and before he could change his mind again. As she passed him, she turned around so she was walking backwards toward the exit. "I'll go fill up with gas. Unless you're ready to go now."

Tracen rose and followed. He walked her all the way to the door, in a face-to-face kind of way. "Oh," he groaned. "I really shouldn't be going at all."

His words might have caused Emily to cringe, except that the way he said them told her he wouldn't be backing out. He held the door open for her. Emily lingered.

Looking down, Tracen paused too. Emily's breath caught as his eyes roamed her face. She studied his in return, noticing laugh lines around his eyes and golden whiskers usually invisible against bronze skin. She couldn't help wondering if the whiskers would tickle or scratch.

She saw his lips moving before the words penetrated her conscious. "I'll be ready when you get back."

* * * * *

Tracen set the pot of water on the breakfast bar and continued past it toward his office. "I'm going to Boise with Emily," he announced, without waiting for a response.

Honey followed him like he knew she would. She stood in the doorway as he sank into his squeaky leather chair and logged onto e-mail.

"What happened to your Bible discussion?"

"We discussed the Bible." Tracen focused on his monitor. Nothing urgent he couldn't ignore for another day. "In fact, Emily was looking up verses on water. It's a theme in her life, she said. That's when I told her my last name."

Honey sank into the chair across from him. "I'm sorry, did you say 'theme,' or did you say 'fling'?"

Ouch. Tracen rifled through a pile of mail. "I thought you liked her."

"I do like her. I also like Howie, but I'm not going to pursue a relationship with him."

Tracen's movements stopped. He focused on the older woman, her frown lines more evident than usual. He hadn't thought about Honey and Howie as a couple until Emily had asked about them, so it took him by surprise to hear Honey's take on their friendship. "Why not?"

Honey threw her arms up. "That's besides the point. We're talking about you and Emily. What do you expect to get out of your little trip today?"

Tracen stood and stuck a pencil in its holder. "I'm getting another wakeboarding lesson, actually. Emily's mom teaches a class at Boise State."

Honey guffawed. "You're meeting her mom?"

No, he was meeting a trampoline instructor. "You're being ridiculous, Honey." With three long strides, Tracen made it to the door and kept going.

He tried to shake Honey's warning words as he joined Emily in her little rented SUV. She looked so cute with her seat scooted as close to the steering wheel as the design allowed. Was he getting in over his head?

He'd chosen to go to Boise because his brothers would give him a bad time if he turned down a day with Emily Van Arsdale. But wasn't that exactly the reason he shouldn't go? She was Emily Van Arsdale and could have any guy she wanted, so why would she choose him? Especially since it would require quitting her career and relocating? He shifted uncomfortably and tried to tell himself that he wasn't the fool he felt. Even if she did have a thing for him now, it surely wouldn't last. He'd just enjoy their friendship—enjoy his chance to practice his wakeboarding tricks.

"So." He cleared his throat, trying to get back to their easy banter. "Do I get to meet your dad too?"

Emily adjusted the speed of the windshield wipers as the car in front of them spit puddles. She focused on the road when responding. "My dad died two years ago. Cancer."

So much for easy banter. But hadn't they talked about cancer before? Oh yeah. Honey's husband. So that's why Emily had gotten emotional on the boat.

"I'm sorry." Tracen couldn't imagine losing his own father. Never again seeing the man's warm smile and lazy eye. Never again battling him in a game of Cribbage or for the last piece of banana cream pie. Never again listening to his preachy words of advice, knowing they came with kind-hearted intentions and unconditional love.

Emily sniffed. She didn't respond, so he tried to fill the silence. "That must have been rough. Did your dad fight it for a long time? Honey has told stories of her husband's chemotherapy and—"

"No." Emily spit the word out. "No, he didn't fight it very long. He didn't fight it at all."

Tracen tried to make sense of her words. "It was sudden?"

Emily's palm slapped the steering wheel. Then, visibly trying to relax, she wrapped her fingers around the wheel and slid both hands wide. "He could have gotten chemo. He could have had more time with me."

Tracen didn't know how to ease her pain, especially since he didn't understand it. "Chemo is pretty scary. Did your dad try a more homeopathic route then?"

Emily sighed. "That's the way he was going to go. All natural. It wasn't covered by insurance, though."

She stared at the road, slowing to take a curve. Tracen waited for her to continue, listening to the tires slurp slick asphalt.

"That's the whole reason I started stunting in the first place. One of Mom's trampoline students got a job for that lifeguard show I told you about. The studio needed more doubles with her skills, so she invited me to share her apartment and work with her. It paid enough to send money to my parents to help with hospital bills."

Tracen sat up a little straighter. Had he heard right? Emily went to Hollywood to help her father fight cancer? That wasn't at all what he would have expected. He wondered what Honey would say about such a revelation. "Very noble of you."

Emily grunted. "It wasn't noble. It was desperate. I didn't want to lose my daddy."

Her voice broke, and Tracen racked his brain for something to ease her pain. What would help him if he'd just lost his dad? Not much. The thought gripped his gut like a vise.

She pressed her lips together. When they parted, her voice became harsher. "But Dad didn't use the money for doctor visits. He spent all I sent him to take Mom on a vacation. He said he wanted to make the most of his last days on Earth."

Tracen twisted to get a better look at Emily's face. Was she for real? She'd tried to save her father's life, and he'd used her act of compassion to live it up? Her expression lacked emotion now. She was spouting facts. Possibly too numb to let herself care anymore.

"Wow," was all he could think to say.

Emily shrugged. "I should have known they would do something like that."

Tracen squinted, still trying to comprehend. Her dad had thrown his life away, and she thought she should have expected it? "Your mom didn't make your father seek medical attention?"

Emily's shoulders sagged. "My mom sees the good in everything. She doesn't deal with pain. She simply pretends it doesn't exist."

Tracen leaned back in his seat, feeling a little of the weight from Emily's burden. He wanted to fight for her. To right a wrong. To make the unjust fair again. But how did one deal with a parent who couldn't see the problem? "You've tried talking to your mom?"

"Oh yeah." Emily kept her eyes firmly on the road. "I talked, I screamed, I begged. I said I wanted my dad to walk me down the aisle when I got married. I said I wanted him to be able to rock his grandchildren. I said I wanted to see him grow old." Her chin quivered. "He never got old. I remember him as vibrant and exciting. He always had so much energy—so much life. I don't understand how he could give that up."

Tracen wanted to reach out and offer comfort, protection. But she was driving. Besides, he'd only known her a week. "That must have been tough."

Emily nodded but didn't respond verbally. The rhythm of the wiper blades filled the silence. What was going on inside her head? Was she reliving memories with her father? Making a list of things they never got to do together?

Finally she glanced his direction. "I think I blame my mom more than anything. That's why I stayed in California. I'd planned to come back, but I couldn't bear to pretend that everything was okay the way she does."

Tracen let Emily's situation sink into him like the warmth from the heater. He slipped his jacket off and wrestled it around the seat belt while planning what to say next. He should reassure her regarding her decision. But what he wanted to do was convince her to move back to Idaho. If only her parents hadn't gone on that ridiculous vacation. Of course, then he might never have met her.

"Where did they go on vacation?" he blurted.

Emily's eyebrows lifted for an instant. "My parents? Oh, they went to the Holy Lands. Israel. It sounds like an amazing place to visit. Someday I'll go, but I don't know if I would want to spend my last days there."

Israel. Tracen had always wanted to see it in person too. He'd done his fourth-grade geography report on the Dead Sea. Apparently you could float in it without a raft. "So what would you do? If you had one day to live, I mean."

Emily rolled her head from shoulder to shoulder, as if she needed to stretch after such a grueling conversation. "One day to live? I don't know. What would you do?"

Tracen rubbed the stubble on his chin. She'd turned the tables on him. But there was no question as to what he would do. "I'd raft a class six." Again.

The respect in Emily's eyes told him she approved. "If you were already going to die, then you would have nothing to fear from the river."

"Yep." Tracen hadn't intended to admit his fear, but Emily knew what he'd been thinking. "Your turn."

"Hmm…" Emily tapped her fingers on the steering wheel. "You know what I fear? Skydiving."

Tracen cocked his head. So she wasn't fearless. "Really? You've thrown yourself off buildings and mountains but never jumped out of a plane?"

Emily scrunched her face up. "No," she said in a tiny voice.

"Char took me last year for my birthday, but I was too chicken. My makeup artist parachuted, but me, the stuntwoman, I panicked."

Tracen slapped his thigh in disbelief. "You're kidding me!"

Emily shrugged, as if embarrassed. "In all my stunts, I still possess a level of control. Leaping into midair with no rope or bungee connected seems too dangerous."

Tracen gaped at her. "I never would have guessed." She became more interesting every moment. "So you would go skydiving if you had one day to live?"

"I would!" Emily declared, as if claiming victory over her fear.

Tracen stuck one finger in his ear and twisted, pretending to have trouble hearing over all her volume.

She giggled, then sent him a demure smile. "Thank you, Tracen. You've helped me to understand my father just a little bit better. Maybe Mom understood all along."

Her smile heated Tracen up even more, though he hadn't meant to justify Emily's mom's actions. He reached over to shut the vent that was starting to feel like a hair dryer. "Your mom still needs to face reality, Emily."

"I know. I can't run away anymore."

Emily rubbed her pretty pink lips together. Tracen tried to avert his gaze so he could concentrate on the conversation, but his rebellious eyes returned to roam her expressive face. Even if his eyes wouldn't obey, hopefully his ears would listen. What was she saying?

"That's what stunting was for me. It kept me busy, so I didn't have to deal with Mom. But now, being back with her, it seems like I've made all the wrong choices. She acts as though she doesn't need anybody, but she's still up here all by herself."

Tracen tried to let the news digest. The fact that Emily moved to Southern California to help her parents out financially was huge in itself. But this. This confession was more shocking than her fear of skydiving. She made it sound like... No, he couldn't let himself think it unless it was fact. "Are you going to move back to Idaho?" His insides sloshed around the way they did when he was rafting. But somehow awaiting Emily's answer was scarier than whitewater.

Emily answered solemnly. "I want to. Mom's going to help me look for a job teaching phys. ed. I have a major in exercise and movement science and a minor in elementary education."

Tracen's laugh echoed through the car. Wonder Woman wanted to teach P.E. And she wanted to teach it in Idaho. He flipped through his mental rolodex to find a contact that could get her hired on at Ernest Hemingway Elementary. Then he could see her every day if he wanted—even eat cafeteria sloppy joes with her on her lunch break.

Emily frowned. "What's so funny?"

Tracen tried to control his enthusiasm. After all, they'd been discussing her father's death. "I'm just"—a grin split his face like he was the guy from the Reach toothbrush commercials—"picturing your students when they find out Wonder Woman is their P.E. teacher."

Emily's frown didn't fade like he thought it would. "You think it's funny that I want a normal job?"

Through the rain, orange construction signs began to appear. Emily tapped the brakes as Tracen attempted a U-turn in their conversation. "No! Absolutely not. I'm sure you'd be a great teacher. It's merely all a little, uh, unexpected."

Emily pulled to a stop behind a row of cars waiting for the

flagger to let them pass. The inconvenience barely registered as Tracen awaited her response. She shifted into park and turned to give Tracen her full attention.

"You don't want to make movies anymore?" He shot a prayer heavenward that her answer would be no.

Emily studied him. What she was looking for, he couldn't be sure. "I've always thought of acting as simply a phase in my life. You know, like high school."

Tracen laughed again, then hurried to explain. He didn't want her to think that he was laughing at her. No, he was laughing at the irony of her situation. How many people moved to Hollywood with dreams of the kind of fame she'd accidentally achieved? People like Serena. Maybe he shouldn't be laughing. But, then, maybe fate was working in his favor this time.

"You surprised me," he began. "But I guess the fact you've been hanging out with rafting guides should have clued me in to who you really are."

The challenge in Emily's eyes turned to a sparkle. "You're missing another pretty obvious clue."

"Oh yeah?" Tracen didn't even try to guess what she was hinting at. He was too intoxicated by her tone. And by the way the apples of her cheeks popped out when she smiled. *Mercy*, he loved her smile. "What's that?"

"*You're* the rafting guide."

Chapter Eleven
....

Emily soared toward the ceiling, muscles tight, waiting for the pull of gravity before tucking into a triple summersault. Cheers arose to welcome her back to the trampoline. She pushed off again, blocking out the crowd that surrounded her and adding a twist to the next layout.

Was it only last week that she'd done the same routine in her mom's class? But this time she felt it all more. Everything was bigger. Almost alive.

She wasn't playing now. She was performing. And it didn't matter that her mother had another student who could execute the exact same moves with better form. It mattered that Tracen was there to see her. And it mattered that Tracen would be eating dinner at her mother's house. She wanted to cut the tramp routine short to join Tracen and her mom with the wakeboard lesson.

Oh, goodness. The drive to Boise had flown by, even with the construction delays. She'd opened up to Tracen, and he'd helped her see her parents in a new light. After that, she hadn't exactly been subtle in her flirting, which could have been a mistake. She didn't want him to think she was one of those girls who threw herself at any cute guy. Because she didn't.

She hadn't even had time for men with her filming schedules, and before that, dealing with her father's illness had drained all her energy. Spending time with Tracen made her feel like Dorothy in the Wizard of Oz—life now had color to it.

Emily rotated through a doubleback summersault with a full twist, the room spinning into a blur. She returned to the trampoline, letting her feet sink, then absorbing the spring into her knees so she wasn't shot back up through the air like a boomerang. The students surrounding the tramp hollered and whistled. She gave a little bow, making sure to face the direction where Tracen was located. Her insides did a flip of their own when he sent her a mock salute. It more than made up for the times he'd ignored her on the wakeboard. Oh yeah, their friendship was definitely growing closer.

"Emily! Emily! Emily!"

She plopped down on the edge of the tramp to sign autographs. Classes were normally quiet during summer sessions, but somehow word had spread that she would be in town. One girl had even donned a red cape in her honor.

As patiently as she could, she answered movie questions and encouraged the young adults to pursue their dreams. For her, the two topics were not related. Yeah, she loved the work. It was challenging and rewarding. But the more time she spent with Tracen, the less stable her life seemed. She wanted what he had. Roots. Friends. Family. A home.

Finally, the class ended, and the students disappeared. Emily half-skipped, half-jogged across the shiny gym floor to join her mom and Tracen.

Tracen bounced awkwardly with a board strapped to his feet. He held up one finger as if to hold her attention. "Watch this."

Emily's mom yanked on the rope looped through the pulley on the ceiling and supporting Tracen's harness just as he threw himself backwards into a tuck. He might have made it over had he angled his board a little more perpendicular to the tramp. Instead, board and man hung in midair, stuck upside-down. Emily's mom slowly lowered him onto his back.

Emily leaped onto the tramp to help Tracen untangle. "I'd love to see you try *that* on Redfish Lake."

Tracen groaned. "I had the trick earlier."

Violet confirmed his declaration. "He got it right away," she assured her daughter. "I think I just wore him out."

Tracen kicked the board away but didn't move from his sprawled-out position. "That you did."

Emily helped him unbuckle the harness so her mom could hoist it up into its resting position. It was a task she'd completed often, but with Tracen as the one harnessed, it suddenly seemed intimate. She focused on slipping the strap out of the buckle and didn't meet his eyes, though she accidentally made contact with his solid stomach. Goodness he was strong, if not exactly graceful.

Only when she'd scooted to the edge once again did she look him in the face. Where did this shyness come from? Tracen seemed to be wondering the same thing as he watched her distance herself. He let her off without comment—probably because her mom was right there.

He turned to Violet. "So when did you get started in this sport?"

Violet draped her forearms along the pad surrounding the apparatus. "I started gymnastics when I was eight. Talked my dad into getting me a trampoline when I turned eleven. I've been jumping ever since. Even when pregnant with Emily, I jumped until the day I delivered."

Tracen chuckled. "No kidding." He turned his disarming smile on Emily. "No wonder she's so athletic."

Emily turned to look at her mom. The woman loved telling the beginning of Emily's career. Most people didn't know the truth.

Violet chuckled. "Actually, Emily was a sickly child. She never had any energy."

Tracen tilted his head.

"I always had a cold and a stomachache," Emily explained.

"She did." Violet took control once again. "I thought she was just lazy. Finally a friend of mine suggested she might have food allergies."

Tracen's head swiveled toward Emily once again. "Milk and wheat."

Violet's voice repeated her words. "Milk and wheat. It took us awhile to figure it out, though. For one whole month she ate nothing but baby food from the jar."

Emily watched for the disgust in Tracen's face. She'd been made fun of at school because of the baby food and spent most of the noon recess in the bathroom hiding her tears. Fourth grade had been the worst year of her young life.

Tracen's eyes didn't bulge like she expected. Instead he looked at her as if she was a present he'd just unwrapped on Christmas morning. "So that's why you didn't eat rolls at The Point. And why you can't eat huckleberry cobbler anymore."

"Yeah." How she missed the sweet zip of huckleberry cobbler.

"Is baby food any good?" Tracen's teasing words were said with enough sensitivity to draw her eyes back up to his.

Salt couldn't even help her creamed turkey dinners. She'd lost eleven pounds—eleven pounds she didn't have to lose. "I will never, ever feed my kids baby food. Not even when they are babies. I'm going to get a baby food grinder, and they will eat whatever we eat."

At her words, Tracen's lips parted, and his eyes squinted. Did she just say *we*? By *we,* she meant her family. She and her husband. She hadn't meant to imply that she'd be eating with Tracen. And she hadn't meant to create the mental image of them parenting together.

"I mean, you know…the baby will eat whatever my family eats."

"Of course that's what you meant." Violet's thick hand gripped her daughter's forearm in support, rescuing her from an uncomfortable situation. "Now Emily eats lots of corn and rice and potatoes and oatmeal. It's an unusual diet, but it keeps her healthy. And as soon as she got healthy, she became unstoppable. She hasn't slowed down since."

Tracen's lips curled up. He blinked lazily at her. "I noticed."

Oh, how contentment flowed through Emily's veins like a sedative. She loved that he noticed her. Not the way others noticed her, but with the perception of a family member. The mental image of dinner with Tracen and a baby food grinder came back.

"Are you coming over to eat, Tracen?" Her mom must have read her thoughts.

* * * * *

Tracen rode with Emily to an older neighborhood, passing houses with wraparound porches and gingerbread detail. Violet's house looked just as old, only hers was peach with blue trim.

"Boise Broncos colors. Mom's idea," Emily stated, her voice wry. "Before Dad died, the fence was painted purple, and we had a totem pole and rainbow flags flying."

Tracen bit back a teasing comment. Apparently Emily's parents hadn't been the kind that tried to fit in, and he could see in her eyes that it had been cause for an embarrassing childhood. Not to mention the baby food thing. The baby food thing that got her talking about having babies—a place where he wouldn't let his thoughts go. So…back to her hippie home. "I'm jealous."

Emily's face broke into a radiant smile. "You are not."

"Actually I am. My childhood home got torn down two years ago." He'd tried to save it. Even applied for a loan to have the house moved onto his land. But the process would have cost much more than for him to build a brand-new home—and he didn't even have enough to do that yet.

"Oh!" Emily gasped. "I'm sorry."

The woman acted as if she were mourning her own home. A kiss on her forehead seemed like the perfect way to calm her down. Tracen resisted, though the desire was growing stronger. He grabbed the door handle to put some distance between the two of them. "Don't be. I've got new plans."

Emily bounced out after him. "Cool!" she called, though he couldn't see her over the hood of the SUV.

They rushed through the drizzle into the warmth of Violet's house. The rooms had high ceilings but felt cramped with all the antique furniture and the plethora of plants. Emily led the way through the jungle into the dining area under a chandelier that would have looked more appropriate in a torture chamber. She shivered as she slid into a high-backed wooden chair. Tracen took a seat in a chair on wheels—vinyl with orange and yellow flowers.

What would the tabloids think of her here? This was *The Simple Life* that divas Paris Hilton and Nicole Ritchie would never know. He leaned his forearms on the scarred butcher block table.

Emily wrinkled her nose at the chair he chose. Her charming, pert, kissable nose.

Violet entered the room from a small hallway that led to the back of the house and, Tracen guessed, by the steaming mugs in her hands, to the kitchen. She placed the mugs in front of Tracen and Emily. "You missing the California sunshine, Emily?"

Emily sipped her drink. "Not today."

Tracen eyed the beverage. It looked like tea, and he was more of a coffee kind of guy. He lifted the mug to his lips. Ew. It tasted like penicillin. He gulped, forcing the liquid down his throat.

Violet watched him as she lowered herself onto a bench on the other side of the table. "Well, I'm glad you kids could visit me today. It's no fun cooking for one."

Tracen let go of his mug for the first and last time. "I'm sorry to hear about your husband, Violet."

"Well." She sat up a little straighter. "He's in heaven now."

Tracen nodded. Though Emily's upbringing was out of the ordinary, he got the impression that she had a strong Christian foundation.

Violet's eyes traveled to her daughter, then back. "Are you a believer, Tracen?"

Tracen blinked at the question. Certainly direct. Was Violet like this with everyone, or was she concerned about her daughter's relationship? If it were the latter, she must have the wrong impression about him. He came for the trampoline lesson. Didn't he?

"Yeah, I grew up in a Christian family. When I was five, I asked Jesus into my heart. I actually said, 'Hey, Jesus, come into my heart.'"

Violet chuckled, but Tracen listened for the tinkle of Emily's laughter. Her sapphire eyes sparkled. "The faith of a child."

Violet stilled and stared as if into the past. "I wish Emily could say the same thing. But we didn't start going to church until she was in fifth grade."

Emily twirled a strand of hair around her index finger. "I remember that. I loved church, because none of the kids knew about the baby food I had to eat the year before."

Tracen reached out and squeezed her shoulder before he could stop himself. He just wanted her to know that he felt for her. That's all. And he left his hand there because he liked the connection. He liked thinking that he could keep her from experiencing any more pain. Her eyes told him she appreciated his gesture.

Violet sighed, as if reminded of the way she used to feel when her husband supported her. "We always believed in God, but we didn't have a relationship with Him. It wasn't until one of Noah's water ski trips, when his boat broke down, and some guy on a jet ski helped him out and told him all about Jesus that—"

"Mom!" Emily's shoulder muscle flexed in his grip. He let his hand fall away as she sat up straighter. Her wide eyes searched his, as if trying to read his thoughts. "You don't think…"

Tracen knew where she was headed. It couldn't be. "Violet, do you remember the man's name?"

Violet's eyes ricocheted between the two of them, her brow wrinkling. "No. I never met him. Why?"

Tracen scooted back on the wheels of his chair. He wanted to call Howie and see if the stories matched up.

Emily's hand flew to her heart. "Mom, one of Tracen's rafting guides used to witness on a jet ski."

Violet's skin began to smooth as she relaxed. "No. The guy who helped Noah out was a pastor. And he would be quite a bit older than you two."

Unbelievable. "Ha *ha*!"

His laugh mingled with Emily's. Her mouth opened wide in an expression Tracen knew mirrored his own.

"Can you believe it?" He was almost shouting.

Emily grabbed his arm and shook it. "You've got to call him."

Violet tilted her head. "You think it was your rafting buddy?"

Tracen dug into his pocket for his cell. "It must have been." Oh man, Howie would be so humbled to hear that he played a part in Emily's childhood—in her whole salvation. He wondered what Honey would have to say about that.

Emily told her mom the whole story while Tracen tried to reach Howie. No answer.

As he finally shoved the phone back into his pocket, Emily quieted down, but her smile was still turned up loud. He didn't need to put his hand on her shoulder to feel the connection anymore.

Violet wiped tears from her eyes. "Tracen, if I can ever meet this friend of yours, I would love to thank him in person. Because of him..." She fished a tissue from her pocket and wipe her nose. "Because of him, I have peace today."

Tracen nodded. Words wouldn't be enough.

In their moment of silence, the noises around them grew louder. A car engine, the refrigerator humming, a constant dripping....

"Ah yes," Violet murmured. "I've got peace and a leaky faucet. I never realized before how much work Noah must have put into this old house."

Emily reached across the table to take her mother's hand. It looked like a little gesture, but Tracen knew how enormous it was from what Emily had shared in the car. She was reaching out to her mom in a way she hadn't since her father died. He felt like an intruder.

"Violet, I can fix your faucet." Yes, he enjoyed fixing things. And usually leaky faucets were much easier to fix than broken relationships.

Violet's eyes slanted his way. "I could get used to having you around."

She showed him to the bathroom and promised to get started on dinner to "repay" him, though he expected his job to be much easier than hers. It didn't take him long. Just a twist of the monkey wrench, and he was good to go. He closed the toolbox and headed toward the kitchen.

"So what's going on between you and Tracen?"

Tracen paused in the hallway. It wasn't that he was eavesdropping exactly. He simply didn't want to embarrass Emily by walking in the moment her mom asked such a personal question.

"Nothing yet." Emily sighed.

Tracen strained to hear over the kitchen noises—the chopping of a knife, the *clink* of glass, the sucking sound of the refrigerator being opened. Okay, now he was eavesdropping.

"Really?" Violet wondered aloud. "Because it seems like there's *something* between you two."

There was something between them, no matter how much Tracen had tried to deny it. Apparently everyone else could see it. Whatever it was, Tracen had rationalized it away. He'd been afraid that *something* wasn't enough. That if he pursued *something*, he'd be wasting his energy. He'd be left wanting more.

But what more could he want? Emily wasn't leaving Idaho in search of fame. She was planning to leave fame and come home. The truth was that she'd never searched for fame. She'd accepted the responsibility at first to make money to help her family. Then she'd stayed in California to cope with the pain that came when her father died. Tracen's heart ached for her. Maybe he could help her heal— he could bring her home.

Emily's response drew all his attention. His hope felt so fragile. If she said anything to discourage him, there would be no hope at all.

"Tracen doesn't seem to want something between us." Her voice lacked the passion he'd come to expect from her. She sounded sad and lonely. He wondered if he could change her tone by telling her how wrong she was.

"What about you?" Violet asked the question he'd been longing to know the answer to.

Every muscle tensed in anticipation. The pulse in his neck throbbed. The pounding in his ears threatened to drown out Emily's words.

"I adore him."

The hard core of fear within his chest burst into a shower of what felt like fireworks. Relief tingled and was swept away by the electric charge of determination. For the first time, he could admit to himself what he wanted.

"I thought so." Emily's mother's voice grew louder, like she was headed Tracen's direction.

Panic might have driven him to retreat and act casual had it not been overpowered by the surprise of Emily's recent revelation. He moved slightly, but not enough. It was as if the emotion churning inside him prevented the proper signals from traveling to his muscles from his brain.

"Tracen!" The water in Violet's stone pitcher sloshed as she came to an abrupt stop in front of him. A loud crash sounded from the kitchen.

Tracen let his arms flop to his sides. He didn't know what his hands had been doing anyway.

"I finished fixing the sink." A lame excuse for not being out of hearing range.

"Wonderful. I appreciate it." Violet moved to step around him. "And if you didn't overhear the conversation in the kitchen, my daughter just said she adores you."

So that's where Emily got her knowing smile. Tracen watched the older woman disappear into the dining room.

Well, if he'd overheard Emily's conversation, she must have overheard his. He stepped onto the black-and-white-checked tile floor to find her wearing oven mitts and staring at him with those round eyes of hers. An irresistible combination.

* * * * *

Emily pulled the Gruyère, leek, and chard frittata out of the oven. It had been awhile since she'd eaten hippie food. It smelled like dill pickles and scrambled eggs. Hopefully Tracen wouldn't mind the organic dinner too much.

"Tracen."

Emily dropped the skillet on the stovetop. Her mom had barely stepped out of the kitchen, yet she was talking to Tracen. How long had the man been standing there? Well, it didn't matter because Mom announced her confession to him to be sure he knew. That was just like her mom—never considering the negative results of her actions. The woman probably thought she was helping out.

Emily's insides suddenly felt like they had the time she'd accidentally flipped off the trampoline and gotten whiplash when her head bounced on the floor. She wasn't in control anymore. She didn't realize she was staring at the doorway until Tracen appeared in it. Goodness, he was gorgeous. And different. He met her gaze with intent. Her heart slammed into her chest. The something between them had just turned into everything.

"I do adore you." There. She said it. Now he couldn't pretend not to know any longer. If only she could have said it at a time when she wasn't wearing orange oven mitts.

But it didn't seem to matter to Tracen. He strode across the room and lifted both his hands to cup her face. The feather-light touch made her whole body feel heavy and helpless. She looked up into eyes that adored her right back. It wasn't the same kind of adoration she got from fans. This was the giving kind. And she would take all he offered.

The warmth of their breath mingled as Tracen leaned down. He moved slowly, giving her a chance to savor every moment. It was pure torture.

She inhaled his scent. He'd brought his woods right into her childhood home. Mmm. She wanted to take it with her everywhere she went—though the only place she wanted to be was closer to Tracen.

Tracen's warm gaze reflected her feelings. Then his eyes dipped down to gaze at her lips. She felt her smile down to her very toes.

Tracen's fingers slid into her hair as he pulled her to him. Oven mitts plopped to the floor when her arms went limp. If she moved, she might accidentally poke herself and wake up from this dream. Finally Tracen's lips brushed hers, claimed hers, traced hers. He pulled back way too soon.

Emily wanted to lean into him. She wanted more. But she also wanted to know that Tracen truly was going to start a relationship with her and wasn't merely being swept away by emotions. "What was that?"

Tracen's hands slid down to her arms as if he didn't want to let her go for a second. He gave a mischievous half-smile. "Something I've been trying not to do for the past week."

Aha! So he had been fighting his feelings. She squirmed in delight. "You gave up?"

"I gave in."

Tracen tipped her chin up, then wrapped his arms behind her back. Emily gripped Tracen's shoulders as he lowered his head to give in once again, but the distance between them reminded Emily of his argument for not dating her. As much as she wanted to surrender to his embrace, she held back.

"I'm not too short for you anymore?"

Tracen's mouth hovered above hers. She expected him to pull away and answer, but instead, his hands slid to her waist. He gripped her hips and lifted her to sit on the countertop. The edge of the Formica bit into her thighs, but since it brought her closer to Tracen, she didn't care. Now her forehead reached as high as his nose. With an excited giggle, she tilted her head to initiate another kiss.

The playfulness turned tender as she ran her hands over his broad chest. It couldn't be a dream. He felt too solid, too real.

Tracen's kisses trailed over her cheekbones, down to her neck. His lips grazed her earlobe. "Is this better?"

As if he didn't know. "The best."

Tracen leaned away to look at her face. "No." He kissed her nose. "The best is yet to come."

With any other guy that would have been a line. With Tracen, it was a promise.

Chapter Twelve

....

Emily leaped over a mud puddle in the dim light. It was only five in the morning, so she should have been yawning and drinking coffee like everybody else. But everybody else did not kiss the rafting guide the day before. She scanned the crew spread out through the trees in the still damp-smelling forest. She'd hoped Tracen would be around, though the scene they had scheduled to shoot didn't actually require much rafting.

The tired mumbling from those around her faded away as Char's vibrant voice called, "There's my Emily." Was she trying to do an Oprah impersonation? "You're on time for a change. But I guess once you've had your face on a box of Wheaties cereal, others have to adjust to your timeline."

Emily squinted hard at a tall shadow next to a tree. Her heart hammered. Tracen? Nope, just the lighting tech. She turned to give the makeup artist her full attention. "Wonder Woman had her picture on the cereal box, not me."

Char motioned her head toward a trailer. "Sure. Come on, Superhero. I need to put your makeup on inside today. Better lighting."

Emily glanced around once more before following Char up the aluminum steps and into the welcome warmth of the trailer. She plopped into her chair and spun around, turning to Char with a grin. She couldn't hold her elation in any longer. "He kissed me."

Char pursed her lips and pulled the tweezers out from her bag of torture instruments. Emily hated those things, but with *her* eyebrows, waxing was never enough.

"Who kissed you?" Char's tone sounded low and disapproving—as if nobody was good enough to kiss Emily.

Emily rubbed her lips together, savoring the memory. The way Tracen caressed her cheekbones. The way he'd lifted her onto the counter. The way her mom found them making out in the kitchen…

What had Char asked? Oh, yeah. "I'll give you one hint. He's tall."

"Hmm." Char focused on the bridge of Emily's nose. "Then it can't be Bruce."

"Ha!" Emily burst into laughter at Char's ridiculous statement, but it quickly turned to tears with the sting of Char's tweezers. "Owie."

Char plucked once more before exchanging the instrument for an eyebrow brush. "So Tracen made a move, huh? I don't know about him, girl. I think he might be too tall for you." Her deadpan voice gave away the joke.

"Char—"

"Ahh!" the makeup artist shrieked. Finally. This was the reaction Emily had been waiting for. "Tracen is perfect for you." She dropped her brush, pulled Emily out of her seat, and gripped her fingers tightly while bouncing up and down.

Emily joined in—she never missed out on a chance to jump. Thank goodness they had the trailer all to themselves. "I know!"

Char led the hopping in a circle. "You two will make such cute babies together."

Planning a pregnancy the week after meeting the man of her

dreams really wasn't mature, but hey, neither was using the trailer like a bounce house. With the way Emily was feeling, she'd probably be drawing hearts on her script before the day was over. "I know!" she shouted again.

"Can I be in your wedding?"

Now Emily screamed with excitement. "Ahh!" And since screaming was to Char what jumping was to Emily, Char joined in. Emily wrapped her arms around her friend, full of joy. So they continued bouncing even in their embrace.

And that's how Tracen found them. Hopping, and hugging, and screaming.

They didn't even notice the door open. "Uh, maybe I'll come back another time."

Emily untangled herself from Char, her eyes on Tracen. She wasn't going to let him go. "Wait. We're done now." She wiped perspiration from her brow and took a calming breath before gliding over to Tracen's side. Again, she'd forgotten how tall he was. The crown of her head barely made it to his shoulder, and she was eye to eye with his—two steaming coffee cups? "Is that for me?"

Tracen held the cups away from her. "One was. But I don't think you need any caffeine right now."

Emily loved the way he could bring a smile to her lips. "Well, it was very sweet of you. But I actually don't drink coffee, anyway."

"I do," Char piped up.

Tracen looked over Emily's head, as if he'd already forgotten they weren't alone. He handed the cup to Char, then settled in the seat across from Emily as Char got back to work with the cosmetics. "Another allergy?"

Oh, he cared. "No, I always burn my tongue and spill on myself."

"She does." Char rummaged through tubes of foundation. "You'd think someone with her coordination would be a little less messy. But nope. The stains drove wardrobe crazy."

Tracen sipped his coffee, a twinkle in his eye. "You two should know about crazy."

Emily met his gaze as Char opened a new tube of mascara. Should she tell him why they'd been so excited? Char took away her options.

"We were just celebrating your first kiss."

Tracen tilted his head as if he hadn't heard right.

"What?" Char demanded. "Boys don't jump and scream over those things?"

Emily knew her face was turning a bright shade of pink by the way it burned, but she was used to Char. Could Tracen handle her?

Tracen winked, as if telling her not to worry. "You didn't see me and Jack dancing down by the river just now?"

Char's laughter practically shook the trailer. "I like this guy, Emily. He's a keeper."

* * * * *

So Emily had apparently been pretty excited about the kisses they'd shared. The thought should have made his day. And it would have, if he hadn't been watching Emily kiss somebody else.

"Cut!" Bruce's voice broke the silence around them.

Emily's eyes flew to Tracen. She seemed to be searching for his support. He gave a lift of his chin—it was supposed to be a nod that he wanted her to continue, but he couldn't quite finish the gesture. Besides, what choice did he have?

Hadn't actress Melanie Griffith thrown an ashtray at her husband when she saw his dancing scene with Catherine Zeta-Jones in *The Mask of Zorro*? No wonder so many marriages failed in this business. But he wouldn't think about that now. Emily wasn't going to be making any more movies after *Whitewater Wedding*. She'd be moving to Sun Valley with him.

If only Jack hadn't confided his interest in Emily. Or, if only Tracen didn't know how soft she felt in a man's arms. Or, if only he didn't have to watch. Maybe he should leave.

"Tracen!" Now Bruce's bullhorn blared at him. "Will you come down here and show Jack how to pull the raft onto shore without jostling Emily all about?"

Tracen took a deep breath and trudged down to the embankment. This was the scene where Emily's character had been knocked unconscious. So cliché. Jack's character rescues the damsel in distress, and they declare their love for each other. It made him want to hurl.

He disconnected himself from the situation, avoiding eye contact with Emily. He couldn't let her see how much the scene was eating at him. It wasn't like they were serious yet. He'd only kissed her once. (Though it made all his kisses with Serena seem like a peck on his cheek from his mother.) He had no reason to feel so possessive.

He pushed the raft with Emily back out into the water, holding onto the rope that encircled the paddleboat. He didn't look at Emily, though he could feel the weight of her body and the heat of her gaze.

He wished she would just do her job and not worry so much about him. It made him feel needy and weak.

"Like this, Jack." He planted his feet on the rocky terrain, pushed with his legs, and twisted through his core, pulling into his arms. The raft swung smoothly onto solid ground.

"That's perfect." Bruce appeared behind his shoulder. "Now, how do you think he should get in, Tracen?"

Was the director serious? Didn't Jack know how to get into a raft?

Tension churned in Tracen's gut as he lifted one leg, then the other, over the edge of the raft. He was going through the moves, showing another man how to advance on Emily.

What was Emily thinking? She lay sprawled at his feet, so he couldn't ignore her now. Her wide eyes watched his every move as if afraid he wouldn't say anything to her—or maybe afraid that he would. She hardly resembled the giddy girl he'd found shrieking in the trailer earlier. She'd never been so still.

"Good, good. Are you watching, Jack?" Bruce motioned the movie star over to get a better look. "Tracen, can you kneel down for us? As if you're checking her pulse?"

Tracen dropped to one knee next to the curve of Emily's hip. He shouldn't focus there. Looking up, he watched Emily's lips part, like she couldn't suck in enough oxygen without opening her mouth. Later those same lips would part for Jack. What had he gotten himself into?

"See, Jack?" Bruce continued the lesson. "You'll want to scramble like you're worried, but be gentle at the same time. Tracen, take her pulse now."

Emily lay silent, awaiting Tracen's next action. How would he feel if the situation were real? If Emily had been knocked unconscious while rafting? Adrenaline surged like the river within him. There was no question that he'd risk his life to keep her safe. Trying to reign in his intensity, he slipped two fingers to the side of her slender neck. Her pulse wasn't hard to find. In fact, the throbbing seemed to speed up at his touch. His own heart began to race, as if trying to beat Emily's to the finish line.

Okay, maybe the scenario wasn't so far-fetched. If he were in Jack's character's shoes, he'd fall for the delicate spitfire, and once finding her alive, he wouldn't be able to keep his fingers from stroking her cheek and slipping into her hair. That's what Tracen wanted to do, and from the way Emily's eyes pleaded with his, that's what she wanted too.

Too bad Bruce was watching so intently. "Emily, that's beautiful. Now when we're filming, I want you to look at Jack with that exact same expression—after you become conscious again, of course."

The guy should have just kicked Tracen in the teeth. It would have been less painful than the thought of Emily begging for Jack's kiss. Emily's muscles stiffened under Tracen's touch, and he pulled away.

"Oh, one more thing, Tracen."

Tracen tensed. What more could the director want?

"You know CPR, right?"

Mercy! Was he going to have to pretend to give Emily mouth-to-mouth?

"Do a quick check to see if Emily is breathing. Jack needs to see how a professional does it."

Tracen looked back down at Emily. She waited innocently—possibly breathlessly. It was his job to check. He gave a little sigh. It wasn't her fault they were in this position. It wasn't her fault she'd momentarily be in the same position with Jack. She was just doing her job. Later on she could dance with Charlene in the trailer about how he'd almost given her CPR. The corners of his lips slipped up. Emily's face relaxed. She really did have a thing for him, didn't she?

Tracen dropped to both knees, tilting Emily's chin up to clear her airway. Bracing himself with one hand at the bottom of the raft, he leaned over to listen and feel for breath with an ear to her mouth. From this position he was also able to watch her chest to see if it rose and fell. And boy, did it.

In the background Bruce explained his every move to Jack, who obviously wouldn't know how to save another's life since he hadn't even been able to save his own. But it wasn't Bruce's words that mattered. From where Emily lay "lifeless" she spoke softly into his ear. "I'm going to pretend I'm kissing you instead of Jack."

The warmth of her whisper fanned over his skin, causing the cool air around him to seem freezing in comparison. A shiver ran down his spine, and goose bumps stretched his skin taut. But the words themselves stirred something inside, heating him up like the cup of coffee he'd hoped to share with Emily that morning. And just as he was addicted to coffee, he'd now become addicted to Emily.

She was going to pretend to be kissing *him*? It would be caught on film forever. From now on, whenever people mentioned the kissing scene between Emily Van Arsdale and Jack Jamison, he could tell them that Emily Van Arsdale had been fantasizing about kissing him. They—whoever they were—would probably laugh in his face. But he would remember this moment. And then, if he had any say in the future of their relationship, he'd simply introduce the skeptics to Emily herself.

It was a fun little daydream. But it didn't change the fact that he had to get out of the raft and let a famous movie star take over where he left off.

Tracen turned his face back to Emily's before standing. Her full lips looked so inviting. He desperately needed to retreat. "I'm going to pretend that you're not kissing anybody," he whispered back.

Then he left. Headed up to The Point. He shouldn't have awakened so early. He'd wanted to see Emily again but had forgotten that he'd have to see her in somebody else's embrace.

Honey hadn't even arrived at work yet. Tracen seated himself on a barstool but left the menu facedown. Food didn't sound that appealing, but it wasn't like he could start returning phone calls for his business yet, since most people were only just getting up at six in the morning. His running shoes were stashed in his truck. Maybe he could go for a jog—sweat out his frustration.

"Where's Emily?" A panting Jor-El dropped into the seat next to him. The kid was dedicated, if nothing else.

"Nice to see you too, Jor-El."

"Um, good morning, Tracen." Jor-El scanned the empty eating area. "Emily called last night to tell me that she's given my name to security so I can watch her film anytime. When does filming start? I want to see her flip out of the raft."

Emily had called Jor-El already? Tracen had only given her the kid's phone number the night before. She sure was sweet. "They've already begun filming today, though I don't know if you're going to want to watch. It's a kissing scene."

"Oh." Jor-El deflated like a flat tire. Was kissing still yucky when you were twelve? "*You're* not going to watch?"

Tracen wondered how much the kid knew about his feelings. He thought he'd been doing a pretty good job of hiding them, but Honey had seen right through him. "They only need me for rafting scenes. I was thinking about going for a run."

Jor-El pulled some change out of his pocket and counted. Not quite enough for breakfast. "I guess I'll go home," he muttered.

Tracen stood and walked with him to the door. A thought struck him. "You brought your unicycle?"

"Yeah. I asked for a bicycle for Christmas last year, but all I got was a winter coat and socks."

Poor guy. Didn't his dad send presents? "A unicycle is cool. Why don't you ride along while I run? Then I'll buy you breakfast."

Jor-El had talent. Underneath the rolls that hid his waist, the kid must possess some awesome core muscles to stay so balanced. Tracen jogged along the pathway that lined the main highway, passing a couple on roller skis. And Jor-El literally rode circles around them all.

They headed back toward The Point when the sun reached the spot in the horizon where it blinded anyone not turned away from it. Tracen got tired of the sneezing fits.

"Bless you," Jor-El called for what must have been the nineteenth time.

"Thanks," Tracen mumbled again, pulling his T-shirt up over his face to wipe his forehead. Yeesh, he smelled like a locker room.

On rubbery legs, he led Jor-El through the dining room. He grabbed sunglasses from his office, then claimed a table on the patio so Gigi wouldn't scold him about his hygiene scaring off her customers. He could shower after he fed the kid.

Tracen tossed a menu across the picnic table. "What do you want, buddy?"

Jor-El's eyes lit up the way they had when Emily invited him to lunch on the first day he met her. The thought drew Tracen's gaze down to the river. The filming continued, but he couldn't see the actress he was looking for. Where was she?

"I'll have the Belgian waffle. With a side of sausage. And maybe some scrambled eggs. I wonder when the next Wonder Woman movie will come out."

Tracen frowned and scanned the menu prices, totaling up Jor-El's breakfast before Jor-El's last sentence penetrated his mind. He looked up. "A sequel to *Wonder Woman*?"

"Yeah. I read about it online yesterday. Though I know they haven't started filming yet because Emily is still up here. But I hope it doesn't take too long."

"*Wonder Woman II*?" Tracen repeated. Emily hadn't mentioned it. "There must be a different actress playing the part." That's the only thing that made sense. "Emily is planning to move back to Idaho and become a P.E. teacher."

"Emily Van Arsdale is going to teach a gym class?" Jor-El asked in disbelief. But he didn't wait for an answer. "That's so cool. Maybe she could be my teacher and would actually give me a passing grade."

Tracen held back a chuckle. He wondered what the phys. ed. teacher would think of Jor-El's moves on a unicycle. The kid had coordination, even if he couldn't climb a rope to the ceiling. "We will see."

Jor-El leaned forward. "What do you mean we? Is Emily moving here to be with you?"

Oops. Tracen had enough trouble not getting his own hopes up. He didn't need to have to reel Jor-El back in, as well. "No. She misses her mom, actually."

Jor-El nodded thoughtfully. "That's right. I forgot she's from around here. But I think she likes you too."

Huh. "What would give you that idea?" Tracen lifted his menu so the kid couldn't read his expression—his eagerness to hear Jor-El's answer.

"Oh..." Jor-El paused dramatically, as if telling a secret. "I talked to her last night on the phone. She laughed a lot when I told her about the time you promised your grandma that if she went rafting with you, she would stay dry."

Not his most impressive moment. Tracen dropped his menu and finished the story for Jor-El. "But then I stayed so close to the bank that when we rounded a bend, an overgrown bush knocked Grandma backwards out of the raft, and all I could see were her feet sticking up out of the water."

"And she got pneumonia."

"You didn't tell Emily that part, did you?"

"I had to. She asked. See, I told you she likes you."

"Yeah. Thanks." Hopefully the kid also shared the part about how his grandmother laughed at the circumstances and how she begged to go rafting every time she'd visited since.

Gigi appeared then, so Tracen and Jor-El could order. As Gigi's stick figure strode away in her nursing shoes, Tracen let his eyes wander back toward the river. He could see Emily now, but he wished he couldn't. Jack had her pressed against a tree. The actor's head dipped down until there was no space between the two of them. The contents of Tracen's stomach curdled.

"She's acting, isn't she?" Jor-El's voice sounded young and worried.

Tracen grunted and turned away. Why did he sit on the patio again? "Kissing scene."

"Have *you* kissed her yet?"

Tracen's spine stiffened, and he tried to remain nonchalant. Maybe the kid wasn't as innocent as he'd thought. He feigned ignorance. "What?"

Jor-El's eyes bored into him. "Maybe if you kiss her, then she won't leave. She'll let another actress play in *Wonder Woman II*, like you said."

Tracen chuckled. "That would be some kiss, kid. But don't worry. She never really wanted to be an actress anyway."

Jor-El's shoulders relaxed as he slouched back down into his seat. "That's good. Because famous people don't usually stay here for long."

Tracen wanted to argue, but all he could do was offer an encouraging smile—a sad smile. Unfortunately, the kid wasn't talking about Serena. He was talking about his dad.

Chapter Thirteen

....

"They're here!" Tracen called, looking out the bay window.

The gravel crunching under tires could barely be heard over Toto's barking. Then another noise joined the symphony. Emily's phone. She pulled the device from her purse in surprise. She so rarely had the phone charged and with her that she wasn't used to the old-fashioned ring.

Tracen planted a kiss on her forehead, and all sounds faded away. "Go ahead and answer it. Then tell whoever is calling that you're spending time with family, and you won't be available for the rest of the day."

Emily enjoyed the warmth that spread through her. He was so sweet. Giving, yet protective at the same time. And she liked the sound of his word *family*. It made her feel like she'd come home.

For privacy, Emily stepped up into the kitchen of the manufactured home from the cozy addition Tracen had built on—she didn't want to seem rude and full of herself the first time she met Tracen's brothers. He had four of them. Growing up in the Lake household must have been a blast.

Emily flipped open the phone to hear Bruce's curt greeting, then his bossy babbling. The man obviously hated holidays, as they kept him from his work.

"Okay, Bruce, okay, okay."

The back door slammed, and a variety of male voices drew her attention away. "Bruce, we'll talk tomorrow."

Bruce kept talking.

"Okay," she said again. Yes, she would be ready to shoot on time. It wasn't like she was always late. Well, maybe she had been since she got to Sun Valley. A small smile played on her lips. Filming seemed so unimportant when Tracen was around.

"All right, Bruce. I'll be there. I'm turning off my phone now."

Whew. She held the power button down and listened to see if Tracen had mentioned her yet.

"So," an unfamiliar voice spoke up, "you're really helping coordinate the rafting scenes for the movie being filmed here?" The tone sounded just a little cocky. She wondered how the guy's attitude would change when she walked into the room.

"Yeah." Emily pictured Tracen leaning against the fireplace mantel with arms crossed. She took a step toward the family room.

A lower voice broke in. "Is that actress Emily Van Arsdale in it?"

That actress? Emily paused and waited for Tracen's response.

"Yeah," was all he said, though she could almost hear his smile.

"Have you met her?" A younger voice now.

Emily covered her mouth to hold back a laugh. What would Tracen's brothers think if they knew *that actress* was listening to their conversation?

Tracen repeated his standard answer. "Yeah." Was he waiting for her to make an entrance?

"No way!" That must have been the young brother.

A commanding voice now. "What's she like in real person?"

Real person. As if actors weren't real people.

"She's adorable."

Ahh. Tracen couldn't have given a better answer. Later she'd thank him properly for such a compliment. She sneaked toward the doorway. Tracen's eyes caught hers, and he gave a barely discernible nod. Two of his brothers sat in her line of sight, but they had their backs toward her.

The cocky voice again. "Can you introduce us?"

A snicker came from the back of the room. "You're engaged, dude."

The young-sounding voice spoke up again. "*I'd* like to meet her."

Tracen's head tilted toward the ceiling, as if he didn't want his brothers to see his expression. He looked back down at the brother with a buzz cut. "Sam, I'm so happy to have you back on American soil safe and sound that I would do anything for you."

Sam's spine shot up straighter. "You mean you'd introduce me to Emily Van Arsdale? You can do that?"

The other brothers chuckled. One tossed a throw pillow at Tracen.

Tracen smiled at the floor now, scratching the back of his neck. He looked up and shook his head. Then he gazed at Emily, eyes twinkling. That was her cue.

Emily stepped forward, her flip-flops squishing against the laminate hardwood flooring. The faces that swiveled to look at her could have come right out of a comic strip—eyes popping out, chins to the floor, cheeks bright red. She made her way to Tracen and slipped her arm through his.

"Welcome home, Sam."

Sam laughed in disbelief. He threw the baseball cap he was holding into the air. "No way."

Tracen slid a solid arm behind Emily's back, his smile just as warm as his touch. He pulled his gaze away from hers to address his brothers. "I told you I'd introduce you to Emily, but keep in mind that she's taken."

"What?"

"You're kidding."

"You mean by *you*?"

Sam leaned forward in his seat, face aglow. "Emily Van Arsdale. Holy buckets! Please tell me you're not dating my dopey brother. You could do so much better."

Tracen kicked the hat back at him. "Thanks a lot, Bro."

Emily squinted as she thought over their short relationship. "Actually…" The room quieted. "I don't think we are dating. You've never asked me out, Tracen."

Tracen turned to face her, playing along. "I haven't?"

"No. Howie invited me to go waterskiing. And then I had to bribe you to get you to go to Boise with me. That's not really dating." Though the thrill from her non-dates had all exceeded any date she'd ever been on.

"Ooh," the cocky brother taunted Tracen. Now Emily could see he had spiky hair and a bright blue dress shirt with an expensive-looking striped tie.

"That's not very romantic, Trace," the oldest brother reprimanded, reigning from a recliner in the corner. His coloring and gruffness reminded her of Kiefer Sutherland.

"Ask her out, Tracen." The second brother in line looked to be the smallest and the sweetest.

Sam piped up, sporting a wicked grin. "Or don't. Then I'd still have a chance."

Emily laughed at all their support. What had she been worried about? Tracen's brothers were the kind of family she'd always imagined.

"So, Em?" Tracen spoke as if offhand. "Would you want to go on a date this weekend? Maybe fishing? And then a rodeo? What do you think?"

The guy in the tie grunted with disapproval. Emily bet he'd worked a little harder when winning the heart of his fiancée. That was one of the things she loved about her relationship with Tracen. It wasn't work.

"I thought you'd never ask." She beamed.

Tracen made the introductions then. His oldest brother Dave ran a Christian retreat center on the coast with his wife and three kids. The next brother, Matt, the sweet one, worked as a private pilot for a wealthy businessman in Portland, Oregon. He'd flown all the brothers down to Sun Valley, landing on Redfish Lake in his boss's new pontoon plane. Josh, the slick sibling, was two years younger than Tracen and worked as a sales director in Chicago. Then there was Sam, who was the youngest, the tallest, and now the buffest from his training duties with the military.

Emily shook hands all around. Sam took advantage of being last. He twirled her close and dipped her. "If I'd have known I was going to get this kind of greeting when I returned to the States, I would have come back sooner."

"You're cute, Sam, but I think you're too tall for me."

Tracen's laugh sounded louder than the rest. He pulled Emily to her feet and out of Sam's grip. His eyes twinkled, telling her he was thinking the same thing she was. They'd come a long way since he'd told her she was too short for him—though she still didn't know what had caused him to avoid her in the first place. He'd practically run away the time she traced the scar on his ribs. And she hadn't even meant anything by it—just wanted to remember his name.

"Wait a minute." She stood up straighter, her back to Tracen, though she couldn't possibly forget he was there with the way his fingertips ran up and down her arms. She pointed from brother to brother as she recited their names. "Dave. Matt. Josh. Sam." She spun to face the guy she was now dating. "Tracen."

Tracen shrugged at his brothers, as if trying to explain her actions. "She's usually bad at names."

"Only names that are hard to remember," she retorted. "Like yours. Only yours." The Sesame Street song "One of These Things Is Not Like the Others" played through her head. "Where did you get your name?"

Dave piped up. "His name was supposed to be Pete."

Emily's face split into a smile. "Pete?" He was no Pete.

Josh joined in. "But see, if he'd been a girl, Mom and Dad were going to name him Tracy."

Emily felt her smile grow wider. She didn't know if she could trust Josh, but that would be pretty funny if he spoke the truth. "Seriously?"

Tracen gave a weak nod.

Matt finished the story. "Mom got tired of waiting for a daughter, so when Dad left the room she wrote the name *Tracen* on his birth certificate."

Emily guffawed. Who would do that? She wanted to dig deeper, but Tracen had his head bent low, so she encouraged him the way she had Jor-El. "Well, I like Tracen. It's a unique name." She added a little more softly, "And it goes with the scar."

Tracen's fingers intertwined with hers, as if he were remembering the first time she'd touched him. "I'm glad you like the name *Tracen*," he said, his eyes finding hers. "But I think it's more important that you like the name *Lake*."

The bubble of excitement that rose within made Emily feel lighter than air—like a helium balloon. She did like the name Lake. She tested it out further. *Emily Lake.* She liked the sound of that too. Was she getting ahead of herself? Moving too fast?

A throat cleared in the silence that surrounded them, reminding Emily that they weren't alone. "So, Tracen, are you still planning on staying in Sun Valley?"

Tracen's head jerked up, their connection cut off. The glare he sent his brother Matt made her wonder what else she didn't know about Tracen Lake. "Of course." The tension in his voice drained away as he continued, and Emily wondered if it was all in her imagination. "I just got the blueprints for my cabin. I'll start building it as soon as the filming of Emily's movie ends. In fact, it's her movie that's paying for my down payment."

Emily tilted her head. Tracen was building a cabin? She wanted to ask more, but not in front of his brothers. Not when everybody else already knew what he was talking about.

"Are the blueprints here?" Dave asked. "Can we see them?"

"Yeah." Tracen pointed toward the kitchen. "They're on the dining room table. I knew you guys would want to look 'em over. I've got a wraparound porch. And dormer windows. The garage will only be attached by a covered walkway."

The men filed out of the room. Emily trailed after Tracen, but as soon as his brothers were out of sight, he turned back and bent low to kiss her. Contentment hummed through her core. She couldn't get enough of this man, and apparently he felt the same way. Wrapping both arms behind his neck, she invited him closer, but before his lips reached hers, Josh walked back in. Tracen slid away.

"Can I grab something to drink? You got soda in the fridge?"

"Sure. Yeah. Go." Tracen waved him away.

Josh sent her one of his arrogant smiles before disappearing back into the kitchen.

Tracen didn't seem to mind the fact that they'd almost gotten caught. He locked his arms behind her back and drew her to him once again. She loved the fact that as much as Tracen missed his brothers, he still wanted to make time for her.

"You're building a cabin?" She spoke quietly, intimately.

"Yeah." He brushed her lips with his.

"Right here by the river?"

"Yeah." His lips pressed against hers longer this time.

Mmm. This was how they should have all their conversations.

Josh interrupted again. "Tracen?"

Tracen broke away slowly, not taking his eyes off Emily. "What?" he barked.

"Mom and Dad are here."

Emily turned to find Mrs. Lake standing at the top of the three wide stairs. She must have come in through the front door, though she looked as if she wished she hadn't.

* * * * *

The ribs Tracen had ordered from The Point practically fell off the bone. Emily licked the last bit of tangy barbecue sauce from her fingers. Too bad she was too full to eat more. Eating had given her something to do, since it wasn't like she had anything to contribute to the conversations around her. Unfortunately, the ribs were the best thing about the picnic dinner.

Tracen ran a hand up and down her back, but with the way his mom watched them, she felt stiff and uncomfortable any time he touched her. The woman probably just disapproved because of the way she'd found them together. Emily took a deep breath and sighed. So much for a good first impression.

The refreshing breeze blew a few strands of hair across Emily's face. She tucked it behind her ear and tried to focus on the story Tracen's dad was telling. He'd become Mrs. Lake's interpreter. Mrs. Lake had just ranted about the humidity in Florida, so Mr. Lake was explaining how they came to move so far away.

He shifted to face Emily from his position beside her on the picnic bench. She had to look up because he was just as tall as Tracen. "So every year we would drive a truck full of Christmas trees cross-country to sell them in Florida."

"Wow," Emily murmured. "You'd think they could get trees from the East Coast or at least somewhere closer."

"Oh, they could." Mr. Lake gave a lazy half-smile. "But then we wouldn't make any money off them…. Driving to Florida was never a problem. It was the coming back home that always depressed Becky. She hated returning to all this rain. Finally, I suggested we not return at all. It's been a nice change of pace for us, hasn't it, dear?"

Mrs. Lake nodded grudgingly. Maybe the woman simply wasn't fond of Emily's relationship with Tracen because she wasn't fond of much at all. She was the exact opposite of Violet. Emily sent up a silent prayer of thanks for her mother's optimism.

"Hey, Emily Van Arsdale!"

Emily smiled over at Tracen's oldest brother. They were all still calling her by her full name. Too cute.

Dave held up an action figure—a female with red boots and a star-spangled cape. "Look what I found in my suitcase. It must belong to one of my daughters."

Tracen held out a hand. "Let me see that."

Dave tossed the doll, and Tracen caught it in his palm. She had to get used to the way the Lake boys threw everything. When she'd asked Josh to pass the ketchup, it had become a football, and she hadn't been quite ready to play receiver.

Emily watched in good humor. The action figure didn't bother her. She'd learned to expect seeing her image everywhere. The mall was the worst—DVD covers in the electronics store, T-shirts in the T-shirt store, even a sketch of Wonder Woman at an artist's booth. Why would she think she could get away from it all in Tracen's backyard?

"If you ask me, her outfit is kind of skimpy." Mrs. Lake sniffed.

Josh quipped, "Why do you think the movie did so well, Mom?"

which started another conversation between the brothers about their favorite actresses.

Emily refused to wilt in embarrassment. "It's a patriotic costume. I actually thought about wearing it this weekend, for the Fourth of July."

She stifled the smile that the image brought, but the brothers hooted in laughter. Mrs. Lake's expression soured like the lemonade Emily had forgotten to add sugar to.

The truth was that it had been like wearing a swimming suit to work when she was filming *Wonder Woman*, but with the way swimming suits were designed anymore, the costume could be considered modest. Relief swept through her as Tracen held the doll next to her face, thus moving on.

"I don't see much resemblance," he said, tilting his head. "The doll's nose is proportionately bigger and her eyebrows are thinner. And she doesn't have the same amazing bone structure."

Emily chuckled. "What do you know about bone structure?"

The expression in Tracen's eyes warmed. "I know I like looking at yours."

Emily wanted to get lost in Tracen's gaze. She liked looking at him too. But the clatter from across the table told her that Mrs. Lake was clearing the dishes. Emily had better help to make up for her last comment. She gave a "thank-you" smile to Tracen before standing.

Making polite small talk, Emily gathered all the condiments onto a tray. She hoped this would be a chance to connect with Tracen's mom, but somehow she ended up loading the dishwasher all by herself. She finished and headed back to the bathroom to look for hand soap. Being the bachelor that he was, Tracen just used dish soap to wash his hands in the kitchen. She stepped into the tiny room and was just about to flick on the water when Tracen's voice outside the open window caught her attention.

"Why don't you like her, Mom?"

Emily's inhale got stuck in her throat. He was talking about her. With his mom. Who obviously wasn't her biggest fan.

"I do like her."

Whew.

"She's beautiful. Sweet. Confident. You said she's a Christian."

All good things, but the woman's tone didn't sound accepting. Emily tensed for the "but" that was coming.

"But?" asked Tracen.

"She's an actress."

Emily frowned. How ridiculous. Tracen's excuse that she'd been too short for him was more of a legitimate reason not to like her. Did the woman think she was acting? That she didn't really care for Tracen?

"Mom, she's from Boise. She's moving back to Idaho."

Quiet. Except for Emily's heart pounding.

"Tracen…" The one word sounded like it had a lot more meaning to the guy she spoke it to. Like they'd had this argument before, and he already knew what she was going to say. Emily, however, had no idea.

Tracen's response filled in the missing pieces. "I know what you're getting at, Mom. And I worried about the same thing at first. But she's not Serena. She's not obsessed with fame. It's different this time."

Emily's chest constricted. Was Serena another actress? Had she left Tracen for Hollywood?

Mrs. Lake's voice softened. Maybe she focused on negatives to protect the ones she loved. "I don't want you to get hurt, Sugar."

* * * * *

Tracen watched the light from the exploding fireworks play over Emily's features. She lay on the roof next to him. Both had their hands behind their heads, but Emily was looking up, while he was looking at her.

Had his mom been right? Or Honey, for that matter? Jor-El's mention of a sequel to *Wonder Woman* played in his mind. But Emily would have told him about it. She said she wanted to come back to Idaho. She fit in here.

Her profile pivoted until she was facing him.

"Did you have a nice day?" His brothers could be a little over-whelming sometimes, but she seemed to enjoy them.

Emily's lashes lowered for a moment so he couldn't see her eyes. She glanced back up, but with the shadows, it was still hard to read her. "Your brothers are great. And your dad too."

At the moment all four of his brothers were down by the water's edge. Dave had a permit to shoot off fireworks that were normally considered illegal in Idaho. (His retreat center put on a display every year for New Year's.) He could hear them now, laughing about Sam's exploits in Iraq. Sam would tell them stuff that he didn't tell their parents—stuff parents didn't want to hear.

He'd hear Sam's stories later. His little brother wanted to stay with Tracen for a while. It had to be hard coming home from serving in the military, only to find that the home you grew up in no longer existed.

Tracen's parents had already left for the night. They were staying at Howie's house. He had Emily all to himself.

"I think Sam's got a crush on you." Sam had to be six years younger than her. It was like having a crush on a babysitter.

"Sam has been surrounded by men for the last year. He'd have a crush on anyone in a skirt."

"Or a cape, for that matter." Tracen grinned and laced her delicate fingers through his, claiming her as his own. He lifted her hand so he could study it, their elbows resting on the rough shingles between them. The booming and whistling of fireworks faded so that the chirping of crickets seemed loud. Satisfaction filled him. There was nowhere else he would rather be.

"Tracen?" Her hesitant voice roused him from rest.

"Yeah?"

"I might be jumping ahead in our relationship, but I want you to know that I can't picture myself ever being with anyone else."

The current of his blood sped up. He rolled to his side and lifted up to an elbow. She was so beautiful bathed in moonbeams. How did he get so lucky?

She continued, as if afraid he might interrupt. "I'm not one of those actresses who meets a new boyfriend with every film. This is new for me."

She watched like she was looking for a sign that he wouldn't believe her. Probably because what she was saying was unbelievable. If he didn't feel the same way, he'd assume she was playing him. Had one of his brothers fallen into a romantic relationship so quickly, he'd wrestle said brother into the shower and blast him with cold water.

But this was different. They couldn't take their time and let things happen naturally. Either they went their separate ways when she finished filming the movie, or they took action now to make sure that they could be together later. Emily was definitely worth taking action for.

Emily curled onto her side to face him, tucking both hands under her cheek like a pillow. Tracen watched her, unsure how to communicate his feelings. Earlier he'd mentioned that it was important she like the last name Lake. Wasn't that enough?

"I'm really glad to hear you say that," he responded at last. There. They were on the same page. Now they could just laugh about the way Toto chewed up the Wonder Woman action figure or the way his brothers kept trying to impress Emily by giving their own reviews to all the movies that had just come out.

"Who is Serena?"

"What?" Tracen blurted. He couldn't have heard her right, and if he did, then his stupid question bought him a little more time to figure out what he was going to say. Did one of his brothers blab about his ex? He was going to kill whoever it was. Unless it was Sam, of course. Sam could probably take Tracen out without even standing up.

"I overheard your mom say she didn't want you to get hurt."

Oh, his mom. Darn that woman for being so protective.

"And I overheard you say that you'd been worried at first that I was like Serena."

She may not be a superhero, but she sure had super hearing. He wondered if his dog whistle would affect her.

Emily wouldn't let it go. "Is she an actress?"

Serena an actress? This conversation wasn't making sense

anymore. But that could be because he wasn't participating in it. "She's a dancer."

"And she went to Hollywood?"

He probably should have told her earlier. But he'd still been trying to figure her out at the time. "Serena was my high school sweetheart. I proposed the week we graduated."

"That's young." Emily sounded like she was making excuses for Serena. He didn't want to hear it.

"We were supposed to go to college together in Moscow, Idaho. Then we were going to take over the tree farm. But halfway through our freshman year she ran off." He still had the letter she left him. The rose-patterned stationery. The scrunched script. The tearstains. His and hers.

Emily spoke quietly. "That was a long time ago."

She didn't get it. She'd never had a fiancé dump her, so she couldn't. "Yeah." He should just leave it there. Emily didn't need to know that, since Serena, he hadn't met a single woman who cared about him enough to stay in Sun Valley.

"So that's really why Honey and Gigi warned that you wouldn't be interested in dating me."

She'd connected the dots, which was better than him having to spill his guts. Couldn't they get serious about each other without such serious conversations?

"Yeah. Though you are pretty short."

Emily giggled, scooting closer.

It took him a moment to realize that she was comparing the length of their legs. With their hips lined up, her feet only reached to his calves. "I think I was your height in sixth grade."

Emily's teeth flashed in the moonlight as she grinned. "Then we were the same height. I haven't grown since I was twelve."

Tracen chuckled and stretched out, feeling his muscles tighten then relax. The heat from the day had followed the sun, but he wasn't going to let the growing chill ruin his moment. In fact, he'd give his sweatshirt to Emily if she suggested going in because she was cold. It surprised him that she hadn't made the suggestion already.

"Tracen?"

"You can have my sweatshirt." He sat to unzip the hoodie and lay it over her.

"Thanks." She snuggled down. "But that's not what I was going to ask."

Goose bumps popped up on his arms, so he used it as an excuse to pull Emily close. Body heat had benefits. He nuzzled his nose into her fruity-smelling hair and considered kissing her, but their lip locks hadn't been turning out well. First her mom found them together. Then his. If he tried anything now, he'd probably roll them right off the roof and into his brothers' laps.

"What'd you wanna ask?" he murmured. His lips were so close to her temple. One little kiss couldn't—

"Do you miss her?"

Ooh, that hurt. Tracen stilled. Why were they still talking about Serena? He pulled a couple strands of Emily's hair from his mouth. *Blech.* "Not really."

Emily tilted her head to look up at his face. It would have been the perfect opportunity for a kiss, were they not still talking about his ex-girlfriend.

"What does that mean?"

Tracen groaned. He thought he'd gotten out of revisiting past pain. But he owed it to her. She'd shared about her father's illness. "I guess I mean that I don't really miss Serena. I just miss what we could have had together. You know, the home-cooked meals every night, the two point five kids, the vacations to Disney World™. I had it all perfectly arranged in my head."

Tracen felt the tender touch before he realized Emily had lifted her fingers to his face. She traced his hairline, then his eyebrows, his cheeks, his chin—as if wanting to memorize his every feature. Tracen hoped her memory of features was as bad as it was for names. He'd enjoy the tingles that her prolonged practice would bring.

"Life is never what we expect it to be."

Tracen lifted his own hand to pull hers to his lips. He brushed a kiss across her fingertips. "Sometimes it's better."

Chapter Fourteen
....

Tracen slowed his rusty old Silverado and pulled off the main road since it was apparently closed for a parade. They detoured around The Days of the Old West, passing a kiddie carnival and art display. Emily decided to check out the local art for a memento when they returned for the rodeo later.

No wonder Bruce had wanted to start filming earlier. The population of the tiny town seemed to have doubled. His scenes would definitely have been compromised by giggly teenagers or curious fans.

Tracen headed down Highway 75 to take her fly fishing at the infamous Silver Creek. The brothers made it sound like she'd be facing a challenge, but she loved the excuse to be alone with Tracen. It beat attending the Weekend of Antiques with his mom. Though she would have enjoyed watching the Summer Ice Show performed on the outdoor rink behind the resort where she stayed.

"You know…" Tracen pulled off the highway, giving Emily a glimpse of the river snaking through the valley ahead. "The first time my dad ever came fishing here, he met Ernest Hemingway."

Was he pulling her leg? "Hemingway fished?"

"Oh yeah. His favorite sport. His son actually persuaded The Nature Conservancy to purchase the Silver Creek Preserve, and Hemingway's wife donated his last house out to them." Tracen nodded toward a stone marker that read THE HEMINGWAY LEGACY as they passed. "He used to also hunt duck from a canoe out here."

Now that intrigued Emily. "I'm staying in the Hemingway Suite at the resort. The concierge made a big deal out of it, but I really don't know anything about the guy."

Tracen slowed and wedged his truck under some trees at the side of the road. "Yeah, the resort used to invite all kinds of celebrities up to gain popularity. You've probably seen the black and white photos lining the hallways."

Emily swung her large door open and slid out. "Yep. Though I was more impressed with the fact that Sun Valley had the first chairlifts. I can't wait to ski Baldy this winter."

Tracen hauled a couple fishing poles out of the truck bed. "I'll take you up there before it snows. You might like paragliding off the top."

Emily's toes curled, and her stomach heaved at the idea of dangling from such height. "Um, that might be too close to skydiving."

Tracen joined her, wrapping an arm around her shoulders. He grinned down at her. "You'd love it, my dear."

"Maybe." Or maybe she just loved the thrill of being close to him. Falling in love could be considered a little like skydiving.

Turning her attention from him for the first time, she surveyed their surroundings. Glistening water shimmied along over rocks and around sagebrush. She felt just as free.

Tracen led her down a beaten path to a muddy embankment. "Have you ever gone fishing before?"

"I have." She avoided Tracen's eyes but didn't miss the twitch that almost turned into a smile on his lips.

"Did you catch anything?"

"I did."

Now Tracen gave her a full grin—a surprised yet approving full grin. "I'm impressed."

Emily grinned back. Hopefully she didn't make too big a fool of herself with his rod and reel.

"When was the last time you fished?"

Apparently real fishermen liked telling their fishing stories. She was not one of them. "I was ten years old, and my dad had just gotten his first boat." She smiled sheepishly. Though he wore his ever-present sunglasses, she could imagine Tracen's hazel eyes sparkling like sunshine reflected off the river. Might as well tell the whole truth. "Dad threw my fish back, which made me mad. Fishing seemed like such a waste of time after that. Especially since all the other boaters got to water ski. I told my dad to take my fishing pole back and get me skis."

"*There* it is." Tracen acted as if her fishing experience were a joke, and he'd been waiting for a punch line.

Her defenses stiffened her spine and lowered her voice. "What?" She lifted her chin as she watched him dig through a little backpack he wore on his chest.

Tracen studied the area, looking for just the right spot to cast from. "I wondered if you would get bored today."

Just past Tracen a fish jumped, causing a small splash and rippling effect. She was so enthralled by the simple beauty, she almost forgot what they'd been discussing. Oh yeah, boredom. She'd definitely not be bored, and his assumption was so off the mark that it didn't even deserve a response. Anything was an adventure with Tracen around.

Digging her cell phone out of her shorts pocket, she delighted in the fact that she'd remembered it for once. "This is all so pretty. I want to take a picture." She pressed the power button, hoping the battery wasn't dead. The responding digital ding let her know she was in luck. She stepped back from the creek. "Stand there, Tracen." She pointed the phone at him to capture the image, but he didn't cooperate and stay still.

By the time she looked up from her camera to figure out what he was doing, he had his arm around her and held the phone out to snap a photo of them together. She smiled, and it wasn't just for the camera.

Tracen brought the phone back down so they could both see the screen. His grin had been as big as hers. He pushed the button to save their photo, then squinted at the phone. "Did you know you have voice mail?"

Emily leaned closer to see what he was looking at. "I do? How do you know?"

Tracen pointed to the blue envelope icon. "Don't you know how to work this thing?"

Emily pulled the phone from his grip and pressed the power button. She wasn't going to spend her time in the great outdoors attached to technology. "I know how to press 911 if I ever have an emergency. And I don't even have to have a service plan to do that."

Tracen shook his head as if in disbelief but focused back on his task. Tossing the line into the water with ease, he handed her the pole.

She gripped the plastic handle part tightly, knowing she must be doing it all wrong. But Tracen didn't seem to mind. He went to work on his own reel.

"This area is so gorgeous."

"Yeah." He glanced up. "There are lots of weddings by this bridge now. And you just missed the first annual Rhythm and Ride. It's a new bike and music festival. You like country music?"

Emily enjoyed a lot of country music. Mixed with the scent of cigarettes, it always reminded her of her line-dancing days in high school. She used to sneak into The Buffalo Club to dance, since at school dances she wasn't allowed to have the guys swing her in the air.

Rhythm and Ride sounded like a blast, but it was the wedding part that held her attention. She pictured Tracen wanting an outdoor wedding. And she pictured herself as the bride. Hey, at an outdoor wedding she could even wear flip-flops with her dress.

It had to be more than a coincidence that the theme in her life was water and his last name was Lake. She hoped the connection hadn't scared him off. She'd been pretty brash in declaring her intentions toward him on his roof the night before. His reaction had been encouraging, but confusing. How could she feel like she knew him so well but not be able to read him?

* * * * *

Tracen couldn't read her. She had no clue how to hold a fishing pole, but that didn't seem to be what was worrying her. She'd gone quiet for some other reason. Was she bored already?

"Did you know that Idaho is known for its fishing?" he asked to keep her engaged.

Emily's gaze flicked to his. "Really?"

"Yeah." Well, that was the end of that conversation. He looked down into the water, but the sun's reflection kept him from seeing anything underneath its surface. A sneeze raked through him before he was able to slide his sunglasses back down onto his nose.

"Bless you."

"Thanks." Tracen watched Emily from behind his shades. Maybe they could just enjoy the silence together. What was it called? A comfortable silence. But if it was supposed to be comfortable, then why was Tracen stressing over it? If he wanted to know what she was thinking, he should just ask. "What are you thinking?"

Emily spun the handle on her reel lazily. If she kept it up, he'd have to cast for her again soon. Or maybe he could teach her how to do it, though she didn't seem to be overly excited about their outing. He'd joked about her getting bored, but the fear was very real. The parade earlier was about as wild as Sun Valley ever got. Could she get used to such a tiny town after living in Tinseltown?

The apples of Emily's cheeks hinted at the smile she hid inside. Whatever she was thinking, it must be good. He'd worry about her leaving Sun Valley later. Right now he'd just enjoy the time he had with her.

"My Bible study on water—this morning I read about how Jesus helped Peter catch a lot of fish. I was just thinking I could use a little help as well."

Tracen loved that story. He should have asked sooner, instead of working himself up over nothing. "You know what's interesting about that miracle?"

Emily's crystal blue eyes lit up like a trivia question on a game show. She was as excited to discuss the Bible with him as contestants were to get their name called for *The Price Is Right*. "What?"

Well, he was just as eager to answer her. "The water." Tracen motioned toward the creek below them. "The water was so clear that the fish could see the net and swim away if anybody tried to fish during the day. That's why they'd been fishing at night."

Emily leaned against the railing on the bridge. "I didn't know that."

Tracen nodded thoughtfully. "They'd been fishing all night—doing it their own way—with no results. Then Jesus tells them to try something different, and against all odds, it works."

Emily's eyes remained on him. "That lesson can apply to all of us somehow. You know, like we try and try and try to do something the way we think it should be done, but if we'd just listen to Jesus and do things His way, He would work miracles in our lives."

Tracen let her analogy sink in. She'd gotten more out of the story than he had. It would be interesting to hear her take on all the other crazy things that happened in the Bible, as well. Of course, that would take a long, long time. He smiled at the idea. "Good stuff, huh?"

Tracen lowered himself to a pile of rocks. This is what he loved about fishing. No mindless distractions. No pressing needs. He could contemplate the wonder that was life. And with Emily around, it was all the more wonderful. No more Lonesome Larry.

Around the same time Serena had left him, not a single sockeye salmon returned to Redfish Lake for spawning. The following year only one fish returned, and the media nicknamed him Lonesome Larry. Tracen had often thought of himself as a Lonesome Larry. But now he had Emily, and she was so worth waiting for.

"I'm going to write down the story of Jesus and the fish in my prayer journal."

What other nuggets of wisdom had she scribbled in her prayer journal? She'd seemed to hide it from him the one time he found her writing in it. Hopefully she'd start to feel comfortable enough to share. And hopefully he'd know her long enough for her to share all the messages from God she got out of her little pink Bible.

"That reminds me of one of my favorite quotes," Emily said. "If you want something you've never had, you have to do something you've never done."

Her quote made sense. Yet it was probably one of the hardest of life's lessons to master. It made one accountable for moving on. "Nice."

Tracen offered to hold her fishing reel while she made herself comfortable on a boulder. He waited for just the right moment to share his favorite quote with her.

"You know the definition of insanity, don't you?" he asked.

Emily didn't pause to think like he expected her to. "When a girl falls in love with a guy she's only just met?"

Her response could have knocked him off his rocks. The L-word was one he hadn't uttered since he was a teen. Maybe she'd voiced his own feelings, but were they ready to be voiced?

By the way Emily bit her lip after blurting out her definition, she was asking herself the same question, not to mention mentally flinching at the possibilities of how he could respond. He didn't want her to have to flinch around him.

"No, that's just the definition of a lucky guy."

Emily's radiant smile made him feel incredibly lucky. She was

Emily Van Arsdale. And she was planning to move back to Idaho to be with him—among other reasons.

Was this love? He did love her humility, her courage, her thoughtfulness, her transparency, and her sense of humor. He loved the way she didn't need to be the center of attention, but she wasn't shy. He loved the way she worked through tough situations, and how those situations made her stronger. He loved the way she challenged him and didn't back down, even when confronted by the judgments of others.

Yes, if he were honest with himself, he knew he was falling in love with her too. But it wasn't like he was ready to propose, so no use in making premature commitments. He'd done that once before, and the whole town knew about it.

Emily let him off the hook. She probably already understood how he felt. Like by the way he couldn't get her alone fast enough that morning. "So, what is the definition of insanity?"

Many definitions came to Tracen's mind. Like being afraid to fall in love. But he answered the questions with Ben Franklin's words instead. "Insanity is doing the same thing over and over and expecting different results."

"Oh, I like that." Emily's eyes revealed the fact that she liked a lot more than his quote.

Mercy, she could heat him up faster than the July sunshine. If they weren't perched so precariously on rocks and boulders he'd show her how he felt rather than tell her.

The definition he'd given to "lucky guy" rang through his head again. Emily could be anywhere she wanted to be, yet here she was fishing with him. "Lucky" wasn't enough. Emily's attention was no less than a miracle.

What was it that everybody told him when Serena left? "There's more fish in the sea." He'd tried everything to catch himself a bride, but it took being open to the unexpected for him to land a woman more amazing than he could have imagined.

Tracen wondered if they'd be grilling fish for dinner as he looked down at the water. Then another thought struck him. "Do you remember Jesus' first miracle?"

"Um…" Emily kicked her feet from where they dangled. It was so cute. And her feet didn't only dangle off boulders. They dangled off couches and chairs. They pretty much dangled any time she sat down. He'd have to add that to the list of things he loved about her. "It was at a wedding, wasn't it?"

"He turned water into wine." Tracen waited for her to make the connection, but her thoughts seemed to be elsewhere. "Water. Jesus used water in His very first miracle. You should read about that in your water Bible study."

Emily smiled softly, a stray curl falling over one eye. "Thanks," she said before falling silent again. This time it was a comfortable silence, as Tracen got lost in thought himself.

He told himself he was thinking about Jesus' first miracle, but really he was thinking about weddings and how he might propose to Emily someday—certainly not by putting the ring on his fishing hook and letting her be the one to unhook the fish. That was the first thing that went wrong with his engagement to Serena.

Tracen glanced at Emily, wondering what she was thinking. But this time he wasn't going to ask—in case she asked to know his thoughts too.

Chapter Fifteen
....

Tracen stood behind Emily, arms corralling her on either side as he held onto the fence in front, chin resting on top of her head. With their height difference, Emily didn't have to worry about him being able to see over her. No, they both had a clear view of the calf scramble going on. But even with as cute as the lil' buckaroos were, chasing calves to pull the ribbons off their tails, Emily's interest lay completely in the man at her back.

"Did you ever do that?" she asked.

Tracen's stomach vibrated against her as he chuckled. "Nope. Never was a cowboy. Though you know who was?"

Emily twisted to read his expression. Lips turned up, eyes twinkled. Whoever it was, it had to be good. "Who?"

"My brother Josh."

Emily guffawed. He was kidding her. "Your corporate, yuppie brother?"

"That's the one."

"No!"

Tracen's grin radiated amusement and warmth. "He may be a business man now, but he's got that cowboy attitude. Can't you see him swaggering around with a big belt buckle, tipping his hat to the ladies?"

The image formed slowly since the guy didn't seem prone to enjoy the dust kicked up by animal hooves or the odor left behind by other parts of their bodies. "So he actually chased calves as a kid?"

"Uh…" Tracen's eyes lifted from hers to watch the event in front of them. "He might have done it once. But he was more into mutton bustin'."

"Say what?"

Tracen's hands slid from the railing in front of her so he could wrap his arms tightly around her waist. Emily leaned back into the solid embrace. This was what she'd been missing all her life.

"Mutton bustin' is when kids try to ride on the backs of sheep. You'll see in a bit." He spoke into her ear, and the warmth of his breath made the hairs at the nape of her neck stand on end.

What were they talking about again? Oh, yeah. "Little aspiring bull riders, huh?"

"Yeah." Their gazes locked again. "You probably would have loved it too."

Emily thought back to her own childhood. She would have loved riding a sheep, had she not been sick. So many things she'd missed out on because of her allergies. But she was making up for it now. "Probably."

A flash of bright light washed over them, disappearing as quickly as it came. Emily blinked and jerked her head in the direction of its origin. A photographer grinned from just down the fence. He must have left his job snapping shots of the calf scramble to get a shot of her in Tracen's arms.

Tracen turned his back to the paparazzi wannabe, causing Emily to trip over his feet. Good thing he still had his arms around her to keep her steady, or she might have given the camera an unflattering photo op.

Goodness. Tracen's whole body seemed to tense as if were about to drop onto the back of a bucking bronco. "Act natural," she advised, running her hands along his flexed forearms in an effort to soothe. If he was going to date her, he needed to get used to the inconveniences of celebrity status.

Though it wasn't as if she was the only tourist from Southern Cali there. The bleachers were littered with Prada-wearing socialites trying to figure out their first rodeo. Definitely a unique mix of classes that could only be found in a Sun Valley crowd.

"Let's go." Tracen stepped to her side and pulled her along with a protective arm around her shoulders.

A few spectators from the bleachers pointed their direction. Emily responded with a benevolent smile, but Tracen ducked his head and picked up the pace.

"You really want to leave?" Emily glanced back at the corral. The rodeo had barely begun. Their first date wasn't supposed to be over yet.

Tracen hesitated, glancing behind them as well.

Maybe we better leave. The first photographer had been joined by two more, and they all aimed their cameras at the retreating couple.

Tracen slipped his arm from her shoulders and grabbed her hand so they could walk faster. He led her out the massive entry doors of the fairgrounds arena and into the fresh air of evening. Emily bet the photographers followed. Too bad she didn't have her baseball cap to hide under. But a baseball cap might stand out at a rodeo anyway. What they needed were—

"Cowboy hats!" Emily gripped Tracen's hand tighter as she

reversed directions, pulling him into a tent where local merchants hawked their goods.

"What?" Tracen had followed her physically, but mentally he was still caught up in their escape. She could tell, because his eyes remained on the tent entrance.

"Here." Emily stood on her toes to plunk a brown leather Stetson with braided cord trim on Tracen's head.

Whoa. With his stubble-covered jaw and steely eyes, the man looked like he'd just stepped off the cover of the latest romance novel. She cleared her throat, hoping to dislodge her heart. "The look suits you." She tried to turn away, but her eyes boomeranged back. "And it's, um, you know, a disguise."

Tracen focused on her now, raising a hand to pull the brim of his new hat lower. Her pulse picked up even more. How could such a wholesome man be so stunningly sexy?

He lifted his chin, motioning to her head. "What about you?"

Emily forced herself to glance down at the display table.

"Wait." Tracen held a hand up to stop her, as his other hand roved from hat to hat, apparently picking one for her.

She wouldn't try to help him. No, she reveled in the chance to watch him longer. With his loose jeans and raft company T-shirt, he didn't fit the typical mold of cowboy, but he was perfect for her. Casual, quietly confident, strong, attentive…

His attention returned to her as he raised a cute straw hat over her head. He lowered it with both hands, as if crowning her rodeo queen. And she certainly felt like she'd won something.

Normally Emily would want to check her appearance in a mirror— sometimes hats made her curls stick out in odd places—but not this time. She didn't want to destroy the fairy-tale feeling of beauty she got from Tracen's gaze.

"How do I look?" She hoped the bold question concealed her sudden shyness.

Tracen studied her, and though he didn't answer right away, the pride in his eyes told her everything she needed to know. "You're gorgeous." He reached for the wallet in his back pocket. "Too bad you're not going to make any more movies, because you could play the perfect cowgirl."

Coming from Tracen, that was a compliment. She mustered up her best Western drawl. "Why thank ya, partner." She whipped her own credit card out. "Now let me pay fer ya hat, since it's my fault we're a-needin' them."

One side of Tracen's mouth tilted up. "No, a gentleman would never let a lady pay. And you definitely sound more like a Southern belle than a cowboy."

Emily laughed at his take on her impression. She made her voice a little breathier this time. "Well, I do declare." She stepped in front of Tracen and handed her Visa to a leathery looking older guy. "I'm paying."

"Emily..."

She turned her back on the warning in Tracen's voice. "You paid to get us in here, and you bought the barbecued chicken for dinner. My turn."

Tracen huffed.

The aged cowboy winked at Emily as he returned with the receipt for her to sign. He looked past her at Tracen and spoke with a gruff but kind voice. "Boy, I suggest you pull in your horns. This is one sweet little filly you got here."

Emily suppressed a smile and twisted to view Tracen's reaction. "Yeah, pull in your horns."

Tracen propped his hands on his hips. "Sweet filly, huh? More like a wild Mustang who needs taming."

The clerk gave a raspy chuckle. "Then you better pony up, son." He lined up Emily's receipt with her credit card and read her name before handing them back. "And you have a hog-killin' time tonight, Miss Emily Van Arsdale. I'm much obliged for your business."

Emily nodded, aware of the hush that fell over the tent as the salesman announced her name. The gentle expression he wore didn't reveal any awareness on his part of who she was, but the curious looks she got from other customers ruined the anonymity she was going for with the hats.

Tracen lifted a brow. "Shall we go now, little filly?"

Emily followed him back out under the stars. Groups of people milled about, waiting for the bigger events to draw them back inside the arena. Emily wondered if she'd missed all the mutton busting by now. She was going to suggest they return to the rodeo when Tracen's fingers dug into the flesh of her upper arm, and he yanked her back behind the tent they had just exited.

"Photographers," he muttered.

Boy, a little attention made him a whole lot grumpy.

"Come on, I think we can get in through a back door." He led the way around the large barn-shaped building.

Laughter and shouting grew louder as they neared the rear of the arena. Turning the corner, they ran into an area sectioned off by hay bales. Inside, Howie bounced around on top of a mechanical bull.

Emily's insides jumped. Scared for Howie, she analyzed his

movements. One hand clutched the horn while the other waved in the air. His legs bounced against the sides of the beast and his head whipped around in a way that made her teeth hurt. All he needed was to squeeze with his inner thighs and relax his upper body—like a tree rooted to the ground and bending in the wind. Howie only lasted another second. Dirt pillowed up around the red air mattress as he landed with a thud. But he was safe. Which was especially important to Emily now that she knew the role he'd played in her father's life.

Tracen gave a belly laugh and waved. "Hope you have a good chiropractor, Travolta," he called.

Honey ushered Howie over. "Leave the urban cowboy alone."

Howie pushed his hips to one side, then the other, stretching his back and grimacing. "It's been awhile since I rode Brutus."

Emily patted him on the arm. "Very entertaining, Howie."

Howie cracked his neck and grinned down at her. "That's what it's all about."

A carnival-like call came from speakers inside the ring. "Who's next? Anybody else brave enough to go for a ride?"

Emily glanced around, already feeling herself buckle and twist along with the machine. There seemed to be no line. Somebody had to step up. And her muscles longed for the challenge.

"Come on, cowboys. If you're not going to ride a *real* bull, at least give this one a try."

Oh, she should let Tracen have a chance. But Howie had all his attention. Other bystanders crowded in little circles to chat, forgetting the action. A few even wandered off. What a waste of a mechanical bull.

"How about a cowgirl?" The voice doubled its dare. "I'll go easier on a lady."

Still no volunteers. Emily couldn't stay away any longer.

* * * * *

"Tracen." Honey leaned in toward him while Howie accepted congratulations from the last rider thrown off Brutus. "I'm afraid Howie might really be hurt, and he's just trying to act tough in front of me."

Ah, wasn't that sweet? With all of Honey's bossiness, her softer side never failed to surprise Tracen. He motioned for her to run off. "Go get a drink or something, and I'll find out for sure."

Tracen ignored the mechanical bull operator calling for another rider and waited for Howie. His friend turned toward him with a grin. "Your turn, Tracen. Gotta impress your lady."

"Yeah." Tracen snorted. "Like you impressed her?" He glanced over his shoulder to check on Emily. She seemed to be engrossed with people watching—probably looking for those annoying photographers to pop up again.

Howie held up his hands in mock defense. "If you're too intimidated to follow my ride, I completely understand. I'd likely make you look bad."

Tracen clicked his tongue. "You took quite a tumble there, Howie. Are you sure you're all right?" *In the head?*

"How would I know if I was alive unless I felt a little pain now and then?" Howie shrugged it off as the guy by the mechanical bull called for a lady to ride. "Hey, there you go, Trace. If you're not too worried about getting your skirt dirty, the ride operator will put the bull on an easier level for you."

"Funny."

"No." Howie shook his head. "This is funny: What was the bull doing in the pasture with his eyes closed?"

Tracen glanced towards the concession booth for Honey. He'd tried to do her a favor, and in return he was ridiculed and subjected to lame jokes. "What?"

"Bull-dozing! Get it? He was sleeping. Kind of like what you're doing now instead of riding the bull."

Fine. Tracen would ride just to get Howie to shut up. It shouldn't be much harder than riding a rapid. And hey, if he got hurt, Emily could nurse his injuries. He opened his mouth to volunteer, but somebody else beat him to it.

"I'll ride," Emily announced in her clear, sweet voice as she leapt to a hay bale. He should have known.

She looked back at Tracen with a splash of excitement in her pool-colored eyes as the man with the microphone grasped her hand and led her toward the metal beast. Tracen pushed through the crowd to follow, to get a closer view of her upcoming performance. She would be fine. She always was. And the guy in charge said he'd put it on an easy level for females. So why did Tracen feel a queasiness in his gut?

"What's your name, darlin'?"

Maybe it was the guy touching and talking to Emily that made him queasy.

Emily leaned closer to him to speak into the microphone. "Emily." Her voice boomed from a couple of static-filled speakers.

The guy's head moved as he perused her up and down. Tracen's stomach clenched as tight as his fists. The jerk better lay off or he would—

"Emily," the man repeated in a D.J.-type baritone. "I thought so."

He knew it. She'd been recognized. If he started a scene now, the news would be sure to spread. He wouldn't be Tracen Lake, rafting guide, anymore. He'd become the guy who got into a fight over Emily Van Arsdale. Deep breath.

"Have you ever gone for a ride before, Emily?" Even the guy's tone sounded sleazy. He held out a waiver for her to sign.

Another deep breath. Maybe she wouldn't sign it.

Emily signed it. "Any advice?"

The operator gripped her waist as she climbed over the air mattress to mount, and Tracen couldn't hear his response, but when the operator released Emily and lifted the microphone back to his lips, his words were intended for everyone to hear. "Emily Van Arsdale, ladies and gentleman. We've got Wonder Woman herself bull riding at our Sun Valley Rodeo. You won't want to miss this."

Warm, fleshy bodies pressed into Tracen from behind. He shifted his feet to keep balanced. That's all he could do. Emily would have to do the rest.

"Are? We? Ready?"

Whoops and hollers rose around him. Emily lifted her hat in the air and smiled, though her eyes seemed to be searching for his. Before he could catch her attention, she smashed the hat back on her head and focused on her task at hand.

The grinding of gears signaled the beginning of the show. The bull leaned forward and then backwards. Emily's hips rocked with the rhythm. A fox whistle split the air. Tracen frowned.

Brutus began to spin. Not in a rush thankfully. The guy in charge really was taking it easy on Emily. Though it might have been better had she been knocked right off. How long would Tracen have to endure such a public display of his date?

Howie sidled up beside him. "She makes it look easy."

"Are you surprised?"

"Well, I'm sure they'll speed it up for her. The thing can rock sixty-five times and spin forty-five times in one minute."

The spinning alone would cause Tracen's dinner to reappear. He glanced at the ride operator to gauge the man's intent. The man wasn't even looking at Emily. He was motioning for someone to join him. Out of the crowd stepped the photographer from the calf scramble. That couldn't be good.

The operator's hands returned to his device as he looked up at Emily with anticipation. Tracen shifted his gaze as well, willing Emily to hang on tighter.

Sure enough, the animal bucked harder. And harder. Emily hung on, focusing just beyond the horn where her fingers gripped.

"Her knuckles are turning white," Howie commentated.

Tracen's muscles coiled, preparing for him to spring into the ring at any moment. Howie getting hurt on a mechanical bull was one thing, but Emily was so tiny and precious.

Brutus began to spin, throwing Emily slightly off balance. Her curls spiraled out behind her. If she let go at any time, she was sure to shoot out past the air mattress.

"Hey," Tracen yelled. He had to do something. "Hey!" This time he stepped over a hay bale and stalked toward the operation controls.

He expected the operator to yell at him and motion for him to leave, but the man was too transfixed on Emily to even notice. He stared past Tracen with a smirk. "She's good," he commented to nobody in particular.

"Hey," Tracen hollered again, hoping to be heard over the cheering that surrounded them. "Slow it down."

The man's smirk turned into a sneer as his eyes slanted toward Tracen for a moment. "Who are you? Her bodyguard?"

"Something like that." Tracen didn't have time to argue. He reached past the other guy for the switches that increased the levels. He flicked the one closest to him, then lifted his head to check on Emily.

Arm waving overhead, she rolled with each buck, focused only on the spot between Brutus's horns. The bull still rocked like a raft in a level six rapid. Tracen needed to slow it down a little more.

The operator blocked his path. "Hands off."

Right. Like Tracen was going to let him put Emily on display and in danger any longer.

But before Tracen could get his hands on the controls, the bull came up hard—just as Emily leaned forward. Emily's body collapsed from the head-on collision. She slid off the saddle.

* * * * *

A swirl of darkness and light separated into the black of night and a few display lights at a fairground. Oh yes, she was at the rodeo. The colors that blended together in her peripheral vision belonged to the faces and clothing of people staring down at her. With this awareness, the roar around her became distinct tones and voices. One stood out above them all.

"Emily, are you okay?"

Tracen. Just the presence of that man gave her a feeling of safety. So why the silly question? "Of course I'm okay." Ooh, a throbbing between her eyes argued with the answer she'd just given. What was going on?

She pressed her hands into the ground behind her to roll into a seated position, but the ground gave way like her parents' old water-bed. And her right hand stung as if it had been fishing around in a cooler of ice for just the right drink.

Tracen's warm arm lifted her from behind. "You were knocked out."

Now she remembered. She'd been on a mechanical bull. And she'd stayed on. "No." Impossible. That stuff only happened in movies. So how did she get to the ground?

Lights flashed in her face. Emily blinked against their brilliance. Photographers. Wouldn't they love to publicize this story? Maybe when *People* magazine came out, she could read their captions and figure out what really happened to her.

"You hit your head." Tracen held out his hand in front of her. "How many fingers am I holding up?"

Was he serious? If he was going to make hand motions, she would much prefer the sign for "I love you" over "peace."

"Two fingers. I'm fine. Though I've got this stabbing headache."

"Yeah." Tracen's fingers now brushed her forehead, creating an explosion of pressure above her right eye. "You've got a little bump."

Emily raised her own hand to test the damage. *Little bump?* She could be a stunt double for the Elephant Man. Images of her makeup artist trying to hide such disfigurement brought laughter to her lips.

Tracen's brows drew together as if he thought the bump on her head had knocked her brains loose.

She giggled harder. Maybe it had. She attempted to explain anyway. "Char's going to kill me."

Tracen's confusion melted into a tiny smile. "Ah, yes—murder. Hilarious."

Honey's face appeared through the jumble of humanity, reminding Emily of her old *Where's Waldo?* books. "Here." She raised a paper cup dripping in condensation and pressed it to Emily's forehead.

Tracen hovered over her like an EMT. "How's that?"

Emily wiped away icy droplets from her eyebrow and blinked at the mass of faces continuing to stare at her. They were so close, she probably couldn't stand up without knocking them over like bowling pins. "I'm feeling suffocated."

Tracen turned his back to her, motioning for people to give them room. Goodness, it was as if she was an accident on the side of the freeway causing drivers to rubberneck.

One guy didn't back off. Rick—the guy who had helped her onto Brutus in the first place and had given her the advice of focusing on a spot on the bull's head. (Was that how she hit her head?) He crossed his thick arms and lifted his dimpled chin in a challenge. "Does the lady want to go for another ride?"

Maybe if she didn't feel like she'd just survived a lobotomy.

Tracen shot to his feet. "You can't be serious, man. I'm having your certification revoked. You're way out of line—"

A bulb flashed. Photographers recorded their every move. And while Tracen had her best interest in mind, the press could spin the situation....

"Tracen." She pushed away Honey's lemonade and gripped his wrist to haul herself to a standing position. And though she'd planted her feet on packed dirt, it seemed to shift underneath her as if she were still on the inflated mattress. *Whoa.* She closed her eyes and focused on staying balanced. The stabbing pain inside her skull didn't help any. At least she'd stopped Tracen's tirade.

Strong hands steadied her on either side. Opening her eyes, Emily found Tracen grimacing down at her as if he were the one in pain. "What do you need?"

"How about a redo?" Not the greatest ending to their first date.

Tracen tilted his head, his cowboy hat shadowing his eyes. "A redo?"

Where did *her* cowboy hat go? Didn't matter. With Tracen so close, she didn't have time to think of anything else.

"A redo?" This time the question came from Rick. "I was hoping you'd say that."

What did Rick care if they went out on a second date? Unless— shoot. He meant redoing her ride. She must have looked like a total spaz flying off the bull. She who was supposed to move gracefully— with athleticism.

Tracen would understand. She'd probably made him feel better about getting stuck in the trampoline harness. But what about everybody else who had witnessed her humiliation? She scanned the crowd watching her. Having her reputation destroyed in the tabloids was one thing. Losing face in front of a tiny town where she wanted to be accepted was something else.

Tracen spun. "Listen here, you—"

"I'll do it." Emily stepped between the faceoff.

"What?" Tracen gaped.

"A–l–l right." Rick dragged out the words. His presumptuous hands moved to assist her toward the beast.

Tracen knocked them away. "Wait. I'll assist her if she's going to ride."

If. Tracen said *if*. The pounding in Emily's temples faded as she prepared her argument. No doubt Tracen planned to stop her from proving herself.

Rick held up hands in mock retreat as he stepped away. Tracen glowered before turning back to her. "Emily, please don't do this."

She didn't have a choice. But she had to make it light. "Haven't you heard of getting back in the saddle?"

Tracen gave a violent shake of his head. "That saying is about climbing back on a horse."

Was it? She didn't know. "Well, how about this saying: I've got to grab the bull by the horns."

She still couldn't see his eyes very well, but if she had to guess, she would say he rolled them. "You already lost to the bull."

The churning in her gut came from his lack of faith in her, not the past failure. "You don't think I can do it."

Tracen ducked his head and lowered his voice, as if suddenly aware of the scene they were creating. "I don't think you *should* do it. Not with an injury."

He cared. So he should understand. "That's why I have to do it, Tracen. To prove to these cameras, and to Sun Valley, that I'm not afraid."

She reached for his hands to connect, so he knew she wasn't just being argumentative and that she needed his support. But her physical plea backfired when his large hands folded around hers as if she were a precious treasure. It might be nice to let him play protector—to forget everything but his touch.

"When you try to prove things"—Tracen drew her hand toward his ribs, reminding her of the first time she'd touched him—"you end up with scars."

Emily stared up at him, wondering if he was reliving his moment on the river. The scar on his side wasn't the only scar left from his wild raft ride.

"I felt so helpless with you up there," he added, defeat ringing throughout his words.

That was it. His biggest fear. Tracen feared letting go of the control.

Emily ran her thumbs over his knuckles. "Will you control the bull for me this time?" she asked simply.

And he did.

Chapter Sixteen

. . . .

"One of your students is really going to the Olympic trials?" Emily plugged her left ear so she could hear better what her mom was saying over the phone on her right. Bruce's bullhorn barking made it hard to hear anything else.

"Yes!" Violet's response sounded as if she were using a bullhorn of her own. "Keilah had an offer to go train in Indianapolis with USA Gymnastics, but she wants to stay and have me train her instead."

Violet always sounded happy, but Emily couldn't remember the last time she'd sounded excited. Probably before her husband died. "Oh, Mom…"

"The Olympics!" Violet shouted.

Emily's heart picked up speed as if she were competing for the spot on the team herself. "If I hadn't seen the girl jump last time I was in Boise, I wouldn't believe you. But she's amazing. You should be so proud." Emily felt her chest puff up a little for her mom. "If she makes it, I'm coming with you to London for the games."

"You better." Violet's voice softened. "I just wish you were closer to Boise, so you could help me train her. I can't do what I used to on a tramp anymore."

The longing surprised Emily. Her mother had never expressed any desire to be closer with Emily before. And while Emily had

---

wanted to be there for her mom, she'd never really felt needed. The woman hadn't even come to watch her film *Whitewater Wedding*, even when she only lived two hours away.

True, it sounded like Violet only wanted an assistant coach, but Emily would give her so much more. "I would like that too, Mom."

A high-pitched beep interrupted the conversation. Stupid phone battery.

"...So maybe I'll come to Sun Valley to see you."

The beep cut off part of her mother's sentence. It sounded like Violet might come for a visit, but that couldn't be right. "What? I couldn't hear what you said, Mom. My phone is beeping at me."

"Oh, never mind, hon. I know you're really busy, and I don't want to get in the way."

So she *had* offered. "Wait. I can make time—"

Beep.

Violet didn't let her finish. "Call me again later, honey—when your cell isn't about to die."

"Okay. And Mom? Just so you know, I'm planning to move back to Idaho."

No answer. But what had she been expecting? A Charlene-sized shriek? Maybe her mom really didn't need her.

Deep breath. Time to get real. "You're probably thinking it's just because of Tracen. And yeah, I want to be closer to him. Like a *lot* closer. But I also want to spend more time with you, Mom. You're all the family I have left. And this doesn't have anything to do with the trampoline training, though that's really cool. I just feel that we've grown apart since I've been gone." Ooh, Mom might think she was blaming her. That would be a big mistake. "It's my fault. And I'm sorry."

Quiet. Could her mother be crying? That wasn't like her. But it also wasn't like Emily to get so sentimental. "Mom?"

Nothing.

"Mom?" She pulled the phone away to look at the screen—blank. Her phone had died.

Shoot. Had her mother heard anything she'd said? She couldn't even call back to find out. Glancing down the bank to see if Bruce was about ready to start filming again, Emily figured she had enough time to run up to her car and plug her phone in. She needed to get into the habit of doing so every day. Not that she talked on the phone every day, but for the times when she did, it would be nice not to have her conversation cut off. Especially when she was pouring her heart out.

Oh well. She'd consider her one-sided conversation a dress rehearsal. Next time she'd really be ready to tell her mom how she felt. And hopefully she could leave out all the extra nervous babbling. Gripping her red flip-phone, she charged up the hill.

"Hey!" A strong hand gripped her wrist and swung her back around to face the opposite direction. Tracen's commanding features smiled down at her—even though she was the one standing on higher ground. "Where are you going? Don't you have a movie to make?"

Emily smiled right back. She couldn't help it. Normally she would play along with the teasing tone, but it was Tracen, and she needed to tell him her good news. "I have to charge my phone." She held up the dead phone to verify her excuse. "I just got cut off from talking to my mom, but guess what!"

Tracen ran a hand over the bump on her forehead before

entwining their fingers and pulling her closer. "You sent your mom a picture of your bruise on the cell phone, and she couldn't even see it?"

Char had really done an amazing job with makeup—though screeching the whole time about Emily's reckless escapade.

Emily's grin grew. "No." She hadn't really meant for Tracen to guess. But she had said "guess what." Silly expression.

"Okay." Tracen looped their connected arms over her head like a scarf as he prepared to try again. "Your mom…won the lottery and wants to buy me a ski boat."

Emily's laugh bubbled up from deep inside. "No. Though I think I want a ski boat now." Maybe she could get one for Tracen as a wedding present. Put a big red bow on the side. Oops. Getting ahead of herself again. "My mom has a student who might qualify to compete in the Olympics!"

"Cool." Tracen frowned. "What sport does he play?"

"*She* jumps."

The frown line between his eyebrows deepened. "Long jump? High jump?"

Emily spun out of Tracen's embrace without letting go of his hand. Their arms stretched between them like a towrope as she tried to pull him up the hill after her. "Trampoline."

Tracen's trudging slowed her down. "Trampoline is a sport?"

Emily grinned back at him. "Gymnastics."

"Isn't that cheating? Aren't you just supposed to learn tricks on the trampoline to perform on the floor—or on a wakeboard?"

Emily dropped Tracen's hand as she stepped onto the flat gravel parking lot from the incline of the hill. "Don't let my mom hear you talk that way." She pressed the remote on her keychain to unlock her SUV before plopping onto the seat and plugging in her phone.

Tracen propped his forearms on the top of the door and leaned over it. "Maybe *I* should try to get into the Olympics. I've almost mastered my back flip."

Emily couldn't keep from giggling at the image of Tracen stuck upside-down in the harness. "I'll suggest it to my mom." Her mom... "Oh, that's the other thing I wanted to say. I'd just started to tell Mom that I'm moving back to Idaho when my phone died. I don't even know if she heard me or not."

Tracen's eyes studied her, as if he expected her to disappear like a mirage. She stared back, enjoying her own examination of his solid jaw and dark lashes. He was such a loyal and honorable man. Were he to commit himself to her, she knew she'd have the unconditional love that all women dreamed of. That Serena girl had no idea what she'd given up.

Tracen cleared his throat, drawing her gaze back to meet his. "I doubt your mom will be as thrilled as I am over the news of your move, but if you want to call her right now, you can. Just leave the phone hooked up to the charger."

"Oh!" He was thrilled that she was moving to Idaho. His ways of expressing his feelings toward her weren't as direct as her spontaneous, overenthusiastic declarations, but they were woven into flirtatious conversations. Like buried treasure, she savored the words meant only for her. "Okay." What had he told her to do? Oh yeah, call her mom.

Fumbling for her phone, she flipped it open and stared at the screen. What was her mom's phone number again? She glanced up at Tracen. Maybe she should call later when she wasn't so distracted.

Tracen's long arm reached toward her, causing her pulse to quicken. Her heart rate slowed down when his fingers only pointed to the blue envelope on her screen. Drat.

"Your mom could have heard what you said and already called back to leave a message."

She hadn't thought of that. Better check first. How did she check voice mail again? Scrolling down the menu list, she clicked on voice mail. There was a little number thirteen next to it, but that couldn't mean thirteen messages, could it? Who had her cell number?

She held the phone to her ear, planning to only listen for a second. Spending time with Tracen was much more important than listening to recordings.

"Emily!" Her agent always spoke quickly as if she had somebody else on hold—and she probably did. "Call me. I've got great news."

Emily pressed the 7 button to delete. "My agent," she explained to Tracen. She'd call Veronica back later—after filming, and maybe after a trip to the hot springs Howie had been telling her about.

Veronica's rapid-fire communication style interrupted Emily's thoughts again. "Emily, I know you're filming, but you're going to want to make some time to call me. It's important."

What could it be? Had the paparazzi printed some pictures of her and Tracen? No, Veronica had said she had good news. Was Emily being asked to do another Revlon commercial? She'd felt so silly doing the last one, but Veronica would consider such an offer "great news."

Third message: "Emily, you're killing me! Answer your stupid phone, will you?"

Emily frowned at the "stupid" phone. What could be so urgent?

Veronica had her imagination in overdrive. Was it just another audition? But Veronica knew she was busy filming. Could it be a magazine spread? A party appearance as Wonder Woman? Was she going to have a whole comic book series modeled after her? Preposterous.

She better just call Veronica back. She moved her finger to the button that she thought would exit voice mail, but apparently she hit speakerphone because Veronica's voice came back on in stereo.

"Okay, Emily. Here's the deal. They want to do a sequel to *Wonder Woman,* and they want you to play Diana Prince again—even though you cut your hair. The studio is offering five times what you made on the first one. We need an answer pronto. Call. Me."

"Oh my…"

Emily dropped the phone and shot to her feet. *A sequel…sequel… sequel.* The word spun through her mind like a tornado, making her a little dizzy. She'd expected the studio to rip apart her acting since she'd never had any formal training. Getting a part in *Whitewater Wedding* had been the pure momentum of her "career." She didn't expect it to go anywhere after that, and she didn't really care. But how fun would it be to make another *Wonder Woman* movie?

Tracen could travel with her to Hollywood for a few months. They could do Sea World and take a cruise out to Catalina Island. Maybe even hike Half Dome in Yosemite National Park. She'd gotten to know his world, and she loved it, but she wanted to share her own world with him—even if she was planning to leave it.

And how could she turn down the money? It would provide financial stability for their future. Maybe she wouldn't even look for a teaching job at all but could just help Tracen with his business—until they started a family. Hey, she could even help her mom out by paying her way to the London Olympics. So many possibilities. What an opportunity.

* * * * *

Tracen watched in amusement as Emily tried to figure out her phone. *Note to self: don't expect to talk to Emily on the phone much.*

He hung on the open SUV door and kicked at the gravel. She was listening to voice mail now, but in just a moment he'd get to hear her tell her mom she was moving to Idaho. That's what he'd been planning on since the moment he first kissed her, but soon it would be official.

Instead of a girlfriend leaving him because he wanted to stay in Sun Valley, he had a girlfriend moving to Sun Valley to be with him. *Girlfriend.* A weird word. Foreign and exciting to him, but at the same time it didn't fully explain their relationship. In only a couple of weeks, Emily had become his best friend. A part of him.

Emily pulled the phone away from her ear and squinted at its buttons before poking one. Her eyebrows shot up when a voice came out of it like she'd tuned in the radio.

"Okay, Emily. Here's the deal." A snippy, business-minded voice. As if the voice belonged to a blackmailer arranging a dirty transaction. Tracen grimaced. "They want to do a sequel to *Wonder Woman*, and they want you to play Diana Prince." Tracen froze.

So Jor-El had been right when he said they were making a sequel. But that didn't mean he was right about Emily accepting the part. Apparently she hadn't even heard the news. He should have mentioned the rumor sooner, but he figured she would have told him about it, and she probably would have, had it been on her agenda.

Tracen couldn't focus on the rest of the message. He just watched Emily's face. With those wide sky-blue eyes, she looked as innocent as one of his nieces' Cabbage Patch dolls. She wouldn't go back to California just to have another chance to see her face on the big screen. She wasn't like that.

So why did his limbs start to shake the way they did every time he drank the extra strong coffee in Howie's thermos? This wasn't anything to be nervous about. Emily would delete the message, then call her mom to say she was moving to Idaho. That's what they'd planned. He was getting worked up over nothing.

"Oh my…"

Tracen didn't even see Emily stand. All he knew was that one second she was sitting in her car, and the next second her springy hair tickled his nose. Tracen pushed up from his relaxed position, the shakiness inside starting to mix up the contents of his stomach. This wasn't happening. This wasn't happening *again*.

Emily squealed. "Did you hear that?"

He wished he hadn't. He wished he could go back in time to the moment when Emily had been about to call her mother, and he'd ignorantly suggested she check her voice messages first. He'd never guessed that the beeping of the phone would be the death knell of their future together.

Or maybe, if he were going to go back in time, he should go all the way back to the moment he told her he couldn't date her—and stick to his guns. He knew then what could happen. He'd risked it anyway. What was Ben Franklin's definition of insanity again?

"Doing the same thing over and over and expecting different results." He'd been insane to let himself fall for Emily.

"Did you hear?" she repeated, eyes shining and glassy. They didn't look so innocent anymore.

"Yeah." Was this it? One phone call was all she needed to forget the declarations she'd made. Like how she didn't see herself with anyone else. No doubt she'd be kissing another guy on the superhero set.

"What do you think?" Her head tilted up to face his.

Tracen looked away. She knew what he thought. And it hurt too much to read the thoughts revealed in her eager expression. But she *was* asking. So maybe he still had a chance.

It must have taken as much energy to rope a calf at the rodeo as it did to reign in his emotions, but he made sure to do so before looking back down. "I think you should call your mom now to tell her you're moving back to Idaho." He'd meant his response to sound nonchalant, but it came out rather gruff.

Emily blinked as if blindsided by his attitude. Then she waved her arms wide. "What if—" she paused dramatically, though it wasn't like she didn't already have his full attention—"I put the move on hold for a few months? You could come with me to Hollywood."

Did she really want him with her? Or was it an empty gesture? A peace offering?

Maybe she only thought she wanted him with her. If he went to California, she'd find out all too quickly how he didn't fit in. Then she'd choose the lifestyle over him. He'd merely be prolonging the good-bye.

"I'm not going to L.A." Too many people. Too many traffic jams. Too much cement, and filth, and desperation. "I've driven Christmas trees down there a couple of times. It's not for me." And besides, he had a cabin to build before the snow started. A cabin he'd been hoping to share with her.

"Oh, but you have to go to the premiere with me."

She grasped one of his hands with both of hers. Her silky skin caressed the calluses on his palms. But her touch almost hurt more than it soothed. She was already planning for the premiere—as if she'd accepted the role.

"So, you're going to do the movie?" Stupid question. But he had to know for sure. He didn't want to let go of the hope that he'd been clinging to since the moment she told him she wanted to move home—to his home.

"They're offering me five times more than they paid me for the first movie. Think about what we could do with that money."

He didn't want to think about it. And he hadn't thought it would matter to her. But she didn't have to convince him to let her take the part. It was her choice to make. He only wished their relationship influenced her choice.

She grabbed both his hands now. Hands he wanted to slide up her velvety arms and cup her face with before kissing some sense back into her. But the woman couldn't stay still. She was practically dancing with the way she hopped about and wiggled.

"Tracen, this is so great. I'll miss you like crazy, but I'll be back up here by Christmas. Our first Christmas together."

If she came back. Serena hadn't.

"What do you think?" She didn't wait for his response. "I think

I *need* to make a second *Wonder Woman*. I have to redeem myself, since you fell asleep during my first movie."

She wiggled closer, making it hard for him to stay focused. Had he really told her that he'd fallen asleep watching her on screen? He'd have to ask God for forgiveness for that lie. And then God would expect him to work harder at telling the truth. But wasn't honesty always the best policy? Might as well start now.

"I don't want you to go, Emily." He sounded so needy and demanding.

Her activity stilled. Her smile slipped. Who was he to hold her back? Dash her dreams? That's not what he wanted. He just had to be real.

"Em, I'm afraid you won't come back."

Emily's head tilted, and her eyebrows dipped. Still hanging onto his hands, she used them to pull herself closer, like she was a fish and he was reeling her in. Their arms bent between them, holding them together—keeping them apart.

"I'll come back," she vowed softly. "You have to believe me. There's nothing I want more."

Except for making another movie. Would it stop then? What about guest appearances on talk shows to promote the release? What about a *Wonder Woman III*?

Tracen wanted to believe her. There was no deception hidden in the depths of her pool-blue eyes. But people didn't come back to Sun Valley. Serena hadn't. Jor-El's father hadn't.

"Emily, do you know where Jor-El's dad is?"

Emily's eyes shifted from side to side as if looking for the man in question. "Should I?" If only she wasn't so cute.

"He's in Vegas. He does a unicycle and juggling show. He left when Jor-El was four years old. He was supposed to come back before Jor-El turned five." *The jerk. No kid deserved a father like that.*

"Oh no." Concern rang through in Emily's tone. She'd been a friend to Jor-El without even realizing how badly he needed one. "I had no idea. Poor Jor-El."

Where was he going with this? Oh yeah. "Jor-El doesn't talk about it. He still hopes his dad will come back. But every time the guy makes any money, he gambles it away. Jor-El's mom barely scrapes by—housekeeping at the Sun Valley Resort."

"That's terrible. No wonder Jor-El is so attached to the unicycle." The creases in her forehead disappeared as her cheekbones popped out. "But see, with the money I make doing *Wonder Woman II*, we can help people like that out. We could buy Jor-El a real bicycle. Buy his mom a new car."

Tracen let out his breath. She'd completely missed his point.

A bullhorn blared from down at the river's edge. "Emily Van Arsdale. Has anybody seen Emily Van Arsdale?"

Emily closed her eyes and leaned her head back. "Bruce is so going to kill me." She pushed up on tiptoe and brushed a quick kiss over his lips. "Hopefully this won't take long. Do you want to go find that hot springs with Howie and Honey when I'm done?"

How did she move on so quickly? He was still talking about Jor-El. He better finish what he had to say before Bruce fired them both. He couldn't let her leave him to make another movie. She'd never come back. He knew it. "I don't want to have to sit around waiting for you."

Emily giggled as she pulled away. "Impatient to see me in a bikini, huh?"

"No," he called out in frustration as she turned her back toward him to scale the hill. That wasn't what he meant at all. "I'm not going to wait for you if you return to Hollywood."

But she was too far away to hear.

Chapter Seventeen

....

Emily followed Tracen down the path through the quiet forest. He'd been kind of quiet himself, but maybe that was part of their serene trip to Frenchman's Bend Hot Springs. Though Howie didn't sound like he knew the meaning of *serene*.

The older man trailed after her with a thick walking stick. "Tracen, did you warn Emily that most people enjoy the hot springs in the buff—even though most of them aren't buff?" he asked.

Emily smiled back at Howie as Tracen answered for her. "Emily knows. Her mom used to be a hippie."

Behind Howie, Honey eyed Emily. "I hope you plan to keep your bathing suit on."

Emily laughed. "Of course! How about you, Honey? You always wear your bathing suit?"

"Um…" Honey paused as their little group arrived at the top pool. Below them more rocky pools cascaded down into the river, steam rising off them into the cooler evening air. She pointed, as if trying to divert the flow of their conversation. "The top pool is the hottest. I usually enjoy the second one best."

"Me too." Howie pulled his T-shirt up over his protruding stomach.

Emily tried to hold back a smile. "You didn't answer the question,

Honey." It wouldn't surprise her in the least if the all-natural woman had once enjoyed a dip *au naturel*.

Honey sat back on a large rock, removing her shoes and avoiding three pairs of eyes. "Edward and I once had the place to ourselves right after we were married. And that's all I'm going to say."

Emily grinned at Tracen, who seemed to be blinking rather rapidly. He eventually smiled, but it was more towards the ground than at her. Strange. She'd expected him to feel the same anticipation stirring within at thoughts of a honeymoon.

She followed him toward the top pool, which happened to be empty. In the lower pool a family splashed, but no other sounds could be heard in the stillness—until Howie started back in on Honey.

"Eddie came up here with you? He hated hot springs. You know, his phobia of germs and all."

Emily sent another smile Tracen's way, but he was busy watching the little boy below perform a cannonball. Pulling her denim shorts down, she slipped into the clear water after him, the heat wrapping itself around her like a liquid blanket. Her muscles relaxed for the first time in days—just what she needed.

Half-floating, she made her way to a large stone next to where Tracen sat. Settling back into the rock wall behind her, she motioned toward Howie and Honey with her head. "You still don't see them getting together?"

Tracen looked over at his arguing friends, his expression blank. "Honey's not looking for a husband. Probably because it would be too hard to love again after having her heart broken by Eddie's death."

"What?" Tracen's response sounded absurd. Hadn't he ever

heard the quote about how it's better to have loved and lost? "Did Honey tell you that?"

Tracen looked down and stirred patterns into the water. "She didn't have to."

Emily watched Tracen's hands, as well. Such strong, capable hands. Tanned and calloused, but oh so gentle. His hands were one of the best things about him. Though if she had to order the qualities she loved about him, they'd all be in the number-one position. They made him who he was, and that was exactly what she wanted. How could Honey keep herself from loving someone who could be all of that to her? "Have you tried talking to her about him?"

Tracen's eyes finally met hers, though they squinted in confusion. "Who?"

Emily splashed him. The guy needed to lighten up. "I'm talking about Howie and Honey. Who are you talking about?"

Tracen wiped droplets of water from his face. "I'm too tired to talk about anybody right now."

The warmth of the water did make one sleepy. Emily snuggled into Tracen's side. They could talk later.

Of course, Howie wasn't done talking. He descended into the pool slowly with arms spread wide, though the way his swimming trunks ballooned up around him ruined the elegance of his entrance.

"Ahh…" He sighed. "People say the sulfur in this water brings healing to the body. I don't know if that's what it is, but I'm feeling something."

Honey wrapped her braid on top of her head and into a knot. "Like Captain Naaman in the Bible?"

Emily sat up a little straighter. Another Bible story about water that she had missed. "That's the guy Elisha told to dip in the Jordan River seven times because he had some kind of rash or something?"

Honey appeared surprised that Emily knew her Bible stories. "Leprosy."

Okay, maybe Emily didn't know her Bible stories well enough. "I'll have to look it up when I get home." She tilted her head to look at Tracen *Lake*. The water theme in her life should remind him how perfect they were for each other.

Tracen stood. "I'm burning up. Howie, you want to go cool off?"

Howie groaned. "I just got in."

Emily missed Tracen's presence already, and he wasn't even out of the pool. "I'll go."

Tracen turned his head as if looking back over his shoulder at her, but their eyes didn't meet. "Howie and I like to jump in the river between soaks in the hot springs."

Howie nodded. "Revitalizing."

Honey grimaced. "Ridiculous."

Tracen climbed out of the pool with Howie dutifully following. "You wouldn't enjoy it, Emily. The river gets pretty cold. We'll be right back."

Emily watched Tracen stroll away. It wasn't like him to leave her behind. What was up? Thinking back over their thirty-minute drive, Emily realized he hadn't been his usual self at all. Howie had kept the conversation going, so she hadn't noticed at the time.

Could the Wonder Woman role be bothering him? At first, he'd said he didn't want her to go back to California, but she explained her thought process, and he hadn't said anymore. Maybe she was making too much of his cooling-off ritual. Maybe he was merely giving her a chance to get to know Honey better.

Honey leaned back, looking toward the dimming sky. The woman had been one of the first people she'd met in Sun Valley. And she'd been the first to warn Emily away from Tracen. They'd never really talked about it, though.

"Honey?"

Honey lifted her head slowly, as if it was heavy. Her eyelids looked heavy too. She'd either been falling asleep or daydreaming.

"Remember when we first met, and you told me Tracen wouldn't be interested in me?"

Honey's laugh echoed off the water. "Guess I was wrong." Her head rolled back once again.

Emily tucked a damp strand of hair behind her ear. "Well…" She needed to know more. "Was it because of Serena?"

Honey remained quiet so long that Emily didn't know if she'd heard. "It was," she finally responded.

Emily took a deep breath. Honey didn't seem to want to talk, but Emily needed to fill in the missing pieces. It wasn't fair that she had to compete with a memory. She swam through the deeper water to join Honey on the opposite side. Crossing her arms over a large boulder, she turned her head to face the other woman.

"Tracen told me he didn't want to get involved at first because of how Serena left him. I overheard his mom say the same thing." Emily's heart still ached for his. How could anybody do that to someone they loved—somebody they'd planned to spend their life with? "Was she really like me?" The image just didn't fit. Emily cared about others. She wasn't filled with selfish ambition. She wanted to return to Hollywood for one more film to have a better platform to help people. Tracen could understand that.

Honey shifted to one side so she could make eye contact. The harsh lines on her face seemed to have melted with the heat. "You're nothing like Serena, Emily. Serena's move to California didn't surprise anyone but Tracen. She never thought twice about standing him up if she got a better opportunity. She might have been with him, but her thoughts were always elsewhere." Honey's mouth curled up softly. "You're the opposite. Even when you're elsewhere, your thoughts are on Tracen."

Emily quirked her lips to one side. Good to hear the comparison, but not good that she'd been so obviously slacking on her job. "Did you overhear the lecture Bruce gave me earlier today?"

The sparkle in Honey's brown eyes told her all she needed to know. "No, but I overheard the film crew talking about it at lunch."

Emily sighed. Not one of her finer moments.

A reassuring squeeze on her shoulder from Honey helped ease the pain. "Emily, before today I didn't think you were a good fit for Tracen. Now I know I was wrong."

* * * * *

Tracen ignored the chill of the air around him. It would soon feel like a sauna compared to the sting of the river. Might as well get it over with. Pushing off the bank, he sailed into its icy grip. Surfacing, he tried to take a breath, but his lungs had become momentarily frozen. Every inch of his skin screamed to return to the hot springs, but Tracen would rather suffer through the burning cold than to have Emily snuggle up to him again when his heart wouldn't let him hold on to her.

He turned to await Howie's splash, but instead the man watched from dry land as Tracen floated on by.

"Howie!" Tracen leaned forward, kicking his legs behind him and fighting the current with long strokes. His teeth chattered as he waded through shallower water to join his friend. "What was that?" he shivered, ripping Howie's towel away so he could cocoon himself in it. It wasn't like Howie was going to use the thing.

Howie chuckled. "I'm older and wiser, man. Besides, I'm not the one who needs a cold shower."

Tracen swung the towel and flicked his buddy before Howie realized what was coming.

"Ye-ouch!"

"I don't need a cold shower." What he needed was a fire and a cup of coffee. And maybe a swift kick to the head for getting himself into an encore performance of the walk-out-on-Tracen-show. Unrolling the towel from the whiplike weapon he'd used it for, he bundled himself back up. "And what was all that talk about being revitalized by a jump in the river? You left me high and dry."

"Nah. I'm the dry one." Howie flinched as Tracen pretended he was going to swing his towel again. "I could tell you needed to talk, though. What's goin' on?"

Tracen turned and plopped onto a rock. He'd wanted to get away from Emily, but he didn't want to talk about it. "Nothing." He pulled the towel over his head to dry his hair—and to veil himself from the counseling session it sounded like Howie had planned.

Howie lowered himself down to sit, as well. "If you don't tell me, I can always ask Emily."

Emily. Just thinking about her caused his muscles to cramp. He wanted to hang onto her and never let go. But he didn't have that power. She was going to leave him just like Serena had.

Looking out over the river, Tracen tried not to relive the moment he'd met Emily. Of how she'd worn a wedding dress at the time, and how he'd started to fantasize that she would someday wear one just for him.

"She's leaving. She's making another movie."

Howie scratched at an ear. "You thought she was going to stay?"

Yes, he'd been stupid enough to think that. "She told me she was going to move back to Idaho. And she still says she's going to, but what will keep her from putting it off again? And again?" Why would she come back at all when she had so much going for her in California?

Howie held up a hand. "Whoa. She's moving up here?"

Tracen shrugged. He didn't know anything anymore.

"She said she's going to give up acting for you?" Howie's jaw hung open, reminding Tracen of a widemouthed bass.

Tracen looked away. He didn't feel like laughing. "She said she can't imagine being with anybody but me."

Howie slapped him on the back. "That's wonderful!"

"Howie." Tracen addressed the other rafting guide as if he were a child. "Serena said the same thing."

"I see," Howie said, but with a voice that implied he saw more than Tracen did. "You're punishing Emily for something somebody else did."

"No." That's not what he was doing. "I'm learning from experience."

"Right."

Was Howie always this sarcastic?

Howie crossed his arms over his Buddha belly. "What if Captain Naaman had learned from experience?"

Tracen slumped lower in his seat. He should have come down to the river by himself. Howie wasn't a pastor anymore, but he had a sermon for everything. And he loved his Bible stories. "Naaman the leper?"

"That's the one." Howie confirmed the analogy. "How many times did he have to go back into the dirty water?"

Tracen rolled his eyes. He hated those fill-in-the-blank Bible studies. "Seven times."

"What if he had stopped at six dips?"

Tracen glared at the river as he recited. "He wouldn't have gotten what he wanted."

"Hmm." Howie gave Tracen time to make the connection verbally. When he didn't, Howie sighed. "Faith is more important than experience. Has Emily given you any reason not to have faith in her?"

Tracen picked up a stick and twirled it through his fingers, its rough bark scratching his skin. He wanted to believe in Emily, but… "I'm afraid she will."

Howie sat in silence with him. Apparently out of arguments. He shook his head as if Tracen was hopeless.

Tracen couldn't handle listening to the unspoken words any longer. "You don't understand, Howie, because you've never been in my shoes."

Howie's face hardened. "You're right."

Tracen was startled. This was a moment to remember—Howie admitting he was wrong.

"You're right, I've never been in your shoes. I've been in Emily's."

Now Tracen was confused. How could Howie possibly be like Emily?

Howie looked up the hill to where the women sat on the edge of the hot springs. Apparently the water had gotten too warm for them, as well. "I proposed to Honey on Valentine's Day this year. She turned me down because she's afraid to love again."

Tracen felt his breath leave him—like the way it did when he jumped into the river. Howie loved Honey? Emily had known. How had he missed it? "You're kidding."

Howie spoke softly. "About which part?"

"I didn't…" Tracen ran a hand through his hair. What kind of friend was he? Complaining about a short romance when Howie had been rejected by his best friend. "I had no idea you loved her."

Now Honey's reaction to Emily made sense. The woman had a guarded heart. And she wanted to guard Tracen's, as well.

Howie pressed his lips together before responding. "Under the circumstances, I'm not really publicizing my feelings."

Tracen thought back to the day when they all picked huckleberries and went skiing. "How can you continue to hang out with her?" He couldn't even enjoy his time with Emily in the hot springs, and she hadn't rejected him yet.

Howie focused back on the women. "How could I *not* hang out with her?"

Tracen followed the other man's line of vision. Emily was now playing with the cannonball kid in the second hot springs. She gave him a piggyback ride from one side to the other. Wait until the little guy was old enough to watch the movie *Wonder Woman*. That would make a great story for him to tell his friends someday.

How could Tracen not hang out with Emily? Was there anything he wanted more? What was he doing down at the river when he could be by her side—maybe even giving *her* a piggyback ride? He knew the two of them could take Howie and Honey in a game of chicken any day.

"Let's go, Howie."

Tracen didn't even wait for his friend to keep up. Using boulders like stairs, he made his way back to the woman he'd fallen for. She looked up hesitantly, as if afraid of more moody behavior, but he didn't let that stop him. No, her hesitation pulled at him harder. Ignoring the heat of the pool, he slid into its scalding depths and sliced through the water with purpose.

She still held the boy on her back, but that didn't bother him either. He wanted to reassure her that they were meant to be together. If he wasn't going to let her go, then he'd use everything he had to fight for her.

Impatient with the weight of the water slowing his pace, he reached forward and dragged Emily to him.

"Wee!" called the kid.

Now expectancy lit her eyes. She wanted to be with him just as much as he wanted her. Her skin slipped against his as he threaded his arms around her then between her back and the kid's stomach. *Mercy*, she felt good.

"Hi," she said, as if she'd been waiting for this side of him to show up all afternoon. And as if there wasn't a child watching their every move from close range.

"Hi," he whispered just before pressing his mouth to hers. The kid could swim away. Nothing was going to stop him from showing Emily how he really felt.

So why did it feel as if he were kissing her good-bye?

Chapter Eighteen

....

Tracen couldn't do it. Even after Howie's sermon and the amazing kiss he laid on Emily the night before, there was no peace with his decision to act as if nothing was bothering him. It had bothered him all night, in fact.

His stomach felt queasy, as if he might be getting the flu, and his body ached with fatigue. How was he supposed to live like this for an undetermined number of months?

Long distance wouldn't work, especially if the distance led Emily back to Hollywood. Some said that distance made the heart grow fonder, but the more accurate saying would be that distance made the heart wander.

He couldn't deal with Emily having a wandering heart. He needed a commitment from her. A tangible commitment. A commitment requiring more than words.

Was it too much to ask for? No, she'd already planned to move. All he wanted was for her to follow through on their plans together. If she cared for him enough, she would.

A few months of playing Wonder Woman couldn't compare to a lifetime of love. That's what people in love did—they compromised to make things work. If she couldn't compromise now, how would he know if their relationship was ever going to work? And giving up the role of Wonder Woman might the best thing she could do—get out while she was ahead. Like Michael Keaton in *Batman*. The first Wonder Woman had been such a hit that it really couldn't get any better for her.

Still, the pending conversation cloaked Tracen in dread. Weakness filled him as if he were Superman wearing a pendant of Kryptonite. How would she react? Would she understand? Or would she crush his one last attempt at hope?

A surge of energy raced through his veins as Emily's rented SUV crunched into the gravel parking lot outside the restaurant window. He'd invited Emily to eat breakfast with him before her filming began for the day. They should continue the tradition even after the film crew left. Breakfast once a week at The Point.

And what kind of car would she drive then? Would she bring up some sporty convertible from California, or would she want a vehicle that complemented his rusty truck in the driveway of their new cabin? He could always fix up an older car for her. Like a vintage Mustang or a classic Thunderbird. Make it a wedding present for her—big red bow and all.

Tracen smiled at the thought. Life would be sweet. Emily knew that. She wouldn't leave him.

The tinkling of a bell announced the opening of the front door. Emily beamed when she spotted him across the room. Tension eased from Tracen's shoulders. This was right—nobody could argue the fact. Not even Honey, who watched with a small smile as Emily sailed across the room toward his table.

"I missed you," she said as she sank into the seat facing his.

Tracen felt the first words out of her mouth soothe his soul as if they were a gentle caress. What had he been worried about? Reaching across the table, he wrapped his fingers over her tiny hand. "I missed you too."

Emily flipped her hand so their palms pressed together, then twisted to lace her fingers with his. "Are you sure you won't come back to California with me? It's going to be so hard to leave you behind."

His stomach turned to lead. Leaving him behind must not be as hard as he'd hoped if she was still planning on making the movie. But at least she'd given him a bridge to broach the subject that haunted him. Otherwise he would probably have put it off until after breakfast. And then until after filming. Possibly until the day she was planning to leave. But this was better. Wasn't it? He could share his concern, and she would reassure him. Then he wouldn't have to live in the shadow of his fears.

"Don't go."

Emily laughed. "Okay." She said the word as if she were doing the voice of Dopey from *The Seven Dwarfs*. "Instead I'll get a job where I could work for the rest of my life and never earn the same amount of money as I could in a few months playing Wonder Woman." Her eyes twinkled just thinking about the opportunity. Her tone returned to normal—sweet and enthusiastic. "It's called *playing* a part. Of course it's hard work, but with as much fun as acting can be, the term *play* really fits."

Tracen froze as Emily slipped her hand from his and picked up a menu. Not quite the reaction he'd been counting on. She made it all into a joke. But he couldn't be more serious.

"Em." He waited for her eyes to rise. Such clear, sky-blue eyes.

Would they cloud and grow stormy when she realized that he wasn't kidding? How could he phrase his thoughts without sounding too demanding? "Which means more to you?" The question came out before he had time to consider the options. Might as well move forward—finish what he started. "Me or the movie?"

Emily's menu dropped. She shifted in her seat and stared, her soft lips parting as if she wanted to reply but didn't know the correct answer. Her hesitation felt like a dagger wound—stabbing into his heart and spilling his blood.

"You should know the answer to that." She spoke carefully, as if he'd laid a trap for her.

But now he held back, afraid he was the one being tricked by her non-answer. "I thought I did." What had he been thinking?

Emily leaned forward, expression earnest. "I told you I don't picture myself with any other man."

He wanted to believe her. Let her draw him back. But… "It's not another man I'm worried about. It's the seduction of Tinseltown."

"Oh." Emily leaned back now, problem solved in her own mind. "I'm moving up here, remember? This movie is one last hurrah. It's not that I'm seeking out fame like…" Some things were best left unsaid. "I'm merely accepting the offer that's been given to me."

Tracen swallowed through a constricted throat. She was accepting. But didn't he get a vote? "What if I ask you not to accept?"

* * * * *

Emily blinked. "Wow." The guy didn't trust her. This was a much bigger issue than he realized, than she realized. How did she respond?

Tracen's eyes grew dark and intense. "I've been looking for teaching jobs for you. I want you to pick out colors for the interior of our cabin. I even looked up your birthday online and bought tickets for a dinner train. But you don't even think twice about leaving all this. You're ready to fly away the moment your agent calls."

Emily's heart fluttered. He'd thought to look up her birthday? And he wanted her to decorate his cabin? Yes, she wanted all of that. But why did he have to wait to spring it on her like a hostage in hostile negotiations?

Darn him. "You're not being fair, Tracen."

Tracen slammed back into his seat. "Fair?" As if noticing Emily scan the room for possible paparazzi, he leaned forward and lowered his voice. "Is expecting you to keep your word unfair?"

Correction. These weren't hostile negotiations. Tracen had simply chosen not to negotiate at all.

Emily lifted her hands into a frozen shrug. What language was Tracen speaking? Her intentions hadn't changed. She wanted everything he offered. But she had to bring her current life to a close before she could start a new one. "I'm going to keep my word."

"Key words: *going to*. That doesn't mean much. I need to know when, Emily."

Tracen shifted his jaw from side to side, his glare demanding. She'd never seen him like this. Was he even talking to her? Or was he seeing Serena when he spoke? Now *that* was unfair.

She needed to reconnect, calm him down. And she'd have to do it before she got too offended. With the way she was starting to feel, she might be able to play the role of another superhero—The Hulk.

Deep breath. They could work this out. The volcano starting to erupt inside her would soon turn dormant. A few years down the road and they'd be laughing at how ridiculous they'd been to almost break up. She just had to give him a timeline to go with her promises. That's all.

Sliding her fingers across the polished log table, she gripped his rough hand once more. Tense, yet lifeless. Waiting before he would respond. She sought words to reassure.

"I told you." She spoke the gentle reminder. "I'll be back by Christmas."

His face didn't relax the way she expected it to. He pulled his hand from hers and looked away. The distance between them grew a disproportionate amount compared to his small movement. "Will you, Emily? You won't be called away for interviews or premieres?"

Now he was asking too much. That was part of the biz. The fun part. Getting to travel and meet new people. Why did it bother him so much? "Yes, I'll have to do some of that stuff. But it works. Demi Moore lives in Idaho, you know."

Tracen's eyes jumped back to meet hers, and she almost jolted in her seat at the impact. "Yes, I know. But it doesn't matter. What works for her isn't going to work for me. I want stability. I want commitment. I don't want to have to change our plans whenever Wonder Woman gets a phone call."

She'd heard of this happening. What drew a couple together became the same thing that pulled them apart. But with the way Tracen kissed her the night before—not caring about the circumstances, such as a little boy on her back—she couldn't believe he would pull such an about-face.

"Tracen, you can't ask me to give up the role of Wonder Woman."

He wouldn't do that. He was falling in love with her. And love was unconditional. She had to make him understand.

Tracen closed his eyes. More distance. He really was pulling away. And as if they'd been glued together, he took part of her with him. The loss shot throbbing pain through her core. Her throat constricted. But she wouldn't cry. Not in front of him anyway.

If he couldn't make compromises, then they never would have worked out anyway. Oh, she had to make it work. They were so close to their happily-ever-after. How could he throw it away like this?

"Emily." He stopped there, as if he couldn't get the rest of his sentence out. And if it was something she didn't want to hear, she hoped it got stuck inside him forever. "Emily," he started again, firmer now. Oh no. She wanted to run away so she didn't have to hear whatever it was that he was having trouble saying. "I can't live my life in limbo. If you—if you choose to make the movie, I can't wait for you."

Emily's stomach rolled over. What did he mean he couldn't? More like *wouldn't*. She must not mean as much to him as she thought she did—as much as he meant to her. "You're giving me an ultimatum?" What a horrible start/end to a relationship.

"No," Tracen said without pausing to consider. After a moment he added, "I'm setting boundaries."

That was a nice spin on things. He threatened to break up with her if she didn't do exactly what he wanted, and then he gave his actions a nice Christian term. "Good idea. You wouldn't want me to mess up the safe little life you have going on here."

She hoped her words hurt. Woke him up to his reality. But not likely. He'd just use her outburst to confirm his decision.

Tracen looked around in exasperation, his lips parting as if he was speechless. Nope. He found his voice. "You said you liked my 'safe little life.' You said you wanted to be part of it."

She did. More than anything. But he was making her choose between his life and who she was created to be. Not that she was created to be Wonder Woman, but she was created to be active and spontaneous. If she let him squelch that part of her now, would it cease to exist completely? Her breathing grew shaky.

"I love Sun Valley, Tracen." She loved the mountains that surrounded it. She loved the rivers that roared through it. She loved the laid-back lifestyle. But more than anything—she loved Tracen. The realization came like a slap in the face. Now that she knew, how could she let him go? "Home is where the heart is. If we are together, then it doesn't matter if we are in Sun Valley or not."

Tracen stiffened even more, if possible. "It matters to me."

It mattered more than her. She could twist this whole conversation on its side. He'd asked her what mattered more, him or the movie. "Which means more to you? Me or Sun Valley?"

Goodness. Now she'd given him an ultimatum. And the worst part was, she already knew his answer. His pause only confirmed her fear.

A chill swept over her, causing her limbs to tremble. But that was nothing compared to the way her insides shivered. Why was she putting herself through this?

Gigi trotted over then, chomping on gum. Emily watched as if from a distance. And Gigi's statement made it sound like she was really on another planet. "You two look so cute over here. What can I get you this morning?"

Anything Emily might consume would certainly make a reappearance with the way her stomach gurgled. And it wasn't like Tracen wanted to spend more time with her anyway.

Shoving backwards, she spoke over the scraping of chair legs on scarred wood flooring. "I'm not hungry anymore. Thanks, Gigi." Standing at attention, she slowly looked back at Tracen. She'd never had to look down to talk to him before, but she got no satisfaction from the fact she was doing so to say good-bye. "Thank you for the conversation, Tracen. I'm really glad we had it now."

Was she? Wouldn't it have been better to live in blissful ignorance for another week? But then it might have hurt even more to realize Tracen had been planning to dump her the moment she made a decision he didn't agree with.

Grabbing her purse, she forced her feet to walk. And he let her go. That's what really hurt. He watched her leave him, and he didn't care to do anything about it.

She yearned to hear him call her back over the pounding of her heart in her ears. She willed him to chase her down. Nothing.

Why hadn't he wanted to work things out? If only he had worded things differently.

She made it to the lobby, not able to continue farther in case he changed his mind. In case she changed her mind.

Sinking onto the couch just out of Tracen's line of sight, she tried to make sense out of her jumbled emotions. Did she really want to be in another movie so badly? At the moment she didn't even want to finish filming the movie she was already in.

If she loved him, and she did, then shouldn't she be the one to compromise? Maybe she'd overreacted. She could look at their situation from his perspective. He had a legitimate reason to fear her leaving. He'd had his heart broken before.

He'd had his heart broken before—and he feared it would happen again. But she would never do that to him.

She was no Serena. And if they were ever going to make a relationship work, she needed to prove it.

She'd give up the movie.

Chapter Nineteen

....

He was going to stick by his decision. It would be too easy to give in. Too easy to let her convince him that living a thousand miles apart could work. Too easy to apologize and ease the pain that she tried to hide by blinking tears away. Too easy to hope that she would come back to Sun Valley.

No. Giving into hope would only lead to heartbreak. Better to rip the Band-Aid off quickly. He could get over her. That's what he told himself, anyway. He'd gotten over Serena. And he hadn't even known Emily a month, whereas he'd dated Serena all through high school. If he could get over his ex in ten years, then he could get over Emily in…ten thousand.

The ache in his chest couldn't be fooled. It filled his entire being with remorse. Which was worse? Letting go of Emily or trying to hold on to her in the first place?

He should have listened to Honey. He should have listened to his mom. They knew that a movie star wasn't likely to move permanently to Sun Valley. No, those mansions were only occupied two months out of the year by the rich and famous. She didn't belong in his tourist town any more than he belonged in her Hollywood.

She was a bird. He was a fish. Lonesome Larry. It wasn't her fault. She wasn't trying to fly away. She was simply created to soar.

She had so much to offer, and it wasn't fair for him to want her all to himself. Though that's what he needed. He needed a friend, a lover, a wife, who would stand by his side. Who would be content rafting and fishing and skiing and raising their children.

It was a good life. Just not the life for a famous actress, no matter how hard they had tried to convince themselves it was. Yeah, she'd been dreaming with him. She'd made it seem so believable.

"Tracen." Honey's voice broke through his thoughts like a sledge-hammer through a wall.

He turned to face her, realizing that though he'd made it to his office, he hadn't sat at his desk yet. He hadn't even stepped behind the desk.

"What are you doing?" Her teasing smile couldn't quite hide the worry in her eyes.

"I'm…" Tracen looked around to figure out what he needed to do. He'd rather shove the computer out the window than turn it on, and if he touched the pile of mail next to the phone, it was going to get ripped in half. He shrugged, forcing himself to look back at Honey. Sooner or later he'd have to admit that she was right. It would pain them both.

She stepped into the room and closed the door. "What happened?" she asked softly. The tenderness tore away his resolve to stay strong.

He rubbed away the moisture in his eyes. Tears were so stupid. Even angry, justified tears. "Emily is going back to California to film a sequel to *Wonder Woman*."

Honey moved toward him slowly. Her strong, weathered hand reached out, but he stepped away.

"You were right," he snapped, angrier at himself than at her. He sank down into his chair, wishing to be alone. He didn't want to talk about it. Announcing Emily's decision out loud would solidify his nightmare as reality.

"Oh no." Honey sat across from him. At least she didn't say, "I told you so."

Tracen leaned his elbows onto the desk and knotted his hands through his hair, feeling the roots resist. "I should have listened to you."

"I wish I'd been wrong, Tracen." Her chair squeaked as she shifted. "Seeing you together this past week, I thought I *was* wrong. She seemed to adore you."

Yeah, Emily adored him. She'd said so herself the first time he kissed her. And then when he'd lifted her up onto the counter she'd said his kisses were the best. They were good together, Emily and him. His kisses had only been the best because he was kissing her. Tracen tugged harder at his hair, trying to rid himself of the memory. "I know." He groaned.

"Are you sure..."

Tracen looked up, willing her to say something that would ease the pressure that seemed to be compacting his internal organs. Was there anything he wasn't sure about? Was there anything else he could do to change Emily's mind? Could there still be hope?

She frowned in confusion. "Are you sure she won't come back?"

A bitter laugh shook him. "She says she will. But so did Serena."

They both knew how that turned out.

"So Emily is planning to come back?" Honey asked. "How long does filming take?"

"Honey!" She wasn't helping. First she fought to keep him away from the actress, and now that he'd finally decided to step away, she wanted to reunite them? He needed her on his side. He needed all the support he could get.

Honey pressed her lips into a thin line before standing. "I'll cover the phones if you want to go home early. Obviously you're not capable of conversing civilly."

Tracen rolled his eyes. Honey's sympathy had its limits. "I'm not going home." What did she expect him to do there? Write poetry and listen to sappy love songs?

No, he needed to take out some aggression. Pound nails or kick in a wall. That was it. He'd rip off the rickety railing on The Point's balcony and rebuild. That way he could watch Emily filming downriver. The pang that shot through him with the idea should have had him admitting defeat and running home to Toto. But he couldn't completely leave Emily, no matter how much he knew he needed to.

"I'll rebuild the railing today."

Honey lifted her chin. "About time." Tracen ignored her comment, and she softened. "If you want to talk about Emily, I'll be patching rafts."

"Thanks." But no thanks. He didn't even want to think about Emily, not that he could stop. The amazing way she flipped on the trampoline. Her second ride on the mechanical bull. The way she teased his brothers.

Oh, boy. His brothers would have something to say about the split.

He grabbed the toolbox from the storage room and tromped out onto the balcony, wondering what Emily was doing right then. Perhaps sitting in Char's makeup chair. Or filming another stunt. Or wrapped in Jack's arms. His stomach lurched despite the fact that it shouldn't matter to him anymore.

Deep breath. He could do this. Mindlessly he pried nails from splintered wood. One nail at a time. One minute, one hour, one day at a time. Eventually they'd all run together, and maybe then he wouldn't be so numb.

Casually he glanced down to the river. Bruce barked into his bullhorn from time to time, but still no Emily. He'd know if she was down there. He'd feel it.

"Tracen." The soft voice came from behind him. It sounded more sultry than Emily's, but if she'd been crying....

He spun around, and his pulse raced to catch up. Deep sigh. It wasn't Emily. Just an emaciated blond who really should have eaten a cracker on her way through the restaurant. Something about her seemed familiar, but it didn't matter to him at the moment. He'd help her as quickly as he could, then—

"Tracen, it's me."

That voice. Those overplucked eyebrows. The mole above her lip. "Serena?" What was she doing here? And why now?

Her face relaxed into a smile, though it seemed more gaunt than he remembered. "I'm back," she announced.

She was back. She was back?

"I told you I'd return someday. I'm going to start a ballet studio here in town."

Tracen felt himself nod and imagined that he resembled a bobblehead. Serena had come home. Everything he'd wanted for so long. Yet now it didn't matter. Fate had twisted, and it was wringing him out like a sponge.

"How are you?" she asked, and he couldn't help hoping that she had come to The Point for another reason besides talking to him.

"Busy," he answered. The one word didn't come close to describing his well-being, but he hoped it was a hint that she should leave him to his work. He couldn't deal with her now.

Serena stepped out onto the deck that was supposed to be closed to guests. She surveyed him, spending more than a little time gazing at the ring finger on his left hand. Just a month before her perusal would have meant something. He would have worried that his appearance didn't measure up or that he'd seem too small-town. Since meeting Emily, the insecurities had disappeared. She'd accepted him just the way he was.

"Are you too busy to join me for lunch? I'd love to catch up with you."

Tracen took in Serena's dangly earrings and low-cut blouse. She'd changed, and he had no desire to "catch up." He stared, not quite able to snap out of his daze. Food had no appeal to him either, but Serena needed to eat. "All right."

That must have been the opening she was waiting for. Her slender fingers wrapped around his bicep. "The salmon smells amazing."

Tracen sniffed. He hadn't noticed the fishy scent before. Must be the special of the day. He let her drag him into the dining room. This was definitely not the way he would have expected to spend his afternoon.

"Nothing has changed," Serena purred, looking around. "Not even you."

Tracen didn't know if she thought that was a good or a bad thing, but he knew it wasn't true. For the first time since he could remember, he ached for a woman besides Serena.

"Why are you here again?" he asked as they made their way to the lobby to wait for Gigi to seat them.

Serena tossed her long hair. He vaguely noticed it wasn't as full as he remembered. "Dancing is hard on a person's body. I've got meniscal damage in both knees, and my back keeps going out."

Tracen thought back to the bump on Emily's head. He'd longed to ease her pain. To keep her from getting hurt again. But her bump was probably nothing to the way he'd made her feel today.

The memory faded, leaving Serena's inquisitive face peering at him. What had she been saying? Oh yeah, knee injuries. "Ouch."

Serena's giggle sounded hollow, like a laugh track on a sitcom. Tracen pictured the way Emily threw her head back in amusement as he'd told her jokes. Big difference.

Serena's breathy voice seemed to read his mind. "Emily Van Arsdale?"

Tracen's spine bolted up straighter. How did she know he'd been dating the actress? Had a picture of him somehow gotten into the tabloids? Is that why Serena was really back?

Serena scooted closer to him and whispered excitedly, "Oh my stars. I think that's Emily Van Arsdale sitting over there."

Tracen jerked his head toward the lounge. Emily. She hadn't made it out of the restaurant after all. She sat so still, staring out the window. Wasn't she supposed to be working? His skin began to tingle with awareness.

Serena's grip tightened. "I heard she was filming a movie up here. She cut her hair. And just look how tiny she is."

"Shh…" Tracen tried to shush her. The last thing he needed

was for Emily to see him with his ex. He scanned the dining room to find Gigi, then motioned for her frantically.

Serena's giggle grated against his nerves. "Let's go meet her!"

"What?" Now Tracen grabbed at Serena's arm to hold her still. "No!" He spoke in a hushed tone, but the intensity poured through.

"What do you think she's doing?" Serena beamed up at him. "Maybe she's waiting for Jack Jamison. Though I heard a rumor that there's some other man in her life now."

Tracen ground his teeth together and turned his head away to keep his emotions in check. His face must not have been recognizable in the tabloid photo. Serena had no idea. With control he responded, "I don't think she's waiting for Jack."

Looking back at Emily, he froze. She'd awakened from her trancelike state to watch him holding Serena in place. The glare she sent him seemed to cool his skin like a cloud blocking the sun. The fight drained from him.

Serena took the opportunity to slip away from his grip. She sashayed across the lobby toward the leather couches flanking the fireplace. Toward Emily. He took a hesitant step forward. How could he explain?

"Oh wow! Emily Van Arsdale. I love you." Serena spouted words that Tracen never would. "I'm so pleased to meet you. My name is Serena St. Clair."

Tracen inhaled, waiting for the explosion when his worlds collided. How had he ever compared the women to each other? His relationship with Serena had been as disastrous as a time bomb, while Emily had lit up his life with the sparkle and fun of a firecracker.

Emily's eyes flicked to Serena, then back to him, questioning his intent. The distrust ripped his heart to shreds. Had she figured out who the other woman was?

"Hello," she said smoothly to Serena.

Serena clasped her hands together. "You are absolutely beautiful. I worked in Southern California for a while, so I've seen lots of famous actresses, but they never look as good as they do in the movies. You, however, look radiant. I swore you wore colored contacts in *Wonder Woman*."

Emily's lips turned up hesitantly, though the smile held little warmth. "Thank you."

Tracen watched the interaction between the only two women who had ever broken his heart. And both for the same reason. But that's where the similarities ended. Emily possessed grace and maturity while Serena...Serena continued gushing.

"Yeah, I was a dancer down there. I danced in a music video with Jack Jamison's ex-girlfriend. It's like the whole six degrees of separation thing, except there are only three degrees between the two of us. Oh, wait a minute. I danced at the Oscars last year. Were you there? Because that means you might have seen me."

Emily sat in silence for a moment. At least she wasn't glaring at him. Though he'd love to look into her eyes again. Feel the connection that drew him to her in the first place.

"No, I've never been to the Oscars," she said to Serena. "You must have done pretty well for yourself to have performed there."

She was being so sweet. If the situation were reversed, he'd rip Emily's ex-boyfriend's head off. He'd almost done that to Jack, and their romance had all been an act.

The memories of his jealous rage caused Tracen to ache for

Emily. He hadn't meant to, but he'd pushed her away, then practically paraded another girlfriend past. He deserved the way she completely ignored him, even if it hurt more than if she were to scream and slap him. Life's color faded to black and white like Dorothy's world after she left Oz.

Serena shrugged with mock humility. "I did pretty well."

Emily looked down at the legs she'd curled underneath herself before looking back up and meeting Serena's eyes. "So what brings you to Sun Valley?" Her gaze flitted to Tracen's, revealing the deeper meaning to her question.

Tracen tried to lift his arms in a shrug and shake his head to convey that he had no clue Serena was returning, but Emily didn't look at him long enough to catch the message.

"Oh, I'm from Sun Valley!" Serena spoke with way too much enthusiasm. Even if she hadn't hated growing up in Sun Valley, her volume still could have been toned down a bit. "I'm back because I can't dance anymore. Injuries from overuse. Plus, I always told Tracen I would come back. Just got in today."

Then Emily's stare leveled on him, and the full weight of it could be felt throughout his every muscle. She remained still, except for the rise and fall of her chest. Chiseled cheekbones stretched her soft skin taut, and her eyes accused of betrayal. He struggled to breathe as if he'd just had the wind knocked out of him.

Tracen felt Serena turn toward him, but he didn't break eye contact with Emily. Serena's voice barely registered over the pulse pounding in his ears. "Oh, this here is Tracen Lake, my high school sweetheart."

If Emily hadn't figured out his connection with the blond before, she knew it now. He looked away, hoping for an escape. Instead, he felt Serena's fingers curl around his wrist and drag him forward.

"Hello, Tracen." Emily's guarded voice could have been wearing boxing gloves with the way it sent him reeling.

"Hi." What else could he say? He pulled his arm away from Serena and shoved his hands into his pockets.

Emily rose from her seat, but even standing to her full height, she was dwarfed by Serena. Shorty, he'd called her. But she'd been the perfect size in his arms.

"We've already met," she informed Serena, her voice vague and distant.

"Oh, you have?" Serena's eyes widened as she shot Tracen a bewildered glance. "Why didn't you tell me?"

Emily's expression echoed Serena's question, chin high.

"We, uh…" Tracen motioned between himself and Emily as if his gesture would explain the relationship. He knew words could not. "I…"

Emily's eyes narrowed before she looked away in disgust. This was it. She'd let loose now. He deserved whatever she said about him. But if she came after him physically, he wouldn't be able to fend her off without pulling her to him, cradling her against his chest, caressing her hair in a soothing motion, whispering into her ear, pressing a kiss to her temple…never letting go.

"What Tracen is trying to say"—Emily's clipped words taunted him, independent and bitter—"is that he's an extra in the movie I'm filming."

What? She wasn't going to do the drama queen routine? It would have let him off the hook. He wouldn't have to maintain the façade of normality, letting the charade continue. Of course, it was probably all a dare. She wanted the truth to come from him.

Serena shrieked. "You're in the movie, Tracen? Of all the…I'm in Hollywood for ten years and come back to find that *you* are in a movie? That's so cool. Hey!" She turned back to Emily. "Do you need any more extras?"

From Emily's expression, he knew she must be wondering what he ever saw in the ambitious airhead. He sure was.

Well, if Emily wanted him to make this right, he would. That's the least he could do for her.

"Actually, Serena…" He rubbed a hand over the rough stubble on his jaw. What was he doing? With the correct words he could have Emily back. He could enjoy a few more days with her and delay the inevitable. It wasn't enough, but it was something. "Emily and I—"

"Emily!" Char panted as she ran up the stairs from the basement. "Why aren't you down at the river? What could possibly be keeping…" The makeup stylist's voice faded as she joined the threesome in the lounge. She didn't try to hide the disbelief in her expression when Tracen's position next to Serena registered, explaining the tension in the room. An over-manicured hand lifted to her hip. "Somebody better tell me what is going on."

The look Emily tossed Tracen before breezing past Char left him cold and empty. "Nothing is going on, Char. I was simply wasting time. Sorry."

Chapter Twenty

....

Tracen blindly followed Serena to a table as she yammered on about Emily. Oh, he could tell her a lot more about Emily, but he didn't want to discuss the extent of their relationship. He'd keep his mistakes to himself.

Serena settled across from him. Hadn't he just been in the same place with Emily only a little while earlier? Now it seemed like ages ago already.

"Look at you, Tracen."

Serena's bubbly comment caused him to blink. What exactly was she looking at? He'd propped his elbows on the table and rested his chin on his interlaced fingers while staring off into space. Was she going to criticize his table manners? Or had she read the attraction he had for the actress?

Serena leaned forward. "You can't believe I'm really here, can you? You're in shock."

The shock had started before Serena's return, though she'd definitely added to it. "You could say that."

"It's so good to see you again, Tracen. I missed you."

Tracen tried not to harrumph. Had she missed him or just the attention he'd given her? The way he'd followed her around like a puppy dog, begging for her to throw him a bone. He sure hadn't done that with Emily. He hadn't had to.

"You must not have missed me too much," he stated, no emotion coloring his tone.

Serena sighed. "I didn't have time to think much about you down there. I was so busy all the time. Just trying to survive."

The wall around his heart crumbled a little. She'd probably worked so hard to make her life better that she missed out on a chance to enjoy what she had.

"The competition was fierce, but I did it, Tracen. You would have been so proud of me."

He reinforced the crumbling section of wall. She'd gotten what she wanted, and that's all that really mattered to her. "Good for you, Serena."

"Where's our waitress?" Serena had lost interest in him already. She twisted her head toward the bar. "Is Gigi still running this place?"

Tracen didn't have the energy to respond. Serena didn't care so much about Gigi as she cared about her service.

The front door to the restaurant slammed open, catching his attention. Jor-El ran in, shining with sweat and panting. He spotted Tracen and maneuvered clumsily through the obstacle course of tables and patrons.

Tracen braced himself. No doubt the boy would talk about Emily.

"Hi, Jor-El," he greeted as the kid screeched to a halt in front of him.

"Tracen." Jor-El looked back and forth between Serena and him. "I overslept. I was hoping to catch Emily before she started filming. She left me a message last night, saying she wants to take me and Mom to the California Mountain Unicycle Weekend. Can you believe it?"

Tracen felt a lump form in his throat. First of all, how did Emily even know of such a thing? And second—second—how completely amazing for her to make such an offer. She really did want to use her money and fame to bless others.

Serena giggled. "Mountain unicycling? That sounds ridiculous."

Jor-El's enthusiasm turned to irritation. "Unicycling is a sport. Emily said she's even seen some people jump on a trampoline while riding a unicycle. I bet she could do it."

Tracen bet she could too. There wasn't much Emily couldn't do. Too bad he wouldn't be around to watch her do it. "That's great, Jor-El."

Jor-El nodded, shaking away his frown.

Serena studied the kid with a confused expression. "How do you know Emily Van Arsdale?"

"She's my friend." Jor-El looked to Tracen, as if wondering why he hadn't already explained. "I honestly haven't seen her much since she's been here. But we talk on the phone sometimes."

Serena gaped. "Emily must really put up with a lot from her fans."

Tracen sat up straighter, ready to defend the kid who was also *his* friend. But Jor-El didn't need his help. Somewhere between the time Emily arrived and their current conversation, he had learned to stand up for himself.

"Do you know Emily?" Jor-El demanded.

"Actually, I just met her." Serena tossed her hair, beaming at the memory.

Jor-El's eyes darted to Tracen's, suspicion reflected there. Tracen cringed, expecting Jor-El's next question.

"And how do you know Tracen?"

A smug smile curved Serena's lips up. "I've known Tracen a long time. In fact, he's even asked me to marry him."

Ten years ago. A different Tracen. It didn't even seem real anymore. But that didn't matter to Jor-El.

The kid backed away, horror blackening his face. "No."

Tracen reached out to stop the kid. He couldn't grab him before Jor-El tripped over a purse strap, but he wasn't down long. He sprang right back up like he'd landed on one of the trampolines at Boise State.

"Jor-El," Tracen called after him, standing for a better chance at drawing the kid's attention.

No matter. Jor-El was already to the lobby, racing down the steps to the basement, which would lead out the back door. Which would lead to the river. Which would lead to Emily.

Tracen slammed a palm to his forehead before dropping back to his seat. "That was stupid, Serena."

Serena's amber eyes widened with innocence. "I didn't mean to imply that we are engaged right now. He just asked how I knew you. Gee, that boy is volatile."

She had no idea. As for volatile, he had something building inside that would likely explode if she tried any more stunts like that.

But maybe it was for the best. Emily would think he left her for his former fiancée, thus preventing him from repeating his previous mistake of thinking he could keep the dynamic actress to himself. He'd started out with the intention of trying to get Emily to stay in Sun Valley. But if he really loved her, he should let her go. *Mercy*, he loved her. And that's why he was going to lose her. She deserved so much more than he could offer.

* * * * *

Emily left the crew behind her as she dried off in the sun. They wouldn't be able to shoot the take again until she stopped dripping. Plus, she couldn't see The Point when she hid behind the grove of trees. Which meant she'd be able to get Tracen out of her mind, right?

Never.

Though he would be focused on the other woman right now. A woman he'd apparently never stopped caring about. Had he really broken up with Emily because Emily was leaving? Or was it all because Serena was returning?

If she couldn't trust him to speak the truth during their last conversation together, then how could she believe anything he'd ever said to her? Had she just imagined being close with him because that's what she wanted? He'd never really repeated her sentiments. She just figured it was because he didn't like to talk about his feelings. The joke he'd made about her needing to like his last name, that could have been nothing but harmless flirtation. But she couldn't have imagined the passion in his kiss.

Would he be kissing Serena like that soon? Her stomach grew warm at the thought. Warm and constricted, as if she needed to vomit.

"Emily!"

Oh, joy, Jor-El. His appearance usually made her smile, but today she had no energy to give. She'd left him the invitation to visit her in California on his mother's answering machine. That's when she'd been thinking Tracen would want to come down with him, as well.

She dredged up a smile from deep within. "Hi, Jor-El."

The boy didn't seem as excited as she thought he would be. He stopped about five feet away and studied her.

"Do you want to go on the mountain unicycling trip this fall?" she asked out of politeness.

Jor-El took a step forward. "That's really nice of you to offer."

He sounded so formal. Maybe he couldn't believe that she really wanted to spend more time with him. "You and your mom could stay with me for a vacation. We could do whatever you want. Disneyland. The beach." It would help distract from the haunting loneliness sure to follow her.

"You're really going back?" Jor-El clasped fleshy hands together.

That's what was worrying him. The sweet kid missed her already. "Just for a little while. Then I'm going to live up here with my mom."

Jor-El didn't move. Maybe he wanted her to keep making comic book movies after all. How could she explain her future to him when she didn't even understand it herself?

"My mom needs me. Kinda like your mom needs you. Making movies was fun while it lasted, but—"

"Did you tell Tracen you're coming back?"

Emily's breath caught at Jor-El's words. Why did they have to talk about Tracen? The man who made her want more than what her life currently offered. Then refused to share it with her.

She looked down. "Yes."

Jor-El rushed forward and grabbed her arms with clammy fingers, the crown of his head reaching to her nose. "Then why did he ask another woman to marry him?"

The ground shifted under Emily's feet. A boulder rose up to cradle her in a sitting position as her legs turned to Jell-O.

Tracen couldn't have proposed to Serena already. "What are you talking about?"

Jor-El crouched in front of her. "There was a skinny woman eating lunch with him. I asked her how she knew Tracen, and she told me that he'd asked her to marry him."

Emily swayed in the breeze yet was unable to inhale any of the air that surrounded her. It wasn't real. It wasn't happening.

Jor-El's face began to fade as feelings of abandonment and betrayal threatened to drown her. But she fought back, rising to the surface as if Jesus were holding out His hand to help her walk on water. Just like Peter in the Bible, she had to separate her feelings from fact.

The first fact was that Jor-El had gotten his information from Serena and not from Tracen. Second, maybe he'd misunderstood. Yes, Tracen had proposed to Serena, but it had been a long time ago.

Jor-El's voice broke through her haze. "Emily? Are you okay?"

She focused on him now—his flushed face, hair slicked back with sweat, uncertainty in his squinty eyes. Scooting over on the rock, she motioned for Jor-El to join her.

"Tracen broke up with me this morning," she explained, her voice sounding even despite the way the admission left her insides jagged and raw.

She'd been dumped before, but she'd always been able to shrug it off. With Tracen, she'd expected so much more—more than an ultimatum. But perhaps it was all an excuse. An escape.

Emily focused on the river rushing by. She used to consider its whitewater a form of entertainment and adventure. But now with the way it hurried past, not caring what devastation it might bring in its haste, the rapids seemed cold and cruel. Fitting that Tracen made a living from them.

Might as well tell Jor-El the whole story. Get it all out. "The woman with Tracen is his former fiancée. But it sounds like they're getting back together, huh?"

It must have been what Tracen wanted all along. He certainly wouldn't have the height issue with Serena the way he'd had with Emily. Though the woman had seemed kind of flighty. How could Tracen ever trust her again?

Emily watched Jor-El slump even lower, as if he were a blob of butter melting in the sun. Poor guy. He hurt for her. Probably because he understood her. His own father had abandoned him.

Slinging an arm around Jor-El's shoulder, she hugged him to her. He felt soft, like a pillow. Which is what gave her the urge to bury her face in him and cry.

Jor-El's beefy arm lifted behind her back. He cleared his throat. "I'd marry you, Emily, if I were fifteen years older."

Such sweet acceptance.

"Thank you, Jor-El," she whispered, her throat clogging with humility. "That means a lot to me."

His childish proposal meant everything to her. Since he was the only man left in her life.

Chapter Twenty-one
....

"Don't look now," Charlene commanded, spinning Emily's makeup chair away from the window of the trailer. "Giant jerk at twelve o'clock."

Emily's stomach blended the fruit she'd had for breakfast into a smoothie.

Rafting scenes were over, so she hadn't been expecting to see Tracen on location anymore. But she'd still hoped, despite the ache that intensified like the beeping of a metal detector anytime he came near.

She craved his attention the way she craved chocolate milk shakes. And she still drank one of those occasionally, even knowing it would cause diarrhea and vomiting.

Emily couldn't help ripping the protective plastic cape from her shoulders and bolting to the window. So much for the nonchalance she'd been planning to portray. Her heart plummeted when all she could find was Jack Jamison attempting to hit on the costume designer.

"Where, Char, where?"

A treacherously long fingernail jabbed the air in front of Emily's nose. "He's up the hill in the little shack where they store all the rafts."

Emily's pulse pounded through her veins as she squinted the

direction Char pointed. No sight of Tracen. He must be hidden behind the stack of blue rubber paddleboats. "That's three o'clock, not twelve o'clock," she admonished her fellow spy.

"Either way." Char's indignation led to one of her protective mama lectures. "But girl, if we're gonna talk about time, then it's time you stopped acting like a stray puppy and turn back into the wildcat America fell in love with."

Emily didn't care about America's love. "It's only been two days, Char. Much more time is needed." *If* she were going to get over him. She still couldn't resign herself to the idea that Tracen would just let her go.

Two days without Tracen meant two sleepless nights in bed reliving every moment they shared together. He'd invited her to spend a holiday with his family. He'd been so protective when she knocked herself out on the mechanical bull. Then there was the kiss with the kindergartner on her back at Cougar Hot Springs. If she remembered nothing else, that kiss would be enough to keep her believing that Tracen's feelings for her had been real.

Maybe he hadn't entirely meant the ultimatum he'd given her. But with the way she'd stormed out of The Point after Serena arrived, he hadn't had a chance to apologize. Oh, who was she kidding? Serena was what he really wanted—always wanted. Still…

"I've got to go talk to him, Char."

Charlene blocked the door with her body before Emily could get to it. "Not on my watch."

Emily sighed. Char was trying to keep her from getting hurt. But she'd rather know for a fact that Tracen didn't love her than to let go without a fight. "This might be my last chance to see him."

"There you go, sounding all needy and desperate. That's not how you get a man," Char admonished. "And if the idiot raft instructor doesn't see how special you are, then you shouldn't want him."

Char was right—the part about Tracen being an idiot was right anyway. The part about Emily not wanting him couldn't be further from the truth. But the makeup artist didn't need to know that. "You're right, Char. Now can I go outside and run my lines with Jack?"

Char moved to the side but must have been watching her because the moment Emily stepped off the steel stairs and veered toward the storage shed, Char jumped in front of her again. "Get back in the trailer, girl. You can't trick me."

Emily kept going, detouring around her roadblock.

Char grabbed her wrist. "It's for your own good, babe."

Emily tried to snatch her arm away, but Char's grip locked on tighter. The woman must have missed her true calling of playing linebacker in the NFL.

"Let *me* decide what's good for me." Emily shook her arm and tried to yank it away.

Char twisted Emily's elbow to pin her arm behind her back, then shoved her to the side of the dirty trailer. Goodness, bounty hunter would have also made a perfect career path.

Emily twisted and ducked out of Char's hold.

The wrestling continued until Tracen stepped out of the shed and glanced their direction. The determination drained away from Emily as she realized how Tracen must see her—with a fistful of Char's hair and a leg wrapped behind Char's knee as if to trip the other woman. He didn't react to their scene, though. Only ducked back into the shed.

Char released her from the chokehold as Emily straightened. "Let me finish this my way," Emily pleaded softly, the word *finish* echoing through her mind as if her body was nothing but an empty shell—hollow and lifeless.

Char raised both hands before walking away. "I tried," she called back over her shoulder. A premature "I-told-you-so." But it was only because she cared so much.

Emily hesitated. She'd definitely be safer following Char.

* * * * *

Tracen ran his hands along smooth rubber, looking for the patches Honey had applied. He didn't have to double-check her work. He just wanted an excuse to be down by the river again. Down by Emily.

She'd made it perfectly clear how she felt about him. And he didn't blame her. But what if seeing him again could change her mind? He'd been wrong to try to force her to give up acting for him. It had to be her choice. And that's why he let her go.

Circling the side of the raft, he followed the inflated tube to the outside of the open-sided shed, preparing to sneak a peek of Emily. She probably wouldn't even know he was there. They were both supposed to be working, after all. Separate jobs. Separate worlds. Hers so sophisticated and…

Tracen gaped at the catfight going on down by Bruce's trailer. A taller African-American woman seemed to be trying to strangle a shorter chick, but the chick was quick and agile. She ripped at the woman's hair and wrapped a leg behind her, ready to knock her to the ground. The chick's wild curls flipped back, and for the first time he was able to see her face. Emily stared back at him with those wide blue eyes of hers.

Tracen retreated. He'd already ticked Emily off once. It wouldn't help for him to get in the middle of her scrape with the makeup artist. He hoped she didn't plan to go after Serena next.

Look at him. Mentally pitting one ex against the other. He should be completely on Emily's side. He should be fighting her battles for her. Though with the way Char wrestled, Emily would have to give him CPR afterward.

Memories of how he'd demonstrated rescue breathing for Jack pushed to his consciousness. CPR might not be so bad. Just thinking about it sped up the pattern of expansion and contraction in his lungs.

"Tracen?"

He whirled. Emily stood there so regally. Poised and controlled. Had she really just taken a beating? Because his stomach clenched like he'd been the one punched in the gut.

"Hi," he managed to greet her. Now what? "Char okay?" Brilliant. Like he didn't care if Emily had been hurt. He surveyed her body to reassure himself that everything was intact. And boy, was it.

A small smile played on Emily's lips. She looked away, examining the rafts across from him. "She's fine. Just a little upset that I'm talking to you right now."

That's what the scuffle had been about? Emily's friend had been trying to protect her from him? Shame heated his core.

He returned to checking rafts rather than face her. "I didn't mean to hurt you, Emily."

Sorry wasn't good enough, was it? He couldn't take back the things he'd said. Their relationship just wouldn't work. They'd been fooling themselves. Fallen in love too quickly maybe. Been too naïve.

Emily spun so that her back was to the rafts. She bounced a little when leaning into them. "Tell me you didn't know Serena was returning."

Tracen shook his head before facing her. The way her eyes pleaded with his, pleaded for hope, caused a protective longing to well up within. His throat constricted. "I would have told you if I'd known," he rasped.

His answer seemed to fill her with new confidence. She stood up taller. "Well, did you tell Serena about us?"

He picked at a plastic patch. "No." Serena didn't matter to him anymore, and it was none of her business anyway. His relationship with Emily was way too personal. Besides, he didn't need more people feeling sorry for him.

"Really?" Emily's voice dripped with condescension now. "So she comes home after ten years to find her former fiancé still pining for her?"

Hardly. The woman he was pining for stood only three feet away. Tracen planted his hands on his waist to keep them from pinning Emily down the way Char had done only moments before. Of course then he would kiss her until she knew the gut-wrenching truth. That he cared for her more than he cared for himself.

"No, I—"

Emily wouldn't let him finish. Apparently she was out for revenge. Char should have kept Emily away to protect *him*.

"You know what I wish? I wish you had broken up with me one hour later. Just one hour. Then Serena would have found you dating me—me, a famous actress, a superhero if you will." Emily paced the narrow walkway between rafts as she ranted, arms flying.

Tracen watched with a twisted fascination. Mesmerized by her passion, enraged by her assumptions.

"Serena couldn't believe you were an extra in my movie. How little does she think of you? It would have just blown her mind to see the way you kissed me. To see that you'd moved on. To see that—"

Tracen's arm shot out, blocking Emily's pacing path, thus ending her tirade. Which was a good thing, since he stopped listening anyway after she'd mentioned kissing.

Emily looked down at his arm, then glared up at him. So angry, yet so close. He could tell she was still steaming by the heat radiating off her skin. Her touch would melt him.

Without thinking, he took a step toward her. She backed up into the pile of rafts. What she needed to do was run. Get away from him before he started something that would be even harder to end. And end it would. She still planned to leave him.

Why couldn't he just let her go? Because he needed to kiss her good-bye, that's why. Resting a hand on the raft next to her head, he leaned forward, enjoying the way she narrowed her eyes.

With the angle at which he had to dip down to reach her, their foreheads were closest to touching. All Emily had to do was lift her chin...

Her chin stayed put, but her fingernails made a zipper sound as she clutched the raft behind her. "I should have listened to Honey and Gigi. I should never have gotten involved with you." Strong words spoken in a shaky voice. The truth of them made Tracen's insides quiver, as well.

"Yes, you should have listened to them." Tracen nuzzled her temple with his nose. A coil of hair tickled and tantalized with its fresh-fruity scent. He lowered his lips to murmur into her ear. "And you should leave right now if you don't want me to kiss you."

He wrapped one hand behind his back, demonstrating her freedom to do as he suggested, even while praying that she would stay. And not just for the kiss, but for a lifetime. One more kiss wouldn't be enough.

"Tracen?" Whispering his name brought her chin higher. It wasn't close enough for contact, but he could seal the deal. She hadn't left, and that was all the encouragement he needed.

Taking his free hand from behind his back, he ran his fingers over her sharp cheekbone and into her hair, tingling at the touch. Had it only been a couple of days since he'd held her? How did he ever think that he could live without her?

Her eyes slid shut. He watched her lips part. At last.

"Tracen!"

Emily's eyes popped open at the call. Tracen willed away the interruption. They could just continue in their own little world. She was all that mattered.

"Traaaa-cen!"

He snapped to attention. He couldn't will away Serena's voice or her form when it appeared at the entrance to the shed. Of all the...

"There you are," her voice tinkled as she peered into the darker, enclosed space.

Tracen stepped forward to protect Emily from embarrassment. It wasn't until he blocked her from Serena's view that he remembered her statement about how she wished Serena had seen him kiss her.

Of course, that didn't matter the way she thought it did. But he hadn't had the chance to tell her. He hadn't had the chance to do anything he wanted.

"Honey told me you were down here." Serena grabbed his hand. "Tracen, you have to come see."

Tracen pulled out of her grip. The woman was touchy-feely with everyone, but Emily didn't know that either. He tried to glance over his shoulder to gauge Emily's reaction, but her expression had gone blank.

Serena clapped her hands together. "I went out looking at buildings this morning for my dance studio, and I found the perfect place. It's an old ballroom above a deserted thrift store downtown. Huge. With wood floors and rows of windows. It needs some work, though. That's why I need you."

Tracen tried to keep up with her monologue. But rather than really listening to her words, he tried to read the way Emily would perceive their conversation. The part about Serena needing him would not translate well. "What?"

"Could you help me with some repairs? You're so handy with construction."

He'd help her. A ballet studio would be good for Sun Valley. Now if he could explain to Emily the platonic friendship he'd resumed with the dance instructor, he might as well just tell Serena about the not-so-platonic friendship he'd had with Emily. That's what Emily had been raving about before he backed her into the rafts in a delicious attempt at shutting her up.

He stepped to the side, revealing Emily to Serena like one of the prizes on a game show. "Serena, you actually interrupted Emily and I—"

"Emily Van Arsdale!" Serena squealed. "Is it true that you're moving to Sun Valley?"

Emily's lips parted like they had when Tracen was about to kiss her. But this time it was from speechlessness. She slanted her eyes Tracen's way, probably trying to figure out how to respond. He wasn't any help in that department. How did Serena know about Emily's plans to move? And what else did she know?

Serena answered his unasked questions. "Honey told me that you're from Boise. And you'd like to teach P.E. That's so cool. You must be good with kids because you obviously won over the heart of that tubby boy with the unicycle."

Emily blinked. "I'm planning to move up here at the end of the year, yes."

Tracen kicked the raft behind him with his heel, his hamstring cramping at its resistance. Why did he keep expecting Emily to change her plans? Just because their almost kiss was enough to make him want to sell the rafting company so he could be with her every day.

Serena pushed past him to focus on the movie star. *That* he should have been expecting.

"Emily, I had this crazy idea. Oh my gosh, it's crazy." Serena giggled in a crazy way, reinforcing her claim. "What if we went into business together? You could start a gymnastics center underneath my ballet studio." She let out an excited scream, startling Emily.

Emily looked past Serena to Tracen. He couldn't exactly read the look. Disbelief? Accusation? A cry for help?

Her gaze shifted back to Serena. "I've never thought about starting a gymnastics center."

"Oh, you'd be great at it," Serena gushed.

And she would. She loved the sport. Loved kids. Everybody loved her, so her celebrity status would bring in tons of business. Not that there were tons of kids in the area, but if she started coaching, it might bring new families to Sun Valley.

Only a couple problems. One, she still thought of Serena as competition. And two, she wouldn't be starting the business until after she filmed *Wonder Woman II*.

What would happen between them if she really did leave him to make another movie, only to return the way she planned? Would she still be interested in him after he broke her heart? Would she have moved on by then? And the most consuming question: was he still going to be living in the same limbo that he'd hoped to avoid by breaking up with her? It hadn't gotten any easier, so far.

Emily sighed as she clutched her fingers together at waist height. "I don't know, Serena." She refused to look Tracen's direction.

"Think about it," Serena begged. "We could use the word *Holly-wood* in the name, since we've both worked there."

Emily's chin lifted. This time not for a kiss, but to assert independence. "Ironic, isn't it?" Her gaze didn't stray from Serena, but Tracen knew the words were meant for him.

He inwardly cringed. Emily saw Serena as the reason he was dumping her—either because his former fiancée had hurt him in the past or because she was back now. And here stood the very woman, offering to become business partners with her. Worse, he couldn't think of anything to do about it.

Chapter Twenty-two

....

Emily curled up under her covers. The coveted Hemingway Suite, with its bronze bust of the writer who once stayed there, now felt stuffy and impersonal. She wanted to go home.

A knock on the door jolted her like the morning wake-up call, even though she hadn't gone to sleep at all.

Tracen? Back to tempt her with more kisses? It wasn't like she could resist. Goodness, she'd never been so weak and needy in her life. But even armed with that disturbing knowledge, she limped across the floor and flipped the lock with a longing to have the man hold her one more time.

Swinging the door open, she trembled with anticipation, then felt her shoulders fall at the sight of Char in a swimming suit, towel draped around her neck.

"Oh, hi." The greeting was as good as she could give. Hobbling back toward the bed, she allowed her friend to follow.

The door slammed behind her, the sound reverberating through her skull. Most people only slammed doors out of anger. Char didn't know how to do anything but. Everything Char did was loud.

Emily so didn't need this. Pressing two fingers to her temple, she fell back onto the inviting mattress.

"What are you doing in bed, girl? It's not even nine o'clock. And why are you walking so funny? Is it from the beating I gave you earlier?"

Emily groaned. Her scuffle with Char could have been the high point of her day. "No, you didn't hurt me, Char. Bruce just made me do the tree-climbing scene repeatedly. And the first time Jack was supposed to catch me, he missed."

Char gasped. "Why didn't they have his stuntman catch you?" Char possessed so much more wisdom than Bruce.

"They did after that." Emily rolled her head side to side, feeling the ache down her spine intensify as she arched her back.

Char motioned for Emily to scoot over so she could join her on the bed. Emily wiggled away before the mattress shifted, and the bed squeaked under the other woman's weight. "If you're sore, you should come join me in the hot tub. Heat is supposed to help the muscles."

Emily snuggled deeper under the down comforter and quilt. She was already warm. And her body resisted the idea of moving. Now if Tracen called to invite her to the hot springs again… "I just want to go to sleep."

Char nodded understanding. "Depression?"

"No," Emily retorted automatically. She didn't get depressed. She just got tired. Weary. Hopeless.

"So what happened with the jerk?"

Emily closed her eyes. It was hard enough thinking about the scene in the shed. She didn't want to have to talk about it too. But then maybe letting Char play "bash the boyfriend" would lift her spirits. Not that she was depressed.

She opened her eyes and shook her head at the memory. Her words were going to sound so ridiculous to her friend's ears.

"Okay, here's what happened. Tracen almost kissed me. Then when Serena showed up he stepped in front of me so that she wouldn't see what was going on." The withdrawal still left her cold. "After that he stood by while the other woman offered to become my business partner, if I decide to open up a gymnastics studio here in town."

Char held up a manicured hand. "Wait a minute. Wait just a minute. The woman—this ex-girlfriend of his—doesn't know about your relationship with Tracen?"

Char was supposed to be bashing the boyfriend, but her comment made Emily feel like the stupid one. She pulled the blanket over her head, not caring if it muffled her answer. "Tracen hasn't told her."

"Of all the…" Char's weight lifted from the bed, rocking Emily back into place. "What does the jerk want? Does he really want you to break your contract for *Wonder Woman II*? Or does he simply want his ex-fiancée back?"

Good question. More precisely, it was the exact question that drove Emily to want to escape into sleep, the question that would make it hard to go to sleep, and the question that would wake her with nightmares once she finally managed to fall asleep.

"Char?" Emily paused, pulling the covers from her head. How would Char take her next admission? Maybe knock some sense into her. That's really what she needed, whether she wanted it or not. "Char, I haven't signed the Wonder Woman contract yet."

Char spun from the window to face her, hands on hips, towel now loose and flying around her like a cape. The makeup artist could make a good superhero in her own right. "Say what? Didn't your agent fax you a copy so you could sign it right away?"

Emily had no excuse. She curled onto her side, tucking both hands under her cheek.

Char threw her head to the side like a bull before it charged. "Don't tell me you're having second thoughts because of a boy. It was cute when you were crushing and everything, but now you're talking about giving up your dreams."

Emily sank lower into her mattress as she exhaled. "It was never a dream, Char. More like a distraction."

"Still, it's an opportunity." Char threw her arms in the air. "If a man loves you, he should want what's best for you."

Char's words stung like a bucket of cold water being bailed out of a paddleboat. Emily couldn't argue. Sure, Tracen had insecurities where Hollywood was concerned, and maybe he even thought that staying in Sun Valley was the best thing for her, but if he loved her, then he would certainly want to work this out. Rather than just trying to steal kisses when his former flame wasn't looking.

He'd been so close to kissing her too. A breath away. At the time she'd hoped it was a step toward reconciliation. Like his way of saying he couldn't bear to be without her.

But no. He'd cooled off the moment Serena came calling. That was practically as bad as the guys who hit on her while wearing wedding rings.

Tracen was probably out with Serena that very moment. While Emily lay in bed considering giving up everything to be with him—grieving the loss of something that so obviously had never been hers.

Her heart twisted at the memory of how he'd had every opportunity to explain their relationship to Serena. Emily had made her desire in that area pretty clear. Yet he'd just stood there while Serena gushed about her new business.

Oh how she wanted to give Tracen an excuse. Like maybe he'd been lost in thought over the idea of Emily moving to his hometown and running a gymnastics center. Or maybe he'd been starting to tell Serena about them when the other woman interrupted. Then there was her favorite excuse: maybe his head had still been fuzzy from almost kissing her, and he'd been struck momentarily speechless.

Goodness, she was a fool.

* * * * *

"You're a fool." Sam swung Tracen's golf club, smacking a pinecone out to the middle of the Salmon River with a long, graceful swing accompanied by a whipping sound.

"Thanks, Bro." Tracen teed up. Taking his aggression out on nature might have been therapeutic, had his little brother not found the need to lecture him.

Sam leaned onto his club with one hand and placed the other hand on his hip. "You're seriously going to let her walk away?"

With control, Tracen rolled another row of pinecones into position using the head of his six-iron. Now to smack them into oblivion. The harder he hit them, the easier it would be to stop thinking about Emily, right? "It's not my choice, Sam."

"Bull." Sam shoved his club to the ground.

Tracen stood up straighter. Would he ever get accustomed to his baby brother's newfound strength? His commanding presence made Tracen a little wary.

Pinecones scattered as Sam slammed his foot into Tracen's neat row. "You'd never make it in the military."

Tracen lifted shoulders into a helpless shrug, golf club hanging from his fingers. How did the conversation change gears so quickly? "What are you talking about?" Did his sibling want to pull a Char and try to wrestle him into agreement?

Sam shook his head and stared out past the river. He turned solemn eyes back toward Tracen—eyes wise beyond Tracen's world. "I'm talking about commitment. Loyalty. Fighting for what you believe in."

The words sank in. But they didn't apply. Tracen tipped at his hips to swipe the club Sam had been using off the ground. "Emily isn't a part of my platoon anymore. She'd gone AWOL."

Sam gave a bitter laugh as he took off toward Tracen's trailer. "She's not AWOL. You gave her a dishonorable discharge."

Tracen strode to keep up, his steps crunching dried pine needles. "Actually, Emily never enlisted."

Sam swung the back door open and held it for Tracen to enter—probably just so Tracen would see his expression of disdain close up.

Tracen glared right back. Two years in the army made Sam seem much older, but it didn't give him the right to pull rank. Tracen still had a few years on him.

He pounded up the short set of stairs to grab a couple of water bottles from the fridge. Tossing one to Sam, he strutted back past him into his family room addition. Soon he'd be building a whole cabin. The thought should have cheered him more.

Tracen sank into his recliner, guzzled cool water down his surprisingly dry throat, and jabbed at the remote to find a baseball game. He needed another distraction. His brother was doing a horrible job.

Sam kicked off his shoes and sprawled across the entire couch. "Come on, *Tracey*. Man up."

Tracen narrowed his eyes at the nickname. Sam was asking for it.

Little brother calmed down. "I saw the way she looked at you, dude."

Tracen turned away and flipped to a different station. Sam's compassion was even worse than his ridicule. Reminding himself that his brothers had only seen Emily the one day, Tracen refused to let the comment reach him. How much could Sam know?

"And you couldn't get enough of her either."

Or maybe he knew too much. But he could be wrong. Infatuation. Tracen had only been infatuated. The fun part of falling in love. Maybe it hadn't gone any deeper than that.

"It doesn't matter anymore, Sam."

"That's right." Sam hugged a throw pillow like he used to hug his teddy bear Pookie. The smaller Sam had been much less threatening. The big one continued. "It doesn't matter because you've got your cabin in Sun Valley to keep you happy. And that's all you've ever wanted."

It used to be. Too bad it wasn't what Tracen wanted anymore.

Chapter Twenty-three
....

Tracen waited for Bruce to climb in the raft. The director had one more week of filming, and most of that was going to be panoramic or nature shots. Today Tracen would be taking the cameramen for a ride so they could get footage of the rapids.

Though he hated to admit it to himself, Tracen had hoped for Emily to be around. He hoped to see her smile or hear her laugh just one more time. Yeah, right. He wanted a lot more than one more moment with her. She was like the Energizer Bunny, and he was running on a dead battery.

He knew he needed her, but it was the hope thing that got him all hung up. Why hope? What had hope ever done for him? Better just to let go and turn the other way so he didn't have to face the fact that Emily would rather pretend to be a superhero than to be with him for real.

And it was real. Scary real. So real he couldn't handle it. Good thing he could pretend too. Pretend that he didn't care if Emily left. Pretend Sam's lecture hadn't pierced him with its accuracy. Pretend his soul wasn't bleeding.

Tracen gazed downstream. He could hear the river's roar, but it sounded distant somehow. Though the current raged past, it didn't affect him. The colors faded, the noise muted. The beauty he so loved lost some of its vibrancy.

It was going to be a long day. He wasn't impatient with Bruce—just disconnected. Achingly numb, Tracen swiveled his head to check on the director. The sooner he got the shooting over with, the sooner he could—what? The sooner he would have to do something else that reminded him of Emily.

"Emily wants to what?" Bruce's voice bellowed into his cell phone, but it wasn't his volume that caused Tracen to pay attention to the one-sided conversation. "Well, we probably won't need her anymore, but even if I were going to let her leave, our plane won't be available for charter for another two days at the least."

Tracen's fingers dug into his palms as he gripped the oar tighter. Muscles flexed reactively in what he'd learned to be the fight or flight syndrome. Normally he was a fighter, but—

"She can try to get a commercial flight. She'd have to fly out of Boise, though, and with their size, they might not have any seats left."

Emily was done in Sun Valley. He'd known the moment was coming, but he hadn't expected the loss to feel so much like a punch to the gut. And he hadn't expected her to be this anxious to take off. That's what hurt the most. He knew she wasn't so much in a hurry to escape Sun Valley as she was to escape him.

She'd said she couldn't imagine being with anybody else. But that's exactly what was going to happen. Their romance would be considered nothing more than a silly fling in her memories.

He couldn't breathe. He needed space. He needed to move forward. He needed to forget this power she had over him.

Yanking the raft back onto shore, he motioned to Bruce that he would be right back. Bruce didn't even look up, so Tracen took off to get his backpack by the trailer. The director might not have appreciated being deserted, but it was the least of Tracen's worries at the moment.

Velcro scraped against the rough canvas material as Tracen ripped open the side compartment holding his cell phone. *Please be there, Matt.* He jabbed the numbers to dial his older brother.

Ringing—then the click of a connection.

"Hey, Tracen." The guy was always even-tempered. With the mood Tracen was in, it ticked him off just a little. "How's life among the elite?" Matt's question ticked him off a little more. But he needed help.

"It's about over for me." Tracen tried to keep his words from sounding too clipped. "Though you could have a chance at rubbing elbows with Emily again."

"Really?" Too peppy. Not quite caring. The clink of tools over the line gave the impression that Matt was in the middle of mechanic work.

"Yeah." Tracen looked down at the dirt. "Emily wants to head back to Hollywood right away, though she probably won't be able to get a flight from here for a few days. I was wondering if you might be able to give her a lift."

The banging of tools on Matt's end ceased. "I'm not sure I follow. Is everything okay? I mean, why is your girlfriend leaving so suddenly?"

Tracen gripped the phone until his knuckles burned. Every time he had to explain the breakup, it was like ripping his heart in half again. The pieces kept getting smaller and smaller. "We're not dating anymore. She wants to keep making movies."

"Ah, man. That's rough."

Rough didn't begin to describe the turbulence he felt within. "Yeah."

It was quiet. Matt had nothing else to say. At least he didn't lecture the way Sam had.

"Maybe…"

Uh-oh. Matt was the one who never interfered. It was easier that way. Easier not to go deeper.

Matt went deeper. "Maybe you should go with the girl this time, Tracen."

He'd resisted the idea from the very beginning. Never even considered it. Been repulsed by Emily's suggestion. And he still hated it, but—no, he couldn't. He'd make a fool of himself in Tinseltown. And by going with Emily he'd only prolong the inevitable.

"It's not that easy, Matt."

His big brother couldn't understand. Everything in Matt's life came easy. Like how his rich boss had just given him two of his used jet skis, while Tracen only ever got to putt around in Howie's ancient ski boat. And that was nothing compared to the way Matt had married his high school sweetheart, while Tracen's had dumped him.

Matt cleared his throat, uncomfortable as always with conflict. "I didn't say it would be easy. I just said it might be the way to go this time."

Matt probably had good intentions, but his use of the term "this time" grated against Tracen's last nerve. Like he was rubbing in the fact that Tracen had already failed where Matt had succeeded. "If you're not going to help me—"

"I'll help you."

Silence again. Tracen wanted to slam the phone down on Matt, but even more he wanted to be able to move on without Emily—without holding his breath every time he turned a corner in case she was there. Without aching when she wasn't there. Without stopping to listen for her, only to hear the echo of his heartbeat in the emptiness that surrounded him. Without worrying that at any moment he could change his mind and run the entire course of his life off track just to spend another day with her.

He needed Matt's help. "I'll text you Emily's cell phone number. Then you can call and make arrangements."

What would Emily think when she found out he'd arranged for her to fly away and leave him behind? Would she be grateful for his help? Disappointed that he sped up the process? Angry he presumed to interfere? He didn't have the strength to call her in person and find out for himself.

Matt's voice rang with concern. "Are you sure you don't want to—"

"No."

No warmth in Matt's tone this time. "All right then. Your home in Sun Valley is more important. Got it."

Where did that come from? Of course, Tracen had started out thinking the same thing, but Matt didn't know his motivations. Anyway, they'd changed. "Matt, it's not like that."

"Right. You're not out getting ready to raft at this very moment?"

Not because he wanted to. "It's my job."

"And acting is hers. Too bad you let it come between you." Matt's sigh practically shook Tracen's phone. "For some reason I thought you cared more for this girl than for the last one. Guess not."

Tracen pushed through the descending heaviness to pack his

phone away and return to the raft. Why did Matt have to bring up Serena? He didn't even know she'd come back to Sun Valley. But that's not what mattered. Tracen's choice to let go of Emily had nothing to do with Serena. Did it?

* * * * *

Emily really didn't want to deal with Serena today. Not after one of Tracen's brothers called to say he could fly her back to Southern California early. Apparently Tracen couldn't get rid of her fast enough. Seeing her probably made him guilty for returning to Serena so quickly. Maybe she should stick around just to make Tracen miserable. But then, she'd be more miserable. She was the single one.

Following the bellhop, she nodded thanks to the doorman and took her keys from the valet. Serena screeched to a halt behind her rental car. There was no way she could slip by undetected. Even with the baseball cap and sunglasses.

Serena popped out of the driver's door to her sleek black coupe. "Emily! Where are you going? You're not leaving Sun Valley already, are you?"

No, she wasn't leaving yet. She was standing in a parking lot answering stupid questions. Throwing her shoulders back, Emily willed herself to breathe normally. Serena didn't know that she'd been dating Tracen. The woman was simply being her enthusiastic self.

Emily pressed the remote to unlock the back gate to her vehicle. "Filming is over."

Serena joined her as the bellboy loaded her luggage. "Did you think about my business proposal anymore?"

Emily focused on her suitcase. "It was a nice idea, Serena, but I don't think it will work out."

"Oh, don't say that." Serena leaned against the back of the hatch after the bellboy slammed it. Emily pictured her chaining herself to the bumper the way environmental activists chained themselves to bulldozers. "If you're coming back to Sun Valley, a gymnastics studio would be a great investment."

That was the thing. She wouldn't ever be coming back to Sun Valley. "I'm not coming back, Serena. This isn't my home." Bitterness crept into her tone as she tipped the men at her service. "I don't have an old high school sweetheart to grow old with."

Serena sighed.

Probably picturing herself rocking next to Tracen on the wraparound porch of the cabin he would be building. No, Emily couldn't come back ever.

The woman persisted. "You're from Boise, though. I bet you have lots of friends there. And it's very close by."

Emily smiled wistfully. "Lots of friends, but no Tracen."

Serena smiled and nodded, but she still didn't get it. "There aren't many Tracens in the world. So strong, so stable. He hasn't changed at all since I left."

"Huh." Emily fidgeted, itching to get in her car and drive away. If she stayed much longer, she'd say something she regretted for sure. "So he's, uh, been pining for you for ten years then?"

Serena tilted her head to one side, causing a waterfall of sleek blond hair to cascade over a bare shoulder. "Tracen has never needed me."

The vise gripping Emily's heart slackened its grip slightly.

She'd wanted to believe that Tracen didn't need Serena. That the other woman had nothing to do with the reason Tracen broke up with her.

"But he adores me."

Pressure returned tenfold.

"Nobody has ever adored me the way Tracen does. Every other guy I dated just wanted something from me. But not Tracen."

Emily knew Serena spoke the truth because she'd experienced it too. She didn't want to share him. She didn't want to give him up. But not because he adored her. Because *she* adored *him*.

"What about you, Serena?" she asked quietly. Maybe she could challenge the woman without getting involved. Give to Tracen through Serena—since she was what he'd wanted all along anyway. "Do you adore Tracen? Or do you just adore the way he adores you?"

Serena's spine straightened. "Oh. You mean, like, do I just want to date him because of the way he makes me feel?"

Emily blinked to keep from rolling her eyes. The woman looked as if she'd never considered the question before. "Yes, that's what I'm asking."

Serena laughed before leaning in conspiratorially. "Honestly, when we were engaged, it was because he made me feel so good about myself. In fact, it was his belief in me that gave me the courage to follow my dream of stardom."

Emily's anger melted a little at the thought of how Tracen would react to the knowledge. If he hadn't been such a great boyfriend, he would be married right now. Poor guy. Hopefully Serena had changed and would make up for the years of pain she'd caused him.

"And now?"

"Now?" Serena sighed. "Now I wish I were you. I'm so jealous. I don't blame you if you never come back to Sun Valley."

Emily's heart clunked against her ribs. Serena didn't care for Tracen. Selfish ambition still ruled her. Tracen was going to get hurt again. Emily couldn't let that happen. Her chin lifted, and her mouth opened before she could think over the words she needed to say. "You are jealous of me?" Hands flailed at her sides. "You have everything I want, Serena. You have Tracen."

Serena's palms rose to her chest. "You want Tracen? Does he-does he know?"

The woman might as well have stabbed her. Her cluelessness was dangerous.

"Yes, he knows." Emily's admission stripped her naked. Humiliation mingled with grief.

Serena leaned forward as if believing was seeing, and she needed to get a better look. "I thought he was just an extra to you."

Either Tracen hid their relationship well, or Serena was so wrapped up in her own feelings that she hadn't noticed the tension that hovered between them. Probably both.

Shaky breath. "Yesterday when you found us in the shed? We weren't filming."

"Oh!" Serena's eyes glazed over as she recalled the moment. "Oh…" Her cheeks flamed pink. "Then why are you leaving? Tracen wouldn't choose me over you." The jealousy that tinged her tone earlier had fizzled away. Only curiosity remained.

Emily eyeballed the woman. What was wrong with her? How could she be so objective?

Moving toward the driver's side door, Emily tried to distance herself from the situation, from her emotions. It felt a little like swimming upstream.

"Tracen chose Sun Valley over me," she replied, giving the explanation that only made sense to Tracen.

Serena stood there, jaw slack, and Emily could think of no other reason to hang around. She tossed her purse to the passenger seat.

It didn't make sense. She was the one who cared so much for Tracen, and she was the one leaving.

Pausing, she looked back at Tracen's former flame. Emily really did want them to be happy together. "I hope you'll grow to adore Tracen the way I do."

Serena faded into the distance as Emily pulled away. Not exactly the way she wanted to remember the resort town, but she didn't want to focus on the more enjoyable memories either. Too fresh. Too naïve. Too depressing at the moment.

Pulling her cell phone out of her pocket, Emily dialed her mom. They hadn't talked since her battery died a few days before. And it looked like the battery was going to die again soon. Why had she packed her charger in her suitcase? Couldn't worry about that now. Better to say good-bye while she had the chance.

Violet picked up after the second ring.

"Hi, Mom." If Tracen hadn't arranged the flight for her, she'd go hang out in Boise for a few more days with her mother. They'd grown so much closer during her visit.

"Sweetie. I was wondering when I'd hear from you again. Especially after you dropped that last bomb."

Oh no. Her mom had heard her say she was moving to Sun Valley? She'd thought they'd lost connection before that.

"I cleaned out your old room for you, so you can stay with me until you get your own place. And I told all my students you want to help out on the trampoline. You wouldn't believe how excited they are."

"Mom, I—"

"As for the Tracen fellow, I couldn't be happier for you. I hope you didn't mind my meddling too much while he was here, but he's a special young man."

Emily slammed her head back into the headrest, letting it bounce off the cushion before repeating the action with more force. No, no, no. She needed a safe place to rest. Her mom was supposed to be that safe place.

"Change of plans, Mom." She spoke calmly, though she planned to scream as soon as she could disconnect the phone call. "Tracen and I broke up because I'm making another movie."

"What? You're—what?" Violet sounded more like a confused senior than an angry mother. But perhaps she had the right to be both. Emily had no justification for abandoning her only living relative again.

"I'm sorry, Mom. I'll come live with you when production for the next movie is over. I promise." Then they would have a chance to reconnect. At the moment, she didn't think she could stay in Idaho without running back to Tracen.

"You're running away again."

Emily barely made out her mother's quiet words. But just because Violet spoke them with resignation didn't make them true.

No, Emily wasn't running away. She was claiming her freedom. She was escaping a controlling relationship. She was refusing to risk her heart.

Okay, she was running away. Again.

Chapter Twenty-four

························

Tracen waved at Gigi to let her know she didn't have to worry about seating him. He led his brother out to the deck and claimed a table in the early morning sunshine. A sneezing fit raked his body before he could slide his shades over his eyes. The Achoo Syndrome refused to grant him any grace.

Sam slid farther down his bench seat to escape airborne germs. "Glad I haven't ordered my food yet, Bro."

"Sorry," Tracen muttered, though sure that the affliction never annoyed anyone else as much as it annoyed him. Memories of how Emily thought his sneezing had been cute surfaced in his consciousness. A sad smile played on his lips.

Gigi sauntered over, pulling a pad of paper from her apron. "You boys ready?"

"Yes, ma'am." Sam practically saluted.

The kid's newfound respectfulness still caught Tracen off guard. He wouldn't be staying single for long if he continued to give women that kind of attention. And if Josh got married soon, Tracen would be the only bachelor left in the family. He'd be the only brother without a family of his own.

"Yeah, I'm ready," Tracen grunted, handing Gigi his menu. He was ready for anything that might be a distraction from his thoughts of Emily.

Gigi tucked his menu under one arm and plucked a pencil from behind her ear. "What do you want?"

What did he want? How could everything that was supposed to distract him from thinking of the actress only reinforce his desire for her? Deep breath. All he had to do was tell Gigi he wanted biscuits and gravy. He opened his mouth...

"Emily Van Arsdale." The breathy voice came from behind.

Tracen clamped his mouth shut and turned to see who had read his mind.

Serena rushed onto the deck, face flushed, hair flying. Tracen tried to remember if he'd ever seen her so frazzled. And why was she talking about Emily? She pushed in front of Gigi.

"Emily Van Arsdale is leaving Sun Valley for good!" Her wild eyes locked onto Tracen.

Tracen leaned back, trying to read Serena's expression. She must have been upset about not getting to do business with the star. "You'll be fine, Serena. A gymnastics center probably would have stolen some of your business anyway. Now all the little girls in Sun Valley will take dance from you."

The table jerked, causing salt and pepper shakers to rattle as Serena slammed both palms onto it. She leaned forward, and Tracen flinched, expecting her to growl or claw at him like some caged animal. What had gotten into her?

"I'm not talking about my business." Her tone erratically covered all octaves.

Tracen glanced around to see how much attention they'd drawn. Gigi had stepped away to take an order from the only other patrons on the patio, thank goodness. But Sam's stare, eyebrows arched as if suspended from the clouds, made up for the lack of attention from anyone else.

Sam had still been in high school when Serena dumped Tracen, but apparently his kid brother remembered her. It hadn't seemed like a wise idea to tell Sam that she was back in town, since Sam would only use it as leverage in their arguments about Emily. Now Tracen regretted his decision.

Scooting farther down the bench, Tracen gripped Serena's wrists and pulled her after him into a seated position. The conversation that was about to come would be much better if he could keep it quiet and calm.

Sam exploded. "Serena St. Claire?"

Serena glanced over at him momentarily. "Hi, Sammy." Her second glance turned into a stare, and her focus seemed to be on his broad shoulders and bulging biceps. "My, my, you've grown up."

Sam preened like a peacock.

Tracen scratched his head, feeling momentarily forgotten. Hadn't Serena come running through the restaurant to talk to him? And about Emily? He gripped the dancer's arm. "What are doing here, Serena?"

She swiveled to face him, resuming her panicked demeanor. "Emily is in love with you."

Tracen jerked back, releasing his hold on her, his grip on reality. Serena knew about his relationship now? How did she find out? And what would make her think Emily loved him? His thoughts slowed like a paddleboat taking on too much water. He fought to bail himself out. "What? Why? Who did you talk to?"

Sam leaned forward, waving Tracen's questions away and

focusing on Serena. "We know Emily loves Tracen. That's old news. The question is, what are *you* doing here?"

Serena slanted her eyes toward Sam, though she continued to face Tracen. "I'm moving back to Sun Valley." Her eyes lingered a moment longer on the younger brother.

Tracen didn't have time for explanations and catching up. He needed facts. They would be the life preserver to keep his feelings from drowning him. "Serena! Who did you talk to?"

The woman jump-started back to life. "Emily, of course. I spoke to Emily. I told her that I was jealous of her, and that's when she said she's jealous of me. Imagine that."

Tracen's heart radiated a heat that fanned out from his core into his fingers and toes. His skin tingled with an itch that couldn't be scratched. Emily was jealous of Serena? Did she think they were back together? That's exactly what he hadn't wanted her to think. Hadn't his attempt at kissing her told her anything?

What if she was leaving for Hollywood, not because she would rather be in a movie, but because she thought he'd chosen Serena over her?

Sam's gray eyes became slits of flint. "Tracen, you told me Emily chose to leave you to make another movie. Why would she be jealous of Serena?"

Tracen ran both hands through his hair, ducking his face to ignore his brother's allegations. Were they true? Had he given Emily a reason to believe he was back with Serena? All he'd wanted was to leave the blond out of it.

Sam's questions only got more heated. "Why didn't you tell me Serena was back, Tracen?"

Serena didn't help. "And he didn't tell me he'd been dating Emily, either. I had no clue I'd gotten in the middle of anything."

How did he make such a mess of things? It had all started out with his fear of being hurt again, and here he'd hurt everybody else. But none of this would have happened if Emily had chosen him over Hollywood. His fear had been realized.

"Stop." He held out both hands. It was over. If Emily loved him, she didn't love him enough. That much was obvious. "Serena had nothing to do with this. I broke up with Emily, because Emily broke her word. She wouldn't stay in Sun Valley like we planned for her to. Happy?"

"Are you?" Sam shot back.

Tracen didn't respond. Sometimes stories didn't have a happily ever after. He just had to deal with it.

"Are you sure I had nothing to do with this?" Serena pleaded. "Emily sure seemed to think that I—"

"No."

"How would you know?" Sam spat out. "You're so wrapped up in your own pain that—"

"Hey!" Serena's manicured hand pointed past Tracen's face. He followed the direction of her finger, down the hill toward the film crew. "Look, there's Emily's makeup artist. She would know. Let's ask her."

Tracen shifted uncomfortably. Charlene was the last person who would want to help him out. "I don't think Char—"

Serena leapt to her feet, waving her arms overhead. "Char! Up here! Char!"

The woman waved back.

Sam took over, leaning over the railing. "We need to ask you a question, ma'am. Can you come up here for a moment?"

Char glanced behind her, as if to make sure it wasn't somebody else they were talking to, then nodded and disappeared underneath them to enter through the basement. Tracen sank lower in his seat. How was he going to make them all understand that he wanted Emily more than anything? But she didn't want him. Could an argument get any more humiliating?

Jor-El stepped onto the balcony. His chubby cheeks dimpled at the commotion. "What's going on?"

Sam scooted over to make room for the kid to sit down. "Emily Van Arsdale left. We think it's because she thought Tracen was in love with Serena and not her."

Jor-El yelped.

Tracen rose to leave. "This is ridiculous."

Jor-El shook his head. "No, it's true. She cried on my shoulder when I told her about your fiancée."

Tracen sank back down. He'd left Emily to cry on a kid's shoulder? His throat clogged with unshed tears of his own. Tears for Emily's heartache.

Serena motioned between herself and Tracen. "We're not engaged."

Char strode out. "I should hope not. Not after all those promises Tracen made to Emily." She stuck a hand on her hip and glared. "Boy, I should kick your butt. Do you know how long I've been praying for Emily to find a good guy? I'm ashamed to admit I thought you were an answer to my prayers."

Tracen half-wished Char would make good on her offer. Having his body beaten to a pulp would be less painful than the emotional torture they were all putting him through. Couldn't they see it would be best if he could forget her and move on?

Jack Jamison strolled onto the deck looking cool in khakis and a polo shirt. Tracen rolled his eyes. The guy would probably love watching him being brought down a peg after he "stole" Emily from the actor.

Jack slapped his hands together and rubbed. "Did I hear correctly? Emily has left already?"

"Yeah," Sam piped up. "Tracen paid to have her flown home early."

Ooh, that sounded bad. He'd only been trying to help. She'd been the one looking for a hasty exit.

Jack walked behind him and pounded him on the back. "Tracen, I'm disappointed. I thought you were a macho man. But macho men don't let the girl go. Not a girl like Emily. And not when the girl looks at you the way she did."

Emily's sparkling blue eyes had always turned him to mush, but didn't they have that effect on everybody?

Gigi returned. "Do we need more menus?"

"You got some humble pie for Tracen?" Char asked.

Tracen could feel the heartburn already.

"Actually..." Gigi leveled her gaze on him. "Free advice is today's special. And, Tracen, I advise you to listen to your friends here. We want what's best for you."

Tracen wavered. They weren't all friends. And he couldn't give in to peer pressure. Emily might have said she was jealous of Serena, but she was the one who left. He glanced at the door. Should he make a break for it? Look for a place to have some quiet time. Beg God to mend his broken heart again.

He glimpsed Honey charging past the door. Her gaze connected with his, and though she disappeared for a moment, she reappeared, brows drawn together as she surveyed the mob that surrounded him. He hoped she would take his side. Drive them all away. If anybody could do that, Honey could.

"Honey," he called, "these people won't leave me alone about Emily."

"She left today," Jor-El announced glumly.

Honey crossed her arms.

"Because she thinks Tracen wanted to get back together with Serena," Sam added.

Honey tilted her head. She looked at Serena.

Serena nervously repeated her whole spiel. "Emily said she was jealous of me. And I had no idea that she'd even been dating Tracen. In fact, I told her that Tracen would never choose me over her, and that's when she said…"

Silence. Serena paused mid-gesture.

Honey prodded, sounding more like Tracen's elementary school principal than his good friend. "What did she say?"

Serena twisted so that she faced Tracen once again. Tracen braced for impact.

"She said that Tracen chose Sun Valley over her."

The *ahs* of enlightenment and the groans of truth filled the air. Tracen felt both deep within his gut. It all came down to his love of the land. But she loved it too. Why would she not want to settle down with him in a cabin on the river?

The crowd parted so Honey could make her way to the table.

"Tracen, it's time to let go," Honey said softly.

Tracen balled his fists, the veins of his arms popping out. He'd been planning to build a log cabin since he was old enough to play with Lincoln Logs.

"You've been afraid from the very beginning. I knew it. I tried to protect you from it."

Tracen looked down. He couldn't face the love in Honey's eyes. But neither could he avoid the memories that came with her words. Memories of how he'd gradually allowed Emily into his heart. His assertion that he was going to do things differently with her the way Peter did when Jesus advised him to cast his net one more time.

"I'm going to miss you, Tracen."

Tracen snapped his head back up. Why was she saying good-bye? "Honey, if she loved me enough, she would have stayed."

Honey shook her head. "Love doesn't work that way, Tracen. It has to start with you."

Honey didn't know what she was asking. His dream was finally about to come true. The life he'd planned for his family—to continue the legacy that his parents had started by raising him in such beautiful country. He was the only one who could keep the name *Lake* local. "You don't understand."

Honey's dry laugh ripped at his pride. There was nothing funny about his situation. "Tracen, I lost more than you ever did. I know the vulnerability it takes to commit to a spouse. The possible pain that might result from it."

Okay, so she did understand. But she wasn't making the same sacrifices she wanted him to make.

"It's worth it." She sent one more laserlike look his way before calling back into the restaurant, "Howie! Can you help me for a second?"

Howie bounded out like Toto might. Except Howie held a bucket of rattling dishes. Apparently he'd been helping out as busboy again.

"What's up?" He glanced from person to person with delight as if he'd walked into a surprise party.

Honey turned and took the bucket from his hands and placed it on the picnic table between Serena and Jor-El. "Our boss Tracen is afraid of following his heart."

Howie nodded sympathetically. "I know. I've tried talking to him about it."

"Talking doesn't seem to be working." Honey sent Tracen an unspoken challenge—a dare in her eyes. "So I thought I'd show him what he needs to do." Gripping both of Howie's hands, she dropped down onto one knee in front of him.

Tracen's arms fell limp by his sides. He had no more rebuttals.

"Howie, I've been trying to fight my feelings for you for some time now."

Serena gasped beside him. She'd always been a little slow on the uptake.

But even though Tracen knew what was happening, he couldn't believe it. Honey was actually proposing to Howie. The man had loved her so much—and kept on loving her despite her rejection. Joy for his friends overwhelmed him.

Honey's strong voice cracked. "I loved you when you proposed to me on Valentine's Day. I loved you when you were too shy to kiss me under the mistletoe at Christmas. I think I even loved you back when you dressed up like Captain Hook on Halloween."

"Shiver me timbers," Howie joked, though his eyes shone bright with tears.

Tracen wiped at his own eyes. Would this have happened if not for Emily? Would any of the joys he'd experienced lately have occurred if not for her?

Honey choked on her laugh. "Howie, I never wanted to love again. But I can't help loving you. Will you marry me?"

Howie whisked Honey to her feet and pressed both of her wrinkled cheeks between his hands. "You don't know how happy you've made me, Honey. Yes, I will marry you." A grin scrunched up his face. "As long as you let me wear the tux. Why couldn't you just let me propose like a normal woman would?"

Sam's wolf whistle split the air. The rest of the group cheered.

Honey beamed at her fiancé. "You don't want a normal woman, Howie."

Howie crushed Honey to him in what must have been their first kiss.

First kiss. Emily in oven mitts. Was there anything Tracen wanted more? He couldn't let Honey outdo him.

Swinging both legs over the bench, he tried to squeeze behind Serena.

"Where you going, big brother?" Sam called.

He was going to let go. He was going to do things differently. He was going to listen to Jesus' direction.

"I'm going fishing."

Chapter Twenty-five

....

Emily pulled into the Redfish Lake Lodge. As she unpacked her luggage, children's laughter wafted from a nearby trailer, and the engines of ski boats thrummed in the distance. Overhead, the sun played hide-and-seek behind a few fluffy white clouds, warming her skin whenever it peeked out.

It was the perfect day for playing on the lake. Too perfect. What she wouldn't give for a dreary drizzle to chase all these happy campers away. Though the last time it rained was the first time Tracen kissed her. If she had known then what she knew now, she would have—she would have savored the moment more.

Or maybe she would have turned down the Wonder Woman offer without a second thought. It wasn't worth this.

Of course, had she agreed to stay in Sun Valley, it might not have changed anything. Not with Serena's return. But then at least she wouldn't have this anchor of guilt weighing her down.

Emily's mom hadn't been any help in that department. With her eternal optimism, she'd advised Emily to stay in Sun Valley and let everything work itself out.

Yeah. The way her little talk in the shed had worked out. Tracen had remained so calm and detached during her tirade. As if he didn't care. He'd attempted kissing her, but that didn't make him any different than Jack Jamison—except for the way it caused her toes to curl in anticipation and her breath to catch in her throat.

It was like Tracen had already said his good-bye. Turned off his feelings. Moved on. And that's what she had to do. It's what he wanted her to do. For goodness' sake, he'd hired his brother to fly her home.

There was the floatplane to prove it. Not much bigger than a boat with one long wing extending over the top of it on both sides, and an old fashioned-looking propeller on the nose. It waited at the dock for her flight.

Flight—also a word used to describe fleeing a situation. As in the way Indiana Jones ran from the natives shooting poisonous arrows in his *Raiders of the Lost Ark* escape to the floatplane. The theme music played through Emily's head. If only a real-life escape were as exciting. With the way she was feeling at the moment, she might have preferred the poisonous arrows.

"Emily Van Arsdale!" Matt stepped out of the resort office and strode toward her.

The use of her full name caused Emily to scan the area to see if anybody had overheard. In the window of the trailer where she'd heard the kids playing, a woman's head popped up. Emily sent her a small smile before stepping into Matt's embrace.

"Matt Lake!" Emily returned his enthusiasm, feeling tall next to him after having gotten used to being in Tracen's arms.

Matt stepped back. "So you want to fly in my little plane? For some reason, I thought you had an invisible jet."

Emily forced herself to laugh at the Wonder Woman reference. Had he made the joke at the Fourth of July picnic, she would have found it hilarious. Now it only reminded her how much she was giving up. She really could have gotten used to four brothers-in-law. "Invisible jets aren't very practical. I forgot where I landed mine, and now I can't find it."

Matt chuckled, grabbing two of her suitcases and leading the way toward the dock. "So how are you doing?"

Emily swung her purse strap over her shoulder and trailed after him with her carry-on. She'd hoped to avoid this conversation. Her attempt at humor had been pathetic, but at least it was safe. Maybe she could pretend Matt was making small talk. She'd give the standard response. "I'm fine." No need to get deep.

Matt's slanted glance told her he didn't buy it. "Well, I'm surprised Sam didn't make a move on you now that Tracen is out of the picture."

Their footsteps echoed on the wood planks floating over the surface of the water. Emily looked down, watching where she walked, avoiding eye contact. She couldn't force herself to make jokes about the breakup yet. "Mmm." Could that be considered a response?

Matt tucked her belongings into a storage compartment. He turned to face her, his narrow gray eyes studying her. "I'm sorry Tracen is such an idiot."

A laugh burst between her lips. She hadn't expected Tracen's family to be on her side. She didn't know how much Matt had been told, but he'd assessed the situation correctly. She'd fallen for an idiot. Which made her a fool for love. They would have been a good pair.

"I knew he had issues going into the relationship. I shouldn't have expected him to change for me." No, she wasn't responsible for the choices of others, but she was responsible for her choices.

"I shouldn't have even considered making another movie after telling him I wanted to move back to Idaho." Why couldn't she have tried to see things from Tracen's perspective?

"I don't think you were wrong, Emily. Tracen needs to get over his obsession with staying in Sun Valley." He crossed and uncrossed his arms. "But if you wish you'd chosen to stick with the idiot, then it's not too late. I'll understand if you don't want me to fly you to California."

Emily clasped her hands together. The offer pulled at her emotions like they were a wakeboarder on the end of a towrope. Picking up speed, cutting across the wake, pulling a 360…wiping out. Adrenaline diluted. "Tracen doesn't need me anymore. Serena came home."

Matt's arms dropped down by his sides. "You're kidding. He's taking her back?"

Emily shrugged and scuffed at an uneven plank with the toe of her flip-flop.

Matt blinked and shook his head. "No wonder he didn't want to talk on the phone. I'll be stopping back here on my return trip to Boise to kick his tushy. Or maybe I'll get Sam to do it. Then I can just watch."

Matt's reaction confirmed her fears. He certainly wasn't trying to convince her to stay in Sun Valley anymore. She'd been replaced. No, worse. She'd been the other woman. Tracen had loved Serena all along.

Tracen's brother stepped forward and gripped her shoulders, firm and hard. "Now I'm really sorry, Emily. You deserve so much better."

Better. When Tracen sat her on the counter at her mom's house, he'd asked if it was better. And she'd replied that it was the best.

There was nobody better for her than Tracen. Her heart knew it, and that's why it felt like a deflated balloon within her chest.

Matt's muttering drew her attention back to him. What had he been talking about? "I've actually got to pick up my boss at LAX this afternoon, so taking you down is not out of my way at all. Just let me do my preflight inspection before we take off. If you want to go get a soda in the office, it would probably be a more comfortable place to wait."

Emily sighed. Prolonging her departure only intensified the longing to stay. "Okay, thanks."

She trudged toward the office where, in a trance, she sipped a soda, signed autographs, and smiled for pictures. The mom from the trailer must have been watching for her chance to pounce. And the receptionist gave Emily so much attention that she didn't even answer the phone when it rang. Emily wondered what they would all think if they knew she'd rather stay in Idaho and become neighbors with them than make a sequel to her hit movie.

* * * * *

Tracen strode to his office and punched in Emily's phone number. His Emily. He laughed. All by himself in his office he laughed.

He'd been such a moron. It took Honey proposing to Howie to snap him out of it. He wanted what they had. Why wait? He'd propose to Emily today if he could.

She would be so shocked. She might even say no. But he still wouldn't let her go. He'd follow her to Tinseltown. Maybe he could even be an extra in *Wonder Woman II*. He had the experience now. Ha! He should make a resume.

Emily's voice mail. Not even a ring. Either the cell battery was dead, or she'd turned it off. That figured. "Hi. You've reached Emily Van Arsdale," her clear voice practically bounced. If she wanted to keep acting after her movie career, maybe she could get a job reading audio books. He'd pay to listen to her. But he had to reach her first.

Shoot. He'd call his brother, but if Matt was in the air, he'd have his cell turned off. Hopefully he hadn't picked Emily up already, and that's why her phone was off. He needed to catch them before they left.

Emily would still have to go make her movie, but she could wait a little longer before she left Sun Valley—before they both left Sun Valley. Oh, it wasn't going to be easy to leave. His dreams had finally fallen into place. But without Emily, his dreams felt more like nightmares.

Grabbing the phone book, he flipped to marinas. Where was his brother landing again? At Redfish Lake the best dock would be at the lodge. P...Q...R...Redfish Lake Lodge.

Holding his breath, he dialed the office. Four rings. Then the answering service.

He slammed down the receiver. Now what? Running both hands through his hair, he tugged in frustration. Could he get the airport to radio Matt's plane? No, he didn't know the call sign.

Pushing to his feet, Tracen glanced at his watch. How much time did he have? Serena had come straight over after talking to Emily at the resort. It would have taken Emily longer to get to the lodge than it would have for Serena to get to The Point. Then Matt would have to load the plane and do his little safety routine before departing. Maybe, if he hurried, he could chase her down in time.

Howie appeared in the doorway with a goofy grin. "How about a double wedding?"

A buzz of energy zapped through Tracen. He had to get his bride back before any wedding talk. But when he did, he didn't know if he could wait for a traditional ceremony. Wouldn't an elopement create a sensation for the tabloids?

He slapped Howie on the shoulder before charging past. "Love ya, Howie. Congratulations. Gotta go."

Howie grabbed his arm to stop him. "Wait!"

Tracen didn't have time to wait. Every fraction of a second counted. His heart ticked them off as a reminder. "We'll talk about the wedding later. Besides, dude, the women will be the ones planning it all anyway."

"What?" Howie squinted in confusion. "I don't want to talk about the wedding. I'm talking about the future Mrs. Lake. Did you call her?"

Tracen huffed. If Emily got away today, he'd make Howie help bring her back from the L.A. area. They'd be the rafting version of the movie *Urban Cowboys*—calling for the taxi driver to row hard right and wearing a life vest to the beach.

"I tried to call her, got her voice mail. I'm going to have to speed over to the marina." And speed he would. He'd take Sam's motorcycle and ride right onto the dock if he had to. He'd come this far, he wasn't going to stop now.

"Stop."

Tracen turned to face Howie, balling his hands into fists. This was ridiculous. The whole restaurant ganged up on him to get him to give up everything for Emily, and then when he finally did, his best friend tried to sabotage their reunion. "This better be good, Howie."

Howie simply pointed to a disgruntled crowd pushing through the entrance. "Highway 75 is closed for construction."

Not good. Worse than not good. Bad.

Unless the road closed before Emily left. Then maybe she was a part of the crowd streaming in. His pulse throbbed, sending blood through his veins with the rush of whitewater. In that case he might have her back within the minute.

Howie snapped his fingers in front of Tracen's face. "It just happened."

Tracen's urgency subsided as the cloud of defeat threatened to rain down on him. He listened to what he could hear of Howie's explanation over the windstorm that blew away his hope.

"Earlier they'd closed down one lane so that east and westbound traffic had to take turns." Howie shrugged. "Then I guess a dump truck accidentally spilled its load across the open lane. It'll be a little while before traffic can get through again, but I'm guessing it happened after Emily left."

Tracen kicked a nearby barstool to keep from spewing negativity. The pressure of the connection jarred his big toe, bringing with it a burning sensation. The stool tilted in slow motion before clattering to the floor. The damage didn't compared to the turmoil inside, and he stepped forward to kick something else.

Howie gripped his arms from behind and spun him back towards the office before he could rip the breakfast bar apart. "Cool it, Trace."

Tracen pulled away. Hands off. He already felt caged. He didn't need to be held down as well.

"There's nothing else I can do, Howie! I'm stuck. Finally I decide to act, and then I don't get my chance."

Howie lifted an eyebrow. "All in God's timing, my friend."

Tracen threw his hands in the air. "God's timing would have been days ago, but I wasn't listening." Now he was being punished. He wasn't as good at spending time in The Word the way Emily was. He could learn so much from her—if he could ever get to her.

Her and her pink Bible. And her study on water.

Water…

Tracen looked out the window toward the river, barely hearing Howie's latest sermon.

"So Samuel anointed David king, but he had to wait on God's timing and trust that—"

"David did a lot of wise things." Tracen interrupted, a plan forming in his head. David also did a lot of foolish things. And Tracen was going to follow David's lead, though he didn't know if it was a wise or foolish choice.

He focused on Howie, wondering how his buddy was going to respond. It didn't matter. If Tracen was going to act, he had to do it quickly.

"Remember how David captured Jerusalem?" Tracen didn't wait for a response. He took off for the stairs.

Howie trotted after him. "Yeah, he used a water tunnel to sneak into the…" Howie doubled his pace and caught up to Tracen on the landing. "What are you doing?"

"I'm using the water route, just like David did." Tracen didn't slow his pace as he thundered down the stairs and out the back door.

Howie didn't follow, thank goodness. Tracen knew he would try to talk some sense into him. Remind him where he got his scar.

Fear whispered in Tracen's ear, but he didn't have time to listen. He owed it to Emily. If she saw him arriving by raft, she would know that he'd done it for her.

Ripping his life vest off the peg in the shed, he snapped the straps shut while grabbing an oar. This was it. The ride of his life. If he survived.

"Tracen Lake!" Honey hollered from the balcony. Apparently Howie hadn't retreated. He'd merely called in reinforcements. "I will not allow you to raft a class six. It's not safe. Come back in."

"Can't, Honey." Tracen pushed the top raft from the pile onto the hard-packed dirt. "If I'm conquering fears today, I might as well beat them all."

Chapter Twenty-six

....

Emily adjusted her stiff seat belt while Matt slammed the flimsy plane door closed. This was it. The end.

She surveyed the confusing panel of dials, gauges, and levers for a moment before turning back toward the window. The beauty of the nature around her made the cockpit seem even stuffier. It only it could suffocate her emotions.

Settling into her melancholy, Emily forced herself to acknowledge Matt's presence as he climbed in and started the ignition. Vibrations thrummed through her in a way that she normally would have found thrilling. Now, however, she was just glad the noise from the engine would prevent conversation.

The sun glistened off the water, almost blinding in its intensity. Memories of her last visit to the lake flooded her thoughts. That had been the first time Tracen had allowed himself to enjoy being with her. He'd joked about Howie and opened up about Honey. Then his mood had changed, and he'd taken off unexpectedly. Why had she expected any more from him this time?

Sure, she was the one actually taking off, but he'd arranged it for her. Maybe she should be thankful. She needed to get away from him. Hiding herself in the Lord hadn't really been working. As she continued her Bible study on water, the verses just taunted her.

"Many waters cannot quench love; rivers cannot wash it away...."

Not quite a hopeful thought when she was trying to get over a broken heart. She never should have even considered opening to Song of Songs. But it wasn't the worst verse. No, the quote from Isaiah that she'd always considered part of her favorite worship song now haunted her.

"Come, all who are thirsty, come to the waters...."

Of course, she shouldn't have taken it so literally, but she couldn't help thinking that she'd come to the waters, and now she had to leave before she drowned.

* * * * *

He was going to drown. Tracen's nose burned as icy water surged up his nostrils. Every gasp for air only choked him with another mouthful of raging whitewater.

What had he been thinking? No helmet. And he was all by himself. If he got thrown out of the raft, there would be nobody to pull him back in. If he got knocked unconscious, who would make sure his head stayed above water? If he got stranded on a rock with his chest sliced open again, nobody would know to call an ambulance. He could soon join statistics by becoming one of the fifty rafters to die every year.

The raft plunged deeper, jerking sideways in the roiling water. Tracen's muscles screamed in anger as he forced them to push harder with the oar. He fought to see downstream over the wild waves that dwarfed him, though he would have barely been able to see through the water spots on his sunglasses had his view been unobstructed.

He realigned his raft moments before he could tell where he was headed, which resulted in a strainer sneaking up on him.

The current pinned him to the rock, pressing against his raft with a force greater than gravity. It was like a fire hose aimed at him, knocking him back, preventing movement, blasting him with a never-ending tsunami.

Memories of his last trip down a class six washed over him. He'd been stupid to attempt it as a fifteen-year-old. He was even stupider now.

How could he get out? Move forward? He had to get to Emily. She'd never forgive him if he killed himself in an attempt to stop her from leaving.

"Lord save me!" he gurgled.

Where had he heard those words before? Who else had called for the Lord to save him? Whoever it was must have been at the brink of death, trapped in a storm of his own making. Did that person get an answer from the Lord? Because Tracen still felt helpless and on his own.

At least the raft hadn't capsized yet. And he had his oar. Gripping tighter with his left hand, he let go with his right, praying the water didn't snatch the paddle from his grip. With his right hand, he resisted the river's control long enough to reach down and grip the rope that encircled the raft through connected tabs. If he could just hang on, he might be able to push to the side of the rock.

Rock. It was Peter, named after a rock, who had cried out to the Lord to save him. Peter had stepped out of the boat to walk on water.

Only last weekend, Tracen read the passage with Emily. He knew that Jesus saved Peter.

And Tracen had been like Peter in his relationship with Emily. He'd made the choice to step off the boat—to date her—but when the waves came, he got scared and sank.

No more. With renewed strength, Tracen shoved his raft parallel to the boulder. It would take another shove. And another. Slow, painful process. But he had hope. Yes, his hope had returned.

He might not feel God's presence, but he had the words of Jesus to reassure himself. *"You of little faith…why did you doubt?"*

The raft bounced, rocked against the edge like a teeter-totter, then shot forward, bringing a rush of wind and a sense of soaring. Tracen held his oar overhead, lifting his hands to his Savior in worship.

"Woo-hoo!"

The next drop tickled his tummy, jarred his teeth, and forced him to refocus on his surroundings. But he'd left his fear back at the rock. He could do this.

* * * * *

Emily shaded her eyes from the sun as the plane tilted upward in takeoff. Wobbling side to side like a toddler learning to walk, the craft made its way into the air.

Emily dropped her hand and gripped the seat, closing her eyes against the momentary brilliance. Sunglasses would have helped. At least she didn't need them as much as Tracen did.

Tracen. She was thinking of him again, though she'd promised not to. But at least it was a distraction from the nausea that swam in her stomach.

"You can open your eyes, Emily," Matt teased over the hum of the engine. "We're up."

Emily pried her eyes open. Blue sky. She loosened her grip on the seat and turned to look out her passenger window.

They weren't that high yet. Emily could still make out people at play. Kids on a tube. A pontoon driver arguing with an officer on a patrol boat. A rafter being spat out of the Salmon River.

Emily focused on the rafter. Wasn't that last stretch of the river a class six? Not many rafters would attempt such a run. And this guy was by himself. Not safe. He couldn't have come from Tracen's rafting company.

The guy waved at the plane. Not just a casual wave. He had both hands overhead, waving wildly. So wild, in fact, that he knocked his sunglasses off. Then he doubled over as if sneezing....

"Ahh!" Emily's arms flew wide as she screamed, smacking Matt. She pressed her nose closer to the window when the plane zipped past Tracen. *Oh no.*

"What in the world?" Matt's voice demanded from behind her.

She spun to face him. "Turn the plane around!" They had to turn around. Because Tracen was coming to stop her. Why else would he raft a class six by himself? He'd risked his life. She couldn't leave him. Joy bubbled within. "Turn around. Tracen's here."

"What?" Matt's eyebrows drew together for the moment he could look at her.

"Tracen. I saw him. He rafted here." She twisted madly to get a look at his fading figure.

"What?" Matt repeated.

She didn't have time to explain. They were already flying over land, headed for California. Her heart ricocheted between her ribs. "Go back. We have to land."

"I can't. I don't have time to do my preflight check all over if I'm going to pick up my boss on time." Matt squinted into the distance, trying to see Tracen for himself. "That can't be Tracen, Emily. He knows better than to raft a class six."

Emily itched to throw off her seat belt. "Exactly. But he's crazy for me." It was the only explanation. She wouldn't have to miss him anymore. Not if Matt would just land the plane.

"He's crazy, all right. But he's too late."

Emily clasped her hands together. "Matt, please." How could she endure an entire flight to California, when Tracen was waiting for her below? Well, more accurately, waiting for her behind. They continued their flight pattern.

"I'm sorry, Emily. I can't land. I'd lose my job."

He couldn't be serious. He knew Tracen's fear. He knew she hadn't wanted to leave in the first place. But now it was out of her control. "Help, Lord."

Maybe God had been trying to tell her to wait through the verses in her head. *"Many waters cannot quench love."* She should have listened.

"Come to the waters."

Emily peered at the lake behind them. The blue speck of Tracen's raft grew fainter. Goodness, he'd really rafted a class six for her. Something he'd only thought he could do if he had but one day to live. A deathly fear. Like jumping out of a plane had been for her.

"Come to the waters."

If she jumped out of the plane, Matt wouldn't have to land and wouldn't be late for picking up his boss.

"Come to the waters."

Tracen wasn't the only crazy one. Grabbing the buckle to her seat belt, she released it from her waist.

Matt's wide eyes did a double take. "Emily!"

"Turn the plane around, Matt."

Blood pounded in her ears, drowning out his argument. Whatever it was, it didn't matter. They weren't that high over the water. It would be like cliff diving. Or so she tried to tell herself.

"I'm crazy for your brother too."

The plane tilted and buzzed around to return the way it came. Excitement warred with anxiety, causing her limbs to tremble. But she couldn't let fear stand in the way. Tracen hadn't.

Matt looked at her like he could hear her thoughts. "Holy cow. I can't believe I'm letting you do this."

Laughter burst from Emily's gut. What a great story it was going to make for Matt's future nephews and nieces.

"Okay, no boats below. Get ready."

Emily took a deep breath, which was a good thing, because as soon as she released the latch, the door snapped open, and the wind froze her lungs. Whoa, this wasn't cliff jumping at all. It was more like jumping from a speeding car. But hey, she'd done that before.

Looking down, she watched the water zip by, the distance causing her skin to feel covered in pinpricks. The dizziness traveled from her head to her stomach.

"I'll count you down," Matt volunteered.

She couldn't think about it. Without looking down, she stuck her legs out the door and positioned her feet upon the pontoon.

A flip-flop slipped from her foot, whirling erratically to the depths below.

"Three…"

O Lord, one miscalculation and she could flail like the flip-flop.

"Two…"

"Come to the waters."

"One!"

This was it. With a giant leap of faith she lined her fingers up together in a prayer position, ducked her head, and leaned forward, letting gravity turn her into a comet.

It took an impossibly long time, yet she stayed tight, chin tucked. The water in the middle of the lake would be deep enough, wouldn't it? Matt wouldn't have let her jump if not. Too late to rethink things.

Bam. Liquid had never felt so solid. The lake slipped over her, slowing her descent, and chilling her to the temperature of an ice sculpture.

Arching her back, she sliced toward the surface, scissoring her legs. Her lungs burned for oxygen. Had she even inhaled after opening the plane door? Almost there. She could do it. Almost there. She hoped. And she'd thought the worst part was over.

Her vision blurred. No, it wasn't her vision. It was the water. Bubbles dispersed, leaving Tracen's image moving toward her through the water.

Oxygen or Tracen? Tracen.

She clawed at the water. Tracen mirrored her actions, air escaping from his wide smile. Reaching out, she caught his hand, and he pulled her to the surface.

Oh, she wanted to kiss him, feel the amazing connection once again. She gasped air—its burn raked through her. She was panting and puffing.

She wrapped her arms around Tracen's neck, then sank down like a buoy bobbing in the waves. Tracen's strong arms lifted her back up. Finally, he'd kiss her. He leaned in…she turned her head away just in time to cough up water.

Tracen laughed, his eyes sparkling down at her. Were they going to get a chance to kiss before a sneezing fit attacked him?

Tracen motioned toward the raft, then led the way in a front crawl, head above water, like he didn't want anything else to possibly come between them. "You're insane," he yelled back at her.

He could call her anything he wanted to. "And you're an idiot."

Tracen grabbed the side of the raft and helped heave Emily into it. She turned and reached back over to pull him after her. He slid to the bottom and sprawled in the sun. Emily couldn't take her eyes off him.

"I *am* an idiot." Rolling to face her, Tracen's smile slipped. "Will you ever forgive me?"

Emily reached for his fingers. The press could have a field day with her final stunt. But all that she cared about was the happy ending. "Forgive you? I just jumped out of a plane for you."

Tracen's lips curled into a half-smile. "You did, didn't you?" He leaned forward, lifting his free hand to cup Emily's face. "You must really love me."

Emily leaned her head toward Tracen's palm, feeling his warmth against her cheek. "I do." It felt so good to say it. And she knew Tracen loved her. Or he wouldn't have rafted to her rescue. Though it didn't make sense why he would wait to the last minute to change his mind. But it didn't matter at the moment. They had the rest of their lives to figure things out.

She looked into his eyes, willing the moment to never end. "Let's start over."

Tracen's thumb lifted and brushed over her lower lip. "I can't think of a better way to start," he murmured.

"I know." She breathed. "You have no idea what your thumb is doing to me right now."

Tracen lifted his thumb, and the corners of his cheeks lifted, as well. "That's not what I meant." He paused. "I'm talking about how we just got washed by the water. Washed clean. Which is a good way to start afresh."

Emily slipped closer to Tracen, enjoying the way his slick skin made it easy. "Mmm...yes, this is a good start. But are you sure you can't think of anything better?"

"Actually, I can." Tracen rolled to his knees, away from her. Where was he going? He kept her hand in his, at least. "Emily, I don't ever want to lose you again. I will follow you anywhere you want to go. If you will marry me, I only have one request."

Emily jerked upright. Tracen wasn't just apologizing. He was proposing. That was definitely better. But... "Another ultimatum?"

Tracen's eyebrows shot up. "Oh, I didn't mean it that way."

He looked so cute. So humble. Like a new man. Her man. "I don't care. I want to be with you. So, yes. I will marry you, Tracen Lake."

Tracen crushed her to him then. His mouth covered hers, drinking her in. And she hoped it was a thirst never quenched. As his lips traced her jawbone and traveled down her neck, she had to know what he almost insisted on.

"What is your one request, Tracen? I'll give up Wonder Woman if you want me to. I'm going to make this work."

"No." Tracen drew back, his eyes dancing. "I just want to make sure you give me some say in our wedding. I've got a great idea for the ceremony."

Was that all? How incredibly sweet. Her wedding day might not be what she had planned, but nothing ever was with Tracen around. And she didn't want it any other way.

Emily launched herself back into his embrace with a little too much exuberance. They splashed overboard into the water. The future Mr. and Mrs. Lake.

Epilogue
....

Late again. And for the wedding this time. But what could she do about it? The chairlift only had one speed. And it might not be as old as the world's first chairlift, which was installed at the resort back in 1936, but it sure felt like it.

Emily smoothed the lacy dress under her faux fur wrap and readjusted her ski poles. No, this sure wouldn't have been her choice for a wedding, but it would definitely be one to remember.

She grinned at the guests gathered below, excited to ski down the aisle. She hoped Jor-El wouldn't crash into anyone as he tobogganed into position as ring bearer.

Almost to the top. This was it.

"Emily! Get over here. They've already started the procession. What took you so long?" Honey motioned frantically.

Emily slid to the ground and took a deep breath. Butterflies accompanied her as if she were about to do a stunt, not casually ski down the bunny hill. "So sorry, Honey. I got mobbed back at the resort. The paparazzi are a little obsessed with getting a picture of me in this getup."

Tracen cut through the snow toward her, his shades and tuxedo giving him a 007 vibe. "Well, you look fabulous." Talk about looking fabulous.

Emily melted—not a common occurrence in such freezing temperature. "Shall we?"

"I think we better. Or Honey is going to be a rogue bride and take off without us."

"Now that's a good idea." Honey pushed off toward the curve of the slope.

Emily wrinkled her nose. "She's a little eager."

A smile flitted across Tracen's lips. "So am I."

She knew he wasn't talking about Howie and Honey's wedding, but about their whitewater wedding coming up in June. She couldn't wait for that wild ride to begin either. "Should we race Honey to the altar?"

Tracen cocked his head. "I'd go anywhere with you."

Leaning forward, Emily started the momentum of gravity and called back over her shoulder, "If you can keep up!"

His simple statement was not an easy one, but she'd make sure she was worth the effort. And she'd have fun doing it.

About the Author

....

Angela Ruth sold her first article to a national magazine while still in high school, which motivated her to study journalism at The University of Oregon. She continued writing as a stay-at-home mom, selling children's stories to such publications as *Hopscotch* and an anthology titled *Summer Shorts*. During that time Angela also founded IDAhope Writers to help other aspiring authors pursue their dreams. Currently she works in marketing at Borderline Publishing and is very excited for the release of her first novel. You can e-mail her at angelameuser@ gmail.com. She'd love to hear from you.

www.angelameuser.com

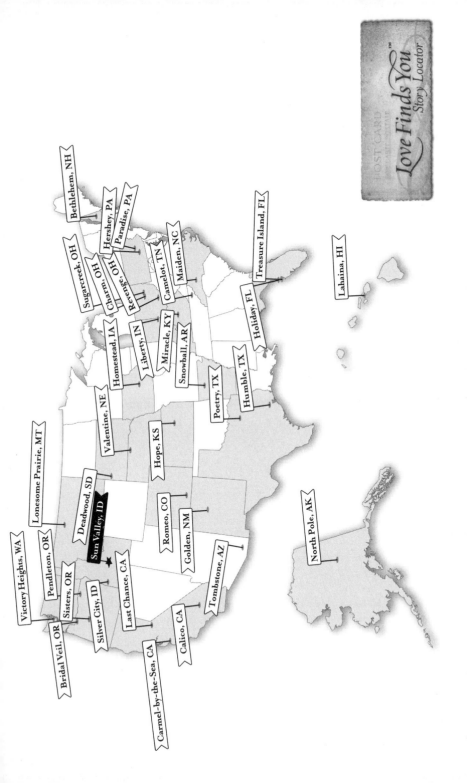

Love Finds You™
Story Locator
POST CARD

Bethlehem, NH

Hershey, PA
Paradise, PA

Sugarcreek, OH
Charm, OH
Revenge, OH
Camelot, TN
Maiden, NC

Treasure Island, FL
Holiday, FL

Lahaina, HI

Homestead, IA
Liberty, IN
Miracle, KY
Snowball, AR

Humble, TX
Poetry, TX

Valentine, NE

Lonesome Prairie, MT

Hope, KS

Deadwood, SD
Sun Valley, ID

Romeo, CO
Golden, NM

North Pole, AK

Victory Heights, WA
Pendleton, OR
Sisters, OR
Bridal Veil, OR
Silver City, ID
Last Chance, CA
Carmel-by-the-Sea, CA
Calico, CA
Tombstone, AZ